# AUSTIN WYRD

## STEVE CURRY

*I owe thanks to some important people in this process. "Ducky" took the first swipe at editing and correcting my work. And my gamer buddies the Crows were kind enough to sacrifice a few of their members and family members to beta reading.*
*I saved the very best for Last. To all of my friends and family that pushed me into believing I was capable of this. Even more thanks go to Cindy. I never would have finished this without your constant encouragement and the occasional eye-roll at my insecurity.*

**WYRD~**

an old Germanic and Viking age concept of fate or destiny
shaped in part by free will but also by complex interactions
of universal necessity and a cosmos beyond the
comprehension of most mortals.

## 1

---

IF YOU TAKE a man's coin then you don't walk away just because things get ugly. It's one of the rules I live by. Well, the corpse in the alley certainly fit the ugly tag. It was ugly enough to make me want to take some vacation time someplace far away. Unfortunately, I'd already cashed my paycheck and despite what some people might say, I have a few standards.

So, there I was paid in full and obligated to talk to the boss. Instead of asking for time off though, I had to tell him the band wouldn't be coming back on since one of them was very messily dead in the garbage behind the bar. When I say messily, I mean it was hard to distinguish where garbage and muck ended, and bits of ex-drummer began.

I assumed it was the drummer from some of the clothes scattered about. There was also the fact that I'd been looking for him out back. One of the barbacks told me he'd seen the guy breaking our rule about bands and clients going out that way. It was supposed to be an insurance risk. It had certainly been risky enough for him. I was already getting a headache when I turned to go back inside.

Canned heavy metal assaulted me as soon as I opened the alley door. It was the same prerecorded stuff that had started when "The Niddhoggs" had left the stage. Pronounced *Nidth,* like width. It was a decent reference to Norse myth and the serpent destroying the world tree. Then again it probably had more to do with the shiny black motorcycles some of them roared in on. They even used their "Hawgs" for musical backup on stage from a pair of Softail Harleys.

First thing through the door I spotted one of the college boys standing there looking impressive and muscle-bound near the dance floor. I waved to get his attention then jerked a thumb towards the door.

We met halfway. "Chet, drag your looming act over by the back door. Nobody goes in or out."

"Sure thing Mouse, what's up?" He adopted his menacing glare as we passed each other.

"Can't say just yet, Chet. You get over and lock down that door. I gotta talk to the boss before I say anything else capiche?" He got the last bit over my shoulder as I dug into the crowd looking for the boss.

I dialed the cops myself when I couldn't find Walter Roy. Walt both co-owns and manages the bar. This means while he's usually in the office, sometimes he has other business to tend to. I left a note with one of the waitresses to have him look for me out back. Yea, the cops were going to want to talk to me since I found the body. The worst part is I work really hard at not being that noticeable to authority figures and such.

I mean sure, the bartenders and especially the waitresses, know who to come to in case of trouble. But to the average clientele, I'm just the polite and kind of stocky guy at the door who cards people and takes the occasional cover charge. There were normally two or three bigger and more noticeable guys in the bar wearing the tight muscle shirts. Sometimes the shirts said security, but usually, it was just the full torso logo of a fantasy-art semi-nude that was half pinup girl and half skeleton where she stood in her boat.

Me? I don't really like black as much as everyone else. It's probably a good thing I'm very proficient at my job. Or maybe it's just that the boss likes me enough to give me some slack on the dress code. I go for khaki, reds or grey, sometimes maybe charcoal but everyone else in the place wears enough black and metal to go around. It's that kind of bar.

Most of the metal-heads and biker wannabe's in the bar wear their tattoos like flags and as much metal in their faces as on those silly dog collars some of them wear. Tonight, I was free of piercings, my ink was covered, and aside from the combat boots, I was fairly conservatively dressed in unwrinkled 501s and a charcoal-colored shirt. So that's what the flashing lights revealed as the first of several police cars and other official vehicles arrived.

When the sirens started to wail even louder than the chaotic sounds coming out of the bar, I stepped forward into the light and walked towards the nearest end of the alley. I figured I might as well flag the police down and show them the way. There was no real hurry anymore, but I wanted to get things moving. Spending time with any type of constabulary is one of those things best done quickly like pulling off a bandage.

The frantic noise of speed-metal rolled out muted but persistent to turn the scene into something out of a mushroom induced dream. The reality factor was already strained by several assaults on the senses; the neon lights flickering from the tattoo parlor at the end of the alley, a sickening stench of bad meat, garbage, and worse. Around it, all the dayglo colors of graffiti hung like a tribute to acid trips. And of course, like most graffiti in Austin, it was bilingual and mostly profane.

The absolute worst of the sensory assaults came from the odor of raw sewage and spilled entrails along with a hint of the coppery scent of blood. Plus there was the blood itself in great splatters and roping rivers of black that betrayed the occasional sheen of red when the tattoo parlor lights shined just right. In the middle of that almost artistic arrangement of blood were the pile of rags and splintered bone, black leather, and metal spikes. There was also an incredible amount of offal as what was normally inside the clothing and skin, was now very much outside and strewn about.

The first officer was young and full of youthful vitality. With an eager look on his face and an energetic bounce, he was halfway into the alley. His approach was textbook. One hand stayed near if not on his handgun. The other hand shined the inevitable heavy-duty flashlight right into my eyes.

"Jesus Chuy, back off the lights. This is the guy who called it in. I doubt he offed somebody in the alley then stood here to wave us in." The second officer was older, thicker in the middle, and obviously in no real hurry to see whatever was down the alley. He also had eyes that said they'd already seen enough. They said scenes like the one behind me were nothing new and lost the appeal of novelty long since. To him, this would probably be less of an adventure and more of an unpleasant job that had to be done. And if he had to do a job, he was going to do it right. That meant he didn't need a young eager beaver tugging on his shirttails. At least that's what I saw in those tired old eyes.

"Look, kid, walk down the alley, don't touch anything,

and don't stand there gawking at the body. Take some tape with you and seal off that end. We'll get this end set-up for the SOCO and the meat wagon." A wave of his meaty hand sent the younger officer jogging down the alley with all of that excess eager energy. "Sorry about the lights. Gomez is a good kid, but this is his first DB. I'm Jackson, what do you have for me?"

Watching the kid run down the alley with his eyes glued to the body instead of his footing seemed likely to provide some entertainment. I figured it was all but a foregone conclusion that the youngster was in for a spill between the light rain beginning to fall, the poor lighting, and a plenitude of debris and garbage. But you don't antagonize the bulls, and ignoring a direct question is about the quickest way to get on their bad side. Turning to face the older officer meant I missed whatever caused the loud bang followed by several fairly profane words in Spanish. I had a good guess though.

Jackson let out a weary sigh and a barely noticeable shake of his head. He raised his voice to carry down the alley. "Officer Gomez, please do not visit devastation on my crime scene and make the forensic people go all frothy at the mouth...Now about that name sir?"

"The name is Magnus, security at Helstyxx. You got it right. I called it in. The DB. Yea I caught that part, Dead Body. What's a SOCO though?" Don't get me wrong. I don't hate cops or anything. In fact, I figure ninety or so out of every hundred of the boys in blue are probably good guys... most of the time. What I *DO* hate, is giving my full name and personal info out to anyone at any time for just about any reason. Thus, the counter-question so maybe he'd move on down the interrogation line of questioning.

"Magnus eh? That a first name or last name? And SOCO

is the Scene of the Crime Officer. The examiners and CSI types." Now he had that little notebook out as well as a body cam pointed my direction. I *really* hate being recorded, or filmed, or pinned down about my identity. I mean I truly despise the notion. But again, it's not a good idea to antagonize the local constabulary when more of them should be arriving at any minute.

"First name, Magnus, last name Gustav. They call me Mouse inside." I jerked a thumb at where the music suddenly crashed out in heavier, almost offensive tones. Just stepping down into the alley and closing the door I could see Walter Roy finally responding to my request to join us. When he got further into the alley he got a good look at the dead drummer from our live music for the night. Even from down the alley I saw him jerk halfway upright after he crouched to see the guy. Maybe it was all the blood and carnage. Somehow though, I got the idea that Walt had seen and made the guy's ID, and he reacted a little funny to it. But then again, there was a lot of blood and carnage. And yea the odors.

We were too far to hear the conversation, but it was visibly apparent that eager young officer Gomez rounded on Walter and fired off a salvo of commands, queries, questions, and suspicious comments. Whatever his wording was, it had the net effect of Walter fishing out an ID and handing it to "Chuy". Jackson noted this with a nod of approval before turning back to me.

"Okay, Mr. Gustaf. What do you do in the club and how did you discover the...victim?" Jackson tried to give the impression that he wasn't looking at me. The tightening around his eyes told me he was watching from his peripheral vision though.

I decided it was probably a good idea to keep the story

simple and try not to make any guilty jumps, break out into fidgets or cold sweats, or anything similar. "I work the door; do a little security here and there. Just try and keep things quiet, Sergeant Jackson."

"Just Officer Jackson." He tapped his shoulder to show me whatever stripe or chevron arrangement indicated his rank. He tilted his head and looked at the open door from which emanated the various throbs, thrums, screeches, and howling.

"Quiet eh?" Good thing the cop looked more amused than skeptical.

"You get used to it." I shrugged. "I just try and keep the bloodshed down to a minimum. Make sure everyone has a good time without any real trouble or damage to more than an ego or two."

As we talked, Jackson had led me deeper, towards the actual carnage itself. As a result, we were close enough to see Walter empty his stomach. It was impossible to say if the younger policeman had already done the same thing. He was definitely a little green beneath his healthy tan.

Walking into full view of the body decorating the alley with its macabre new color scheme, I saw Officer Jackson gulp just once to keep down what was probably the last chili-dog or burrito he'd consumed. "Keep the bloodshed down huh? Great job, Mouse."

IT WAS PRACTICALLY daylight by the time Jackson and a series of other law enforcement types were through asking and re-asking a lot of questions I couldn't answer. Good thing Bouncer and Doorman is by definition a night-job. I was only a couple of hours later than normal in getting home. It was probably a good thing that I was between girlfriends too. I've discovered that no matter how normal and otherwise sane she might appear; almost any woman becomes irrational when her boyfriend comes home late from working in a bar.

Pets are much more practical. They generally don't know how to read a clock. They also don't give a single damn about what perfume you might smell like. That's why I had pets to take care of instead of a lady friend before I went to bed. Rafe is what they call a brown necked Raven. He's honestly more of a crow, kind of muddy black with a few spots of white but almost as big as some of the American breeds of Raven. He's also a bit of a jerk. I haven't let him out of the house or his own run in years. Not since the '09 Flagstaff missing cat epidemic.

Rafe acknowledged my servitude with a customarily rough Kawr or two. Then he proceeded to shred one of the phone books I keep to entertain him. While his attention was diverted I managed to sneak a couple of mice and some grasshoppers into the sawdust of his aviary. Once he realizes they're in there he'll spend hours hunting them down and ensuring their demise. Not that I enjoy their suffering or death. A live diet just seems to keep him happier and healthier. Something to do with hunting and calcium I think.

By contrast, the dog is a breeze. Feed him, change his water, let him run around in the grass or maybe chase a tennis ball, and then share most of a queen size bed with him. It's amazing that an eighty-pound dog can take up three times as much bed as a good-sized healthy adult male human being. I can't explain it. Grimmr doesn't care though.

Grimmr is a Catahoula Leopard Dog. Don't be too surprised if you haven't heard of them. Outside of the wilds in Louisiana, few people know about the breed. Suffice to say that he can track, fight, hunt, herd, and take up more than half of a large bed. He also has an excess of energy sometimes.

Despite my late hours and fatigue, I met his greeting with a few minutes of rough play at the door. Sometimes such play is rougher on me than the mutt. He got a decent shot at my chin with oversized paws and that was that for roughhousing. When I pushed him away he bounced merrily down the hallway without much concern for my aching red jaw.

In fact, he seemed in fine spirits and was scampering about when I got to the kitchen. Grimmr bounded about in his heavy, wall-shaking mode, with a small red fox dodging nimbly between the lummox's feet. The fox was too small to stand up to even a casual thump of those massive paws, but he was just too fast for those paws to thump even casually. The sight of that damned red fox with the sprinkling of snowy white on his muzzle, chest, and legs was deflating. That damned fox seldom shows up with good news. Even as I watched, I felt the spring leave my step. All at once, the air became heavy, grey, and sour in my lungs. The fox seemed to grin at me and then was gone in a cinnamon-colored flash. He came to an abrupt stop next to a barstool supporting a sharply dressed older man with a long greying ponytail and a flawlessly groomed grey speckled beard.

We're not talking about fashion jeans or a cardigan. This guy started with Italian leather shoes, wool socks in a distinctly unpleasant greenish tartan, and a dark suit from Savile Row. A silver chased walking stick finished the look along with a Burberry overcoat worth a dozen of my favorite London Fog. Picture a middle-aged, stocky, slightly more modern, and less in shape version of Steed or maybe Sean Connery to go with the mild brogue.

"Morning, Eachan." I started to settle atop my barstool but was cut short by a wave of his hand.

"Yes Magnus, it is indeed morning. I suspect it shall not be a *good* morning, however. You should, perhaps, brace yourself. And since it is indeed morning and not a more appropriate hour, I'd suggest making a pot of the coffee I left on the counter. Get that started and we shall talk of portents and omens. Else I fear you shall find yourself facing death and waves of scarlet." No kidding. He really talks like that. I assume it's from burying his erudite nose in way too many books that are older than Keith Richards.

"Too late Doc. Your portents and omens should have watched the late news. I've already been embroiled with death and waves of scarlet. Drummer from The Niddhoggs got iced last night. I was lucky enough to be the one that found him right outside the bar. In fact, I'm just getting back from questioning. Doesn't pay to discover a body anymore. You can't even loot 'em these days."

Doctor Eachan Currie, professor of antiquities and Germanic culture, barely seemed fazed by my comment. "Truly? I wonder why the runes showed me today. At least that explains why you are coming in so late of a morn. Not that I was prying into your secrets or anything!"

That got a raised eyebrow. "If you weren't snooping about me, what makes you think your runes were talking about me?"

"That is the thing is it not?" The prof's tone had gone curious, but I had no doubt it would find its way to a properly tutoresque state before he was done. That's just Eachan. "I was in the act of casting my runes of a morning just as I always do. I had drawn a random handful and dropped them on the small square of fur I keep for the purpose. I expected the position of the runes on the field to tell me such things as purposes, various impacts each rune might have on others in the spread and such. This time, however, all six runes fell in a perfectly straight line that, when interpreted purely by their alphabetic symbolism, spelled out MAGNUS."

That got my attention. Runes are tools that don't receive half as much respect as they deserve. Precise, however, they are not. To perfectly spell out my name like that indicated something more than a rune reading to me. Somebody seemed to be fudging with the dice. I truly *hate* being fudged with.

"Okay, that's pretty plain. Honestly, I can't say I've ever heard anything like it. Not that I doubt you Doc, but are you *sure* it was a straight line spelling my name? That hardly seems likely."

"I tell you lad," surprisingly he'd stayed away from a lecturing tone so far, "I was as skeptical and shocked as you. Spit a currant clear across the room. I dare say boy; let that be a lesson to you about reading of the runes while breaking your fast. There were oats and red currants all over the table. Of course, I couldn't leave it at that and did a second casting. That's the one that came up with death and waves of red."

With the coffee brewing, we sat and discussed the exact orientation and location of each of the runes in his spread. That discussion was interrupted once when I realized that Grimmrr was dozing on the bed again. I swear it's his bed more than mine. And a second realization was that the damned fox was gone. "Doc where'd the damned fox go? He's not in there trying to eat my bird again?"

I was already at the doorway peering in to see Rafe stalking one of the grasshoppers when the professor answered. "What fox?"

That's one of his games I hate. I've seen that fox dozens of times, always with the professor, and he has never once admitted that it exists.

"Besides he only grabbed one flight feather. Rafe is already flying again. No harm done." Consistency was never part of conversations about the fox. I did not doubt that if I tried to follow up the inconsistency of a nonexistent fox only taking one feather, Eachan would once more reply with *"what fox?"*

Enough is enough. I shook my head and grabbed a couple of thick stone mugs. Filling each with the rich aromatic coffee, I placed one in front of the professor and sat down with my own. Brown sugar and a smaller pitcher of heavy cream were already on the table along with some scones the prof had brought along. That occasioned a lengthy and pleasant lull in conversation as the scones and red-brown coffee with cream required a certain level of commitment and concentration. It left me just enough free will to divert my thoughts to the runic revelations as well as Eachan's restraint in questioning me.

Eachan knows I have a strange and shadowed history. He's always had the courtesy not to press me too much about it though. Perhaps his old-world manners come from being a modern pagan and educator. The curiosity probably ate at him on a minute by minute basis. Would it have surprised me to find out he'd been delving into my past with his runes? Not particularly. Would it have upset me? Again, not particularly. However, it might have surprised me if he'd uncovered anything too deeply hidden.

I'm no slouch with those same runes. That's possibly what had drawn us into our odd little friendship. We'd bumped into each other at a coffee shop and he had noticed and remarked on a bit of runic work in one of my earrings. Normally, I'm better about concealing runes, tattoos, symbols, and identifying marks, you know? I guess Verdandi or one of the other two Norns had given me a little nudge. I mean, I doubt I'm completely hidden from *those* three. All-seeing goddesses of destiny are hellaciously hard to hide from. Norns have an unfair advantage, just like ancestral watchers called Disir or a couple of Ravens I don't even want to think about, much less name and a similar pair of wolves. The only reason I don't worry about the Big Eye-patch in the sky is...I'm probably not worth his time.

Eachan was the first to break the silence. Of course, he'd admitted to already having breakfasted on oatmeal, hadn't he? "You like the coffee? It's my own blend. A mix of chicory and coffee from New Orleans mixed with a bright Kona from Hawaii. It gives it the reddish tint and the subtle layering of flavors. It is one of my favorites."

The coffee really was top shelf but I was still more taken by the scone. "Very good stuff Doc. And thanks for the warning even if it's a tad late. However, I have to run an errand and then get some much-needed sleep. Call you later with updates?"

I could see that his curiosity was in full bay for the story of my little discovery of the previous evening. However, the doc was raised with a healthy dose of the aforementioned old-world values. He would never impose on a host after such a polite dismissal. It simply was not done. He might break into one's home armed with scones and coffee, but the prof would never outstay his welcome.

Once I was sure the professor was well and truly gone, I chucked clothes randomly around the bedroom and dove under a thick Dutch quilt. Sure, I had errands to run. But that could just as well come later,in fact, they would have to.

Fortunately, nothing occurred to disturb a sinfully rewarding bit of sleep. I mean sure, I can go without sleep. I can go without sleep for what might seem like extreme lengths of time. But I like to sleep. It makes me less grumpy. Tends to sharpen the old grey matter. Generally makes me a better person to be around. Like the attention of a beautiful woman, like coffee.

## 3

I WOKE up with enough time to grab a quick bite and a checkup for my bike. Enfields are fun. I like the vintage look of the motorcycle and honestly, the small engine is quite enough for me most of the time. On the other hand, you have to keep on top of them or pay a king's ransom for replacement parts. Fortunately, I know a guy who had worked on them extensively in India. He gave my turquoise-colored single-seater a thorough check every few months and I rewarded him with a thick wad of cash. I like cash almost as much as sleep. They don't put your picture or name on cash. Just this nice green stuff that works almost as good as gold used to, or chickens. Hey, there was a time when you could get anything you wanted if you had enough chickens.

Not that I had chickens. Dirty creatures. Peck food out of their leavings. But that's food for a different conversation. I topped off the bike and rode down Mopac to pick up one of the waitresses.

Connie was as cute as they come and probably a ton of fun in the right circumstances. Her hair was thick and approximately the color of midnight. Her eyelashes were the same black but thick, long, and able to send various signals from "come over here" to "I'll be right over there" and several other statements I can't mention in polite company. She wasn't very tall, but what height she had was filled out with more female than most ladies a foot taller. She was curvy and soft and sweet and a feast for the eyes. That doesn't even consider the rather magical way she moved. Whether she was walking or just sitting still, little Connie seemed like she was ready to begin the steps to a fast and hot salsa number. Yea she was cute and looked like a ton of fun alright.

But she had a tendency to talk. She talked a lot. She talked a lot and she talked really fast. She talked a lot really fast and she never stopped. Thus, my offer of a ride to work had been charitable and not the opening ploy in any type of seduction or other overly friendly overture.

Somehow, between a barrage of information about her wardrobe, her puppy, her shoes, her makeup, the movie she watched the previous evening, and her sick aunt, I managed to mention the excitement at the club and tried to avoid any anxiety for her if the police showed up. It was just as we were pulling into the parking lot and started removing our helmets that I finally mentioned it was the drummer whose name I still hadn't caught.

"ABEL!?" For a very long and stunning few seconds, there was silence behind me on the bike. I kicked the stand down and turned to look at a Connie gone waxy gray around some impressively wide eyes. "Dios, I went out with him three nights ago. He was cute and a ton of fun. We did the whole dinner and dance thing and...well, we had a good time okay? But he didn't seem like no drug dealer or gang banger! You said he was all cut up or something not shot right? Who the hell does that?"

Before I could answer her, she was off the bike and clicking away on five-inch heels toward the doors of the club and then inside. Something about her reaction bugged mee. There was a time I would have jumped on that intuition and wrestled it down. That was back when any distraction might be fatal though. These days I was more alert for guys who got too boisterous with their tequila. Hardly life-threatening.

Still, I couldn't figure out what that little voice was trying to tell me. As it turned out, I didn't have time to be thinking about her reaction. I should have been worrying about my own. Maybe it was all those thoughts going through my head, but I never even heard a whistle.

And that baseball bat just had to be whistling with the speed it was moving when it clipped my head. Later I would wish that I had kept my helmet on a little longer. Right then though all I was concerned with was how I got off my bike and why was I laying in a puddle of cold rainwater getting my favorite navy pea coat all muddy. Thick PVC combat boots with chains dangling kicked the icy water into my face and helped me wake up just as the bat prodded me painfully in the ribs.

"Where's your boss midget?" The voice was deep and gravelly. I was pretty sure I should recognize it. Of course, that would require knowing where both of my ears were and I suspected that one or both of those ears had been knocked off with the impact of wood on my bat, or the bat on my wooden head. That didn't seem quite right, but the second kick of water into my face brought me a little more into focus.

"I asked you a question, moron. Where's the boss?"

Frankly, I was better with *moron*. It's generic. You know it's more about getting a rise out of you than any truth about a sensitive subject like your height. Midget was just painful. Is it my fault I look almost as broad across the shoulders as I am tall? My whole life I'd put up with scorn and laughing from six-footers. At least they always tried with the laughing and sometimes worse abuse. Maybe that's why I had learned a few things about self-defense here and there.

Behind the first set of boots, I saw three more pairs. That made eight boots. Unless we had some peg legs out there or some of them were rehearsing like ballerinas that meant I had four guys to deal with. See? That last splash helped a lot. I was even doing math again. I moaned and rolled a little. That should make the bully happy. Guys like that enjoy seeing the little guy scared, hurt, and thrashing about in pain. Of course, that wasn't exactly what was going on under my bat-assisted improvisation.

In the middle of rolling, I got my knees under me. I also got one hand planted pretty well. From the size of the boots and the positions, I knew a few things. One was, the guy standing above me with the bat was probably well over six feet tall and weighed half as much as my bike. The second thing I knew was the relative positioning of his buddies.

I was pretty sure I could bounce up and have this guy dealt with before his friends showed up to dance. If I did it right I could use his unconscious slab of meat to ward off the two on my left while I dealt with the guy closest. The problem was, I didn't know if they had more bats or maybe even something a little more decisive. In my saddlebag, I had a ten shot Glock that would have made the whole issue something entirely different. But that was in my saddle-bags. I was in a world of hurt if they had guns out. Hel with my bells still ringing they'd probably have time to pull guns out of their bags and load them before I could get to mine.

Still, you don't get my job for being indecisive or backing down once the confrontation is underway. I came up from both knees and gave Mr. Batter a rough and rock-hard bunch of knuckles right between his thighs where it would do him the least amount of good. Before he could fall, I had my other hand on his chest and shoved with both legs and that arm.

When I say I look almost as broad as I am tall, it's not entirely because I'm only seven inches over five feet. It's helped a little bit by the fact that I have a fifty-one-inch chest and shoulders to match. Not much of that is fat. Mostly it's good lean corn-fed beef. The guy I'd hit was probably six-four and little under two hundred. Those artistic types rarely carry much excess muscle. He had some nicely sculpted tone and just enough definition to impress the girls. But for the most part, he was a spruce to my oak stump.

He might have been built more like a pin but when I shoved him, he rolled into his accomplices or maybe cheer-leaders like a bowling ball. And they weren't even close to a seven-ten split. Both of those supporting actors went down hard trying to catch him. I was about to do some rough and ready dental work on the remaining guy when a bellow split the air from behind me. I winced and scrunched my neck down. It was truly a Herculean bellow but that wasn't what got me. No, I recognized the voice. It was Jackson, the cop from the previous evening. That's when the concussion-related fog faded enough for me to recognize these guys.

Freaking metal bands, why do they insist on trying to be tough? The soundboard guy was backing away from me with both hands up and a lot of white showing around his eyes.

Off to my left, the bass was helping lead guitar hold up their vocalist while he yarfed up breakfast burrito and maybe some of his own gonads. That first punch was a pretty good shot. I was wondering if he'd still have that god-of-death hate-metal voice tonight, provided he could go on stage at all.

I still had some decent adrenalin going from the bat to the head. Besides, my old dad had always said you don't have to win every fight. You *do* have to make damned sure the other guy doesn't want to do it ever again even if he does end up the victor. I took a long stride forward and got one hand wrapped up in the singer's shirt with my other fist somewhere waaay back behind me when I heard that bellow again.

"Gustaf, stand down!" Now that was a good strong bass, full of authority and character. I bet Jackson would have been center stage even yacking up testicles and he'd still be roaring like some primeval beast.

I tried to look meek and even more wounded when I let go and turned around. Face it, the guys from the band had lost any steam they had to cause trouble. Now I just needed to get back on the officer's good side. "Good evening Officer Jackson. What can I do for you?"

If I ignored the guy tossing his toenails behind me, maybe the cop would too? Yea right. Jackson looked over my shoulder with a streetwise eyeball." Looks like he ate something that didn't agree with him. Or at least bit off something he couldn't chew. Get him off the street guys. Use the club bathroom and clean him up."

He punctuated his directions by picking up the dropped bat and slapping it into his meaty palm with a distinct and unsettling splat. "Don't leave the building again until we talk, gents. I'll be in after I have a word with the bully here."

He stepped around to face me with his back to the four of them. "Bully." The word was just loud enough for me to hear it. I doubt the band even knew he'd spoken. He grinned so wide that it made me struggle to keep from laughing as well. I figured I'd already hurt enough feelings without throwing salt on their wounded pride.

"So how much trouble am I in?" I tried not to sound resigned and maybe a little bitter. It has been my experience that the police look unkindly upon those of us with both a propensity and talent for violence. I felt the grimace taking shape despite my efforts.

Jackson stopped me with a raised hand and looked over his shoulder to make sure the musicians were filing through the door. "Not a lick. Saw the whole thing. Saw you pull up and talk to the girl. Saw her go all pale and scared. Saw the guys come slinking up behind you and watched him clip you with the bat."

"And it never occurred to you to say something? No *"Watch out there's a bat!"* or Even a friendly *"head's up"*. Hell even *"Batter batter batter swing!"* Would have been appreciated." I had the leisure to poke at the lump rising all along the back of my head while scowling and delivering my frustration to the police officer.

He stepped up and pushed my fingers away to look for himself. "Hell, I wanted to see the swing. And frankly, I wanted to see why the bouncers in there all admit they're more for show and you handle the rough stuff. For a minute I thought you were pretty overrated. Just stood there with a dumb look on your face while guys jangling chains and stomping prissy boots walked up and clocked you. You came up fast enough that I didn't have to interfere right away. Not bad by the way. I'm not sure I've seen the martial arts school that goes straight for the nads. Seemed pretty effective though."

"Yea I call that one Punch Junk Dough. If you do it right, first their nethers go all soft and doughy, and then the guy goes all white and doughy and collapses. I thought about calling it the Pillsbury Punch. I was afraid there might be licensing and trademark issues though."

"Good call" Jackson kept his face straight, but again those eyes gave him away. "Those bakers can be kinda yeasty."

I had to admit defeat. It isn't often I find someone who can out-pun me. But then again, he hadn't been knocked for an infield double within the last few minutes. "You're not out here to hold my hand or bandage my boo-boos. Apparently, you're not arresting me for assaulting all four of them and their bat with the back of my head. So, what did you want to talk about Officer Jackson?"

"The young lady you just dropped off. That wouldn't be a server named..." He flipped open his book again. "One Pilar Consuelo aka Connie?"

He returned my nod with one of his own. "Were you aware that Ms. Consuelo had been seeing... and sleeping with, the deceased?"

He got the same nod again. His look told me I should probably explain. "She more or less told me just before she got off the bike and went inside."

He scribbled that down in his book and then looked up with shrewd eyes. "Did you know she'd been living with your boss Walter Roy in there off and on for the last few months?"

Ain't that a Son-of-a-bitch.

When we got inside, the band was sitting over by the stage and glaring at me with more coordinated and harmonious hate than they usually displayed in their music. The singer was done tossing cookies at least. He held a wet rag across his forehead and looked away from glaring at me to stare at the ceiling and gulp a few times. The others maintained their stare despite the lack of any obvious doom or despair on my part.

Closer to the door and thus closer to us as we entered, little "Pilar" was crying softly onto Walter's shoulder and he had both arms around her while he rubbed her back and spoke into her ear. I tried not to notice the sharp glance and nod Jackson gave at the sight.

Walter looked over at the sound of the door opening and caught sight of both the officer and myself. "What the hell happened out there Mouse? Connie came in crying too much to explain and then the band came in cursing you up a blue streak while that singer ran over and threw up in the trash can. They just came back out of the bathroom."

Walt's look spoke more disgust and anger than it did confusion. But the confusion gained ground when the policeman answered rather than letting me. "Your employee was just assaulted by friends of last night's victim. It seemed like they were looking for you and he, umm, forestalled them. Care to tell me why the victim's associates seem very angry with you Mr. Roy? Or would you like to discuss the video footage that shows you walking out of Walmart two days ago with a shiny new machete?"

For a bar that regularly hosted some of the most raucous and rowdy music around, this one was as silent as a crypt after that statement. The bass player across the room broke the silence with a single particularly crude word. An instant later Connie shoved herself away from Walter and looked back and forth between him and the constable. "Walter, what in the world is he talking about? Why did you buy a machete? And why is the band looking for you? And why did they beat up Mouse? All he did was give me a ride. Sangre de Cristo! Are you all loco?"

The girl, with tear tracks still stark against her face, turned from one person to another before taking a few steps that put her closer to the cop and me than anyone else in the bar. "Mouse? Do you know what's happening here? Will you tell me please?"

I didn't go as far as Walter. She needed some reassurance but I decided a good pat on the shoulder would do as well as any public embraces. For one thing, I didn't need any more interest from this particularly curious cop. He was already too suspicious and seemed sharper than most. Grabbing the girl like another contender for her attention would have just put me near the top of the suspect list. I hate being suspected. It's always just another worry when you get people poking into your secrets and origins.

Holding onto Connie's hand, I gave her an avuncular pat and then pushed her towards the ladies' room down the hall. "I'm not positive, Chica. I'll find out while you go wash your face and maybe get a drink, okay?"

Of course, it wasn't that easy. First, we all filed into Walt's office. The cop perched himself on a corner of the desk and I took one end of the couch. There was plenty of room on that long plush leather couch for Walt to sit. Instead, he tried to take a nonchalant stance leaning on the filing cabinet. The whole pose was awkward enough to even make a loyal employee like me want to start suspecting him. Even worse was when he tried to feign some of that cool indifference by shaking a cig out of the pack and lighting it. After he picked up the three or four smokes that had sprayed across the floor, he repackaged all but one. He finally managed to get that one lit despite a visibly shaking hand.

"Now what can I do for you Officer?" Walter probably thought he was going to take control of the situation since we were in the haven of his office in his club. That, however, was a short-lived belief. Jackson disabused him almost instantly of his error.

"Well, you could confess and save me a lot of trouble. Chances are that's not going to happen though. So why don't we start with an explanation about the chainsaw, the machete, your feelings about a drummer sneaking one over on you with the girl out there? Oh, and whatever you have for an alibi would be good too. Start talking about whatever you want. I'll organize the notes when you're done." Once more the good constable pulled his little booklet out and started scratching even before anyone else started talking.

"Look, this is ridiculous. I was here at the bar all night. Everyone here can vouch for me." Walter seemed to be trying for annoyed and firm. What he got was anxious and maybe just a little bit panicked. "Surely you have other suspects or clues to look for. I repeat I was here At. The. Bar."

"Right" Jackson's tone, by comparison, was very cool and very much contained. Perhaps there was a touch of sarcasm in it, but not enough to cause him any trouble from public relations or anything. "You were here at the bar, the bar the body was found behind."

"What? But...that's ridiculous! I was inside the bar working. Ask anyone...ask Magnus! Mouse, you were here. You saw me." Any hint of control was gone as my boss started to realize he was in real trouble here and that it was not going to go away with a little casual bluster.

I hated admitting that I couldn't help his growing fear very much. With a slow shake of the head, I answered. "Walt, I only had eyes on you a total of thirty or forty minutes all night. Well once the crowd started filling in at least. I doubt anyone else could say they'd had eyes on you any longer. It was a busy night."

I very carefully did not add the next thoughts. The girls were all handling more tables than normal. The bartenders and bar backs were running to keep up and my guys had been circling with their eyes on the crowd. It was all but a forgone conclusion that nobody had been looking for Roy except to put out a brush fire. I couldn't remember any brush fires that would have provided an alibi though.

I learned loyalty in an older and different school of thought. In another day and age, they would have called him the Master of the business. Maybe even the lord of his small castle. This was my chief slowly melting before me. It wasn't an easy thing to watch. Maybe there was a way to help though. "So, I guess we better do everything we can to make sure they get the right guy and don't arrest someone just because of a weak alibi."

This time something in my voice caught the drowning man's attention. Walter's head snapped up and he locked his eyes on mine. "That's right. Somewhere out there is the man who did it. We find him and we don't have to worry about me. All they have is a weak alibi and a weak motive over one of my waitresses."

It did me good to see how much it helped the chief to think of something other than a looming jail cell. And then I watched him come crashing to earth.

"A weak motive, a weak alibi, and a shiny new machete on video." I could have given Jackson the same Punch Junk Dough maneuver he'd seen me use outside. Even then I don't think he would have looked as sick and as stricken as Walter suddenly did.

## 4

THE "QUESTIONING" only lasted a few more minutes. Walt explained that he'd bought the chainsaw and the machete to work on the lot next door. Apparently, he had managed to acquire another large lot next to the bar. It had previously belonged to an eccentric small mom and pop operation. They specialized in home and garden stuff. Grew a lot of their own plants, shrubs, even some small trees in the lot behind their small shop. Walt got a quick sale from their estate and managed to keep word from getting out until the deal was accomplished. The real estate wasn't exactly a prime location, but it was good enough that there might have been other interested buyers if word got out.

He said he intended to expand the bar out into that area, maybe even make an outside bar and patio on part of the new land. He'd picked up the tools to clear out some of the old dead and dying brush as well as the thick grove of small trees. Of course, a good cop was going to check all of that out and do just what Jackson did when he pointed it out. "Just because you used them on wood doesn't mean they weren't used on a musician that got a little too friendly with your girlfriend."

Before anyone could jump on that little explosive bit of dialogue, a snarl of loud voices intruded through the closed door. Almost at the same instant all three of us moved for the door.

When we got back onto the main floor, we saw the band bunched up around two women who were the main source of all the noise.

One of the two was Ms. Consuelo, whom I believe I've pointed out was not at all deficient in the physical charms department. However, she stood on her proverbial pedestal several steps below that of the woman at whom she was yelling in full voice.

This one had the same coffee and cream coloring as her rival. Her hair was darker than a raven's wing and gleamed almost blue in the lighting of the stage. Even with the briefest of glimpses, I could tell she had a figure that probably took attention from swimsuit models. Skintight denim shorts hugged a tight waist and ended high enough to reveal almost the entirety of the kind of legs that dancers work most of their lives in hopes of achieving. At the end of the legs were wide little ankle boots with more chains wrapped around them and studs sparkling along spike heels at least four or five inches long. She also wore a leather vest that ended a few inches above a low slung black leather belt that sported shining metal studs and spikes that matched her leather wristbands and dog collar. The vest itself was open except for the very bottom button which was an inch or two above her pierced navel. Underneath the vest, there was nothing except a shiny metallic-looking bra and a whole lot of very warm and inviting girl.

Smoldering eyes were startlingly dark-chocolate colored

in a face that made you think of jungles and pyramids and maybe wanton drum-fueled rituals under a moonlit sky. The centerpieces of that orgiastic face were lips that looked full and ripe and capable of anything from nuzzling an ear to launching osculatory fireworks. At present they were erupting like some Latin American Vesuvius in a tirade comprised of equal parts Spanish, English, and venom.

Before we got across the dance floor, the volcano had gone from rumbles and spitting to a full-blown eruption. Connie went straight for the hair with one hand and the face with the other claw. She missed the rake which was probably for the best. They were both mad enough to kill without someone getting their face messed up.

For her own part, the newcomer was doing her best to keep those nails away from her eyes and fancy makeup. She slapped the offending hand away and sidestepped but was brought up short by her trapped and entangled tresses. Connie snatched her head hard enough that I half expected the sound of some vertebrae popping. Instead, I got a very loud word in Spanish that I didn't know but could guess at with a reasonable degree of success. It would be a word used more often by sailors and stevedores and less often in a church or garden party.

Little Ms. "duck and slide so far" didn't like the hair pulling. She spun and got her hand into Connie's hair. That's where it usually turns into a painful if comedic looking game of ponytail tug-of-war. Connie's opponent had other ideas. She drove a few inches of spike heel at my waitress's instep. Consuela's reflexes were barely enough to get her out of that one. She spun to the side and met an incoming fist. It wasn't a slap or a flash of the claws. This was a semi-professional looking left hook. The stranger even got her shoulders and hip into it. From several feet away, it resounded like a shot. It was one helluva punch. It was good enough for Connie to stumble back and for both of them to release the hair. Despite the slight glaze to her eyes, Consuela lurched back towards the other girl with the clear intention of perpetrating something more serious than a hair tug this time.

Walter got a grip on one side of Connie at the same time Jackson got her by the opposite arm. The band seemed to have their collective hands full restraining the other girl. Some of our other staff had arrived as well since I could see a flash of color here and there behind all of the black denim and leather that signified the band. As for good old Mouse aka Magnus? I'll take on bikers all day long. Sometimes I'll handle two or three of the Harley crowd at a time. But it takes a lot of incentive for me to get involved between a metal groupie and a bar waitress. Double that amount of incentive if they are both fiery Latinas.

Jackson's Bellow of Doom came down like a word from on high and stopped both girls in their tracks. Out of the corner of my eye, I saw Connie get one last vindictive little shove in as the other started to turn away. For a breath or two, it looked like hostilities were going to resume. But the other waitresses intervened as well as the least experienced of my security guys. They were big, young, muscular fellows; probably second or third-string linebackers. The first-string guys don't usually work in bars. We politely ignore any rumors about under the table scholarships and other financial transactions. If these inexperienced second-stringers stayed with the job around here they'd learn when not to put their hands in the beehive. Men you can predict. Angry women, well they can be...questionable.

Once the girls were firmly isolated from each other and surrounded by their various camps of followers, supporters, or restrainers, I walked over to see what Jackson had planned next.

"About time hotshot. I thought you were the heavy muscle around here. Why did the band and college kids have to separate those two?" Even the hardened eyes of the portly policeman looked a little stunned and wary as he gazed back and forth between the two simmering beauties.

"I know what you mean" My voice was intentionally a shade frustrated. "It was just a waitress and a groupie that had barely got to slapping. They weren't even to *serious* hair pulling yet. The waitresses should have handled it. I save my guys for bigger fish."

I held the face as long as I could while the cop slowly craned his head around to look me in the eye. Finally, his stunned expression was too much and I felt a broad grin spread recklessly across my face. "Next time warn me when I have bats coming at my head and maybe I won't jack with you in return."

"Next time I'll be swinging the bat." His snort was at least tempered with a chuckle so I guess I wasn't too far off in my guess about his sense of humor. "I'll take your waitress first. You make sure the other one doesn't go anywhere." He chuckle snorted one more time as he hooked both thumbs behind the wide utility belt straining to hold in his burgeoning paunch and moved towards the Connie camp. Is that a snuckle or a chort? Maybe the root of the word chortle even? Hey, look at that. You can learn grammar and English in the middle of the afternoon in a bar.

Jackson was still snuckling when I turned towards the table with ticked off band members and an even angrier senorita. I won't say I approached the other table gingerly. I also won't try and claim I was comfortable with the whole scenario. Not only was there the insanely hot and hot-headed Hispanic to deal with, but I also hadn't forgotten that one of those guys at her table had taken a bat to my skull very recently. Nor had I forgotten the hate he'd shot at me after his buddies cleaned the knacker-knock induced yarf off of his face.

The vocalist was still shooting me plenty of hate. But I hardly noticed. My attention was at least temporarily shanghaied by the girl sitting behind his right shoulder. I don't mean she jumped up and demanded attention. I mean from the moment my eyes landed on this *new* newcomer, I lost interest in everything else including the two lovelies who had been fighting just moments earlier.

I already mentioned Connie's placement on the pedestal scale relative to the other Latina lovely. Either of them could have held their own in a room full of swimsuit models. The new one was up on the celestial balcony looking down at the other two poor girls on their plain pedestals. Where they were all dark-chocolate, ebon black, and cappuccino; she was cream and strawberries and ginger and cinnamon and everything a man dreams about finding and never expects or even hopes that he will. Even sitting I could tell she would be a good several inches taller than the other two. Instead of gleaming blue-black, she had hair that barely missed being brick red. It wasn't auburn, or bronze or strawberry blond or anything in between. If anything, I'd say it was scarlet polished amber, maybe a blood amber? I've never heard of such a stone but that's what I'd call this color. The eyes sealed my fate when I got closer. They snuck over and ambushed me in the middle of the same head that a bat had failed to even significantly dent.

Her eyes were probably what people would call hazel. I don't know though, to me they were malachite and jade and amber and sapphire and topaz all together or maybe shifting into and out of one another constantly. They were sun-warmed kisses and laughter on a summer breeze and a roaring fireplace on a cold rainy day. They were just... magick. I barely saw the rest of her enough to register that she too was built to a scale that other women shouldn't have to compete with. Her waist was just right to support everything above it. And there was plenty of interesting stuff above it. Below the waist was invisible behind the table.

Wait? Behind the table? Wasn't there a glaring leather-clad vocalist in front of her before? Yea you guessed it. He wasn't in front of her. He was in front of me. Clenched teeth and a big blue throbbing vein in his forehead told me this guy had neither forgotten nor forgiven that dirty punch in the parking lot. Oh well, looked like we weren't going to be friends I guess.

"We got unfinished business runt. Why don't we settle while the cop's not looking?!" He sprayed the hate more than spoke it. I felt a little mist of spittle close the space between us. A little yack flavored breath wafted along with it. Both of his hands were knotted into fists tight enough to whiten his knuckles.

That's okay. I've dealt with some anger, some rage, even a little true heart-deep hate in my time. I do not, however, like the spitting part. After the first outburst, I started to brush past him. It was just bad luck that the space was narrow and as has been already mentioned I am not even slightly narrow. I guess that's why my shoulder and more importantly a muscle reinforced forearm and elbow "bumped" into his solar plexus and sent that next breath out rather precipitously and without any of the intended vitriol spewing forth.

It also had the happy coincidence of being relatively invisible to his friends behind him. From my angle, he turned a little purple from lack of air and abruptly sat down. That was fine with me as long as hostilities were temporarily in abeyance. I tried to get another look at the red-haired amazon as I went past, but she had turned around to get a glass of water for her poor bullied friend. I guess maybe she either saw or guessed that there was more to the incident than a sudden decision on his part to have a seat.

Before I caught her eye, I felt a hand on my sleeve. When I looked down, I saw long and artistic looking fingers that belonged to Connie's new nemesis. "Hey cholo, you ain't coming to give me trouble too are you?"

She neither looked nor sounded particularly worried about the idea of more trouble from my quarter. As a matter of fact, I got the idea she would welcome a little more diversion. This one had the temper that would have gone with the other one's red hair. I opted for discretion in the face of superior numbers and hostility this time. "No trouble ma'am. The policeman over there sent me to come ask ever so politely if you would stay right here until he gets a chance to hear your story. So you can count on no trouble from me at all. I'm just a simple messenger."

She looked me openly in the eyes as if seeking to divine the truth or fiction in my statement. Then her eyes went over to where the other groupie was administering water to her sputtering band member. For a minute when she looked back at me I thought I saw something like approval. I definitely saw a smile and an arched eyebrow. "A meek and mild sheep delivering the sheepdog's message? I do not think so mister wolf."

For a minute I felt my spine stiffen. Was there a spark in those eyes of something else? Apparently, she'd seen through my charade about brushing past the idiot singer.

What else had she seen with those witchlit eyes? For witchlit they were. Behind the dark chocolate was a fire, an inferno of faith or passion or creativity. Or maybe knowledge and wisdom and what people in other times and places have called Magic or witchcraft.

I forced myself to breathe normally and let my spine loosen up again. The first order of business was to ignore her odd references and knowing gaze. The second was to divert her from whatever delving or seeking she was doing. Looking at a spot just below those entrancing eyes I dug up a reply.

"Sorry, that's me. Just another sheep obeying the law." I worked hard to keep my eyes from hers while trying to sound inoffensive and maybe a little less than bright. "Hey just between the two of us though. What was the beef about?"

It seemed that if diversion was the goal, that question worked perfectly. "That puta got my husband killed! She's going to admit it. She's going to admit everything. She cheated with my husband and then she got him killed by the dirty old goat over there. I want them both to pay! That's what the beef is!"

Oh yea, we really needed another angle to this mess. A wife ought to murk things up even more. The worst part was, the murkier it got, the less chance I had of sorting things out. And if things didn't get sorted out, my boss would likely spend the golden years of his life in prison.

## 5

I WAS SAVED from having to come up with anything witty to say in response to the newly widowed Mrs. Brewster's revelations. Yea that was the drummer. I was informed later that our band was comprised of: Abel Brewster on drums, Seamus McKinnon lead vocals and backup guitar, wee brother Sean McKinnon on bass and backup vocals, and Tavi Raske playing guitar on the ragged edge of disastrously fast. There was now a new local guy sitting in on the drums.

I knew Brian from around the clubs. He was decent and played some of the same metal stuff as the band. Most importantly from their standpoint, he was immediately available. I was skeptical, but the sound guy assured me he had enough recorded stuff to overlay the drummer's parts. If Brian couldn't cut it the sound guy would lower his volume and lay the old drum track over it. It sounded kind of like cheating to me. But then again I had never liked Milli Vanilli and liked looking at Jessica Simpson more than I liked her little sister singing.

I also found out Brewster's widow was Jacqueline Brewster, maiden name of Quintero. She was from somewhere down in central or South America. The tale of her travels was convoluted and I only got to hear part of what she had to tell Officer Jackson.

Most of my time was spent either repeating reassurances or answering questions fielded by little Pilar aka Connie and her on-again-off-again boyfriend, my boss. I might have spent most of that time trying to get another glimpse of the redhead who had turned to sit with her back to me. So I was totally frustrated in my compulsive attempts to garner further and more revealing looks at the captivating young lady.

In maybe a quarter of an hour that seemed a great deal longer, everyone was settled down and Jackson was on his way out of the door with a final obligatory comment about staying where he could find us all. I saw the band head back to their RV to get ready for the show. The widow and the redhead went with them. That left me very little to do until the place got busier.

I considered doing a little investigating on my own. Don't get me wrong. I'm no Hawaiian hotshot investigator. I'm just a plain everyday fellow who's been around the block more than once. Maybe a lot more than once.

When I told Walt that I was headed out he adamantly refused to let me go. Between the body, the cops, his role as the prime suspect, and a very distraught Pilar Consuelo, poor Walter was at the end of his rope. He wanted me handy and he wanted to sit and cry his woes out to me until opening time. Oh well, he writes the paychecks and it was his fate on the line. For the time being, I let him vent.

By the time Walter had gone over everything he could think of a dozen or so times, I knew very little more than I did when I went into his office. Only the fact that the bar was starting to fill up got me out of babysitting duty. Walter didn't really have any choice. There weren't enough people to go around. Nobody could stand in for me at the door. More to the point, most of my guys were good at corralling people but none of them would be the best replacement for me in any kind of serious conflict. The Norns must have turned a kindly eye my way. Not only did everyone behave like responsible little partiers, I got to meet the redhead.

She came through the side door with the rest of the band's crew. I think she might have even carried some cables and gear in for them to make it legit. Once the lights came up though and Tavi hit the opening notes to their first number, Red went her own way. I was at the door when I felt a tap on my shoulder and turned around to fall into those eyes again. With all of the lights of a decent amateur stage show going off behind her it was even harder to tell what color they were, or rather what colors. Just like before, the colors of her eyes seemed to swirl and shift and interact with each other in a whole spectrum of greens and blues and golden browns. Again, I got the impact or maybe just the idea, that they were deep and thoughtful and humorous all at the same time.

The humorous part was plain to see. Before I recovered from the surprise at seeing her up close, she waved her hand in front of my eyes. There was just the slightest hint of some British or Irish or maybe Scottish in her voice. "Are the stage lights about to give you seizures or something? I hear those strobes and flashing ones can make people have fits. Or maybe you're just a little slow of wit eh? I must say you didn't seem this slow when you put Seamus down with that cheap shot to the brisket earlier today."

I winced. I mean I had wondered at the time if anybody noticed. In particular, I suspected that she was aware of the brief jab to McKinnon's wind. Well, there was no more question about it. Before I could start to explain she waved long fingers at me again. I idly noticed an elaborate design of some sort on her manicured nails. "No explanations or apologies. I've seen him sprayin' spittle and raging about like some crazed bull before. Many's the time I've wanted to put one in his breadbasket and sit him down to simmer a while. It was a pleasure to see someone else do it for once."

The silent laughter in her voice was enough to calm my surprise. I caught my breath and then I found my own tongue. "I was really hoping nobody saw that. We'd just had a little tiff shortly before. To be honest, I probably should have avoided him altogether, but the cop sent me to relay a message. For some reason, I completely forgot about him until he was in my face. I probably overreacted too. It's not been a great couple of days."

Her grimace matched mine at the mutual reminder of last night's shocking tragedy. "I can understand that. Have the police told you anything yet? Do they believe that witch Jacque? For that matter what do you think?"

What did I think? I thought there was a lot going on here that didn't make sense to me. I also thought there was potential to cause misery to a lot of folks. It also promised me an immeasurable headache in the process. Living off the radar is possible even in a town like Austin. Keeping out of sight in the middle of a murder investigation is something else entirely. But the most important rule of keeping to the shadows is, don't talk too much.

While I was trying to think of a polite and innocent way of answering that question, an almost apologetic look came over her face. "Oh, I am so sorry. Sometimes words just come tumbling out before I get a chance to think about them. Of course, you're on your boss's side and don't want to say anything one way or the other to someone with the band. Forget I asked."

The contrition in her eyes was real and plucked at something deep inside me. That's another thing that does not go well with living like I do. Internal plucking is contraindicated when you live with as many secrets as me. She stepped forward and I had the distinct impression that she was about to hug me. She might have had the same impression because she stopped rather awkwardly and then her face turned a shade or two lighter than the red in her hair.

"Oh! I forgot what I came over for." She waved that intriguingly expressive hand in front of me again, the hand with the odd decorations on long and slender fingers. "They told me you'd stamp my hand so I could get back in. I need to run out and grab a couple of things but wanted to make sure I got back in."

I opened the door behind my stool for her. I sit beside a side entrance. The line from the front door comes down a fairly long hall and stops where someone at the inner door can check IDs and collect a cover charge when applicable. Beside that inner door is the one leading out to the back of the parking lot. Before she worked around me and out though I reached and laid a hand on her wrist. With my other hand, I signaled one of the big linebackers over. "Don't worry about a stamp. You just come back any time with or without the band. If anyone tries to stop you or asks any questions tell them to take it up with Mouse."

My sharp young bouncer-in-training popped over as quickly as possible at my signal. It might have been out of respect for my nebulous authority. It was more likely a result of the girl I was talking to. His eyes glazed over a little as he got a closer look at the tall lovely lady waiting by the door. She was probably several years older than him. And from the look on his face that didn't matter a single bit. Well, I couldn't blame him. I'm quite a bit older and have seen a veritable cornucopia of truly beautiful women. Austin is home to more than its share of finely built and even better maintained young ladies. And Austin is just one of many cities I've been in for one reason or another. If this girl could reach down and steal my breath, there's no way of knowing just how badly she was affecting the youngster's ability to breathe.

He was resilient though. Maybe it was all the hard training in weight rooms and practice fields. "Sup Mouse?"

"Bodie, I want you to take the young lady out to her car and make sure she's safe. If she wants to come back in, you stay with her until she grabs what she needs, then bring her back. If she has to leave the lot..." When I looked she shook her head with a solemn look that was utterly at odds with the twinkle of merriment in her eyes. "Okay, you don't have to come back without her. Just provide an escort back in when she's done with her errands."

When she put her warm hand on his forearm I felt something in myself both snarl at the other male, and sigh at the loss of her wrist under my own hand. She perked my spirits back up by turning to offer her hand for something more like a squeeze than a shake. "Thank you both. I'm sure it's not necessary but thanks. And I'll only keep him a moment or two."

After that, they were gone. In an atypical reaction, I was instantly impatient for them to get back. My impatience was short-lived. I had only turned away three or four minors and admitted a dozen times that many young partiers when there was a knock on the side door. I let them back in and saw her give him a friendly finger squeeze too. That inner voice grumbled at me when I saw him grin down at her and say something I couldn't hear over some whining seventeen-year-old trying to con his way past me. Whatever Bodie said, she laughed and gave him another of those interesting squeezes before kissing the big oaf on the cheek and pushing him back towards the main floor of the club.

It took a minute before I could stop planning exactly how to most effectively humiliate a large athletic and good-natured kid that had never done anything to me that I can recall. Yea, the girl had an unprecedented effect on me. When I got my eyes uncrossed I saw her standing nearby again. She seemed to be looking at me and laughing. "Did I keep him too long? You look about ready to teach him that lesson all young men must learn about age and treachery. Don't blame him. I had a hard time finding everything I needed. All done and in my bag though!"

She hefted a rather formidable piece of leather that was somewhat short of a full-sized suitcase, but not much. "Speaking of which. Do you mind if I tuck it behind the counter here? It's a tad unwieldy for toting in crowded rooms much less crowded dance floors."

"Go ahead, tuck away." I refrained from growling or saying anything imprudent about the lunkhead athlete. She seemed to accept my silence for assent though and quit worrying about her escort's demise.

"My name is Maureen. You can call me Mary. That's what the boys in the band call me." Her smile was wide and absolutely without guile or any resentment for the trouble I'd had with the singer. She didn't even appear to care that we seemed to be sitting on two different sides when it came to the band and my boss. Most of all, her smile was directed just at me and not everyone else or even anyone else in the room. I liked it. I liked that smile and her complete attention quite a bit.

Something about that was supposed to bother me. I told that little "something" to mind its own business as she continued. "And I know they call you Mouse right?"

At my nod, she smiled anew and asked the inevitable question. "Umm. Mouse doesn't sound very tough for a bouncer does it?"

I'd heard that question, or variations upon that question, dozens of times. Maybe someday I'll print up business cards with the entire explanation. But then again probably not... shadowed past and paranoia, remember?

"One of the waitresses did it. She never could get Magnus right. Started calling me Dormouse since Mouse sounds like Magnus. I sit quietly at the door and never say anything or bother anyone unless I am absolutely forced to. Hence, Dormouse. The others picked it up and shortened it down to Mouse." Maybe I could make a brief concise note card without all the secrecy.

Leaning forward with her elbows on the top of my little podium she nodded. It wasn't necessarily eager but it was an attentive nod and her eyes were locked on mine for the brief explanation. That look made me wish I'd cleaned up a little more after the scuffle. Maybe even changed my shirt.

I had to turn away and stop one youngster that couldn't have been over fifteen or sixteen trying to take advantage of my distraction. That's never been effective that I know of. Then again, I've never had quite as effective a distraction as Maureen. With my open hand blocking him at chest height I shook my head. "Nope, friend. We already discussed the ID that claims you're a thirty-something Marine veteran."

She gave him a smile that was well worth the disappointment of not getting in the bar. At least I thought it was worth the price of dismissal. Once he was gone and there was a pause my redhead leaned down to a level with me.

She whispered in a voice almost as enticing as her perfume. "Aren't you ashamed of destroying a young man's dreams of alcohol and loose women?"

I found us looking eye to eye despite her stooped posture. Despite the proximity, I managed a reply. "Some dreams have to ripen a little bit. I'm probably doing a public service by keeping the youngsters from embarrassing themselves before they're ready for the big league."

"Oh, so it's for their own good you're telling me?" Her laugh was warm and comfortable. And I discovered that I was dismayingly comfortable with her as well. I rarely minded when a woman was taller than me. Let's face it. A towering giant I ain't. A number of women do not enjoy being around shorter men. Maureen was not one of them. Standing side by side it was immediately apparent that she topped me by a good three or four inches. I fervently hoped that that fact wouldn't bother her. I truly *appreciated* when she didn't act bothered or even aware of the difference.

We were interrupted by another group coming in. These were visibly old enough to drink. Age verification was only part of my job though. Maureen seemed amused by my check of bandanas hanging from back pockets on two of the men. Her voice was dripping with barely contained amusement. "So you're a fashion consultant as well as a public servant to police teenage embarrassment?"

"It has nothing to do with fashion." I couldn't tell if she was making fun, so I decided to put her straight rather than take umbrage.

"The bandanas are sometimes tied to a padlock or something similar." I fished one out to show her. "It works like an old flail or ball and chain type weapon. The bandana gives it flexibility and range plus it ends up having a very fast swing speed. A simple little one-pound lock at the end of a foot-long chain or bandana hits hard enough to dent metal or crush bone."

It took some effort, but I restrained myself from whacking anything nearby to illustrate the point. I was long past the age when young men strut like bantams for a pretty girl. Yea, sure I was. Instead of giving the improvised weapon an impressive slash through the air I handed it to her and let her swing it gently a few times with a shake of her head. "And people try to bring these into a pub for a few drinks and a dance?"

"I've seen folks attempt to smuggle just about anything short of a bazooka into the club." I'd like to think my shrug was eloquent. What can you say to people from a different culture though? "The guys with a gun are usually the easiest to persuade. They either weren't thinking about it being a bar or didn't remember they were carrying the damned thing. This is Texas after all and half of them carry weapons just for tradition's sake I think."

I wasn't in the mood to start talking politics with a citizen of merry old disarmed Britain. Politics gets messy too easily and more than anything I wanted Maureen to like me. For that matter, I probably wouldn't volunteer that I have a license for my own guns and often have one handy.

She accepted my exaggeration with only a slight reservation. "So Texas is as rowdy as they all say? Cowboys and horses and shootouts even in this day and age?"

That wasn't exactly what I meant. It also came close to that whole political topic I was trying to avoid. Rather than answer and risk stepping on my chances I pulled out the box with the night's haul. "Let's see. No guns or saddles. Not even a spur in here from those rowdy Tejas cowhands. Mostly I've got a bunch of knives idiots forgot they were carrying. Let's see, there are a couple of wallets on chains and no less than three pepper spray canisters. Not a single colt peacemaker to be found."

"How utterly disappointing. You've gone from crushing teenage boy dreams to ruining my image of you raucous and untamed Texans. However will you repay me?" Her grin hinted at amusement as well as something a little warmer and closer to our baser human nature. Or maybe that was my own baser human instincts putting in their tuppence worth. There seemed just enough slack in the pace of customers that I thought maybe I could take a few minutes to investigate that train of thought.

I called Bodie over and gave him the little clicker that let us know how close we were to being in trouble with the fire marshal. We might go over the limit once or twice in a blue moon. But the club was too important to shut down just because we wanted to let in a score or two extra clientele. To the younger guys, taking over the door was a different kind of responsibility. It's not that way in every bar. But in 'Styxx it was a mark of honor to watch the door. Bodie swelled up to his full impressive, young, good-looking, muscular height and smiled his gratitude. I wasn't jealous there for a minute. Nor was I immature enough to pop him in those perfect teeth. Barely mature enough, but I quelled the urge.

"Okay Lady, Maureen I mean. I am now on break. Care to take a walk and get away from the smoke and the racket?" When I recalled that she was *with* the band in question I mentally winced. Perhaps "racket" was not the proper word. It didn't seem to bother her too much though. She bent over to tuck that big overnight bag or yeti sized purse further out of sight then straightened up to nod. For a second I thought she was going to take my arm. But then again maybe she too was recalling that she was with the band. An almost undetectable shake of the head told me that we wouldn't be holding hands tonight.

That was probably for the best. This one had gotten through my defenses much too easily. A brisk walk in the cool air seemed in order. Once outside we did just that. At least we started the walk briskly. Soon enough though we were just sauntering and enjoying a very clear and bright sky under one of those rare Texas moons that look close enough to reach up and polish. Somehow, we stayed on the quieter side of the club.

We talked very little at first. The night was nice enough to simply enjoy. And I fancy that the company just made it better. In short order we found ourselves strolling past the fence of the overgrown lot Walter recently purchased.

Several sections of the fence had already been removed between the two properties. That gave us access to a surprisingly comfortable little grotto. If I were a girl alone I might not go into the shadows there. But on a night where the full moon has turned all the surfaces into pools of black or silver-lined silhouettes, the place was enchanting. A running stream wandered and murmured its way through the lot to empty into a small pond.

The water there barely stirred from the current. It was inky black and reflected the heavens above as if a section of the night sky had been trapped in a hole for us to look down on. The trees themselves barely rustled in the infrequent gust of wind. Yet those same slight breezes lifted the aroma of dozens of different flowers into a provocative perfume that any cosmetic company would pay a small fortune to duplicate. Nights like that are few and far between. Somehow we found ourselves face to face in a little bit of grey shadow just inside the missing fence.

I couldn't help myself. I'm not sure I would have tried to

stop the moment even if she'd said something. But she didn't say anything; she just flowed into my arms as if it was her idea instead of mine. Who knows, maybe it was. All I knew was one minute we were walking and talking quietly, and the next minute our lips were together and there wasn't a building nearby or even a city around us. For one long breathless minute, there were just two people with two mouths telling each other much more than had been said previously. Or maybe not...maybe I was the only one getting messages. But I'd like to think differently. A moment like that should last forever. They never do. This one sure didn't.

"Madailéin Maureen!" The voice was deep and loud and absurdly angry. It was also familiar. I turned with a weary sigh as she stepped instantly back and away from me to face none other than the same man I punched into doughy junk earlier in the day. While I waited for whatever was to come, he snarled something at her in Irish Gaelic.

Now there was a time when I understood and even spoke passable Gaelic. That Gaelic and this version had little in common. Oh, some of the words still made sense, but he was speaking so fast and with such an accent that I could barely make out half the words that weren't profanities. I'm pretty sure I caught all the profanities. She snapped a few words back just as fast and furious.

When he reached for her I shifted between them. For my efforts, I received an icy glare of feminine disdain that did more damage than the singer, his band, and their bat all together had accomplished. I may not be a genius, but even I know when it's time to take a step back. So I stepped back. He reached for her next and got more than the glare. She slapped his hand aside and shoved him away.

Then with a fit of very deliberate and calculating anger, she reached for a pen poking out of one of her pockets.

Taking her sweet time, Maureen wrote her name and a cell phone number on the back of my hand before she stalked across the empty space between two properties and disappeared towards the parking lot. My protective urge was to follow her. Nightclub parking lots are not the best place to be a female alone near closing time.

I never got the chance. Vocals there shoved me back and snarled something that stopped me in my tracks. "Did she even bother telling you her last name was McKinnon? Or didn't you care that you were stepping in where you had no right?"

When he said it, I remembered her hand when she'd almost reached for mine. There was no band, but there was a line where one had been worn for quite some time. I guess it was something I hadn't wanted to notice. While I sat there and stewed in my own thoughts, he made his move. This time it wasn't a bat, it was the padlock on the bandana. He must have picked it up from my stash at the podium, because he also had one of the knives.

I was still reeling from the thunderous impact behind my ear when I felt the knife go in. Either he was very lucky, or someone had taught him a thing or two. The slender blade went between my fourth and fifth ribs on the right side. It went in slick as a whistle, blade lined up parallel to the ribs so it wouldn't get stuck on a bone.

I felt the little pop when the lung went. There was no mistaking the weird wet wheezing that started when he pulled the knife out. That's when my breath started to fade fast as I lost the volume in that part of the lung. Sucking chest wounds are an undeniable pain in more places than the chest. I firmly believe they're called "sucking" chest wounds less because they pull air in and collapse the lung and more because it just sucks to have one.

The immediate danger was from panic. If I panicked, this guy could pick me apart at his leisure while I flailed around and lost consciousness. Panic is pretty natural though. In most branches of the military, they cover chest wounds in basic first aid. Every jarhead, squid, and flatfoot is taught what to do in the event of a sucking chest wound. The problem is, reading about a lung collapsing does not compare with the feel of your breath fading, the eerie sensation of a shift within your chest as the unequal pressure moves stuff around. Even your throat shifts in response to the changing air pressure. Then there's the approach of good ole mister unconsciousness.

Things start to slow down around you in response to the adrenalin. You, however, can't move as fast as your thoughts, so your own actions become sluggish and frustrating. That makes you feel just a tad helpless since you've been *taught* that you're seconds away from fading to black. Like I said, panic is natural when you've never done more than read about the wound. So I guess it's macabrely humorous or maybe just ironic...that I know precisely what a sucking chest wound feels like.

That means I didn't panic. I didn't flail around or start searching blindly for help that wasn't around. No, I was certain that I had a good thirty or forty second interval before I lost track of everything. That gave me time to take care of the asshole with the sticker.

I have perhaps hinted or insinuated that I am built like an oak stump knotted with muscle. I don't know that I've mentioned how much training I have in various forms of violence. Given the weapons in my opponent's hands, he would have been dead within seconds had I wanted his corpse on my hands. I did not have his weapons but I still had years of experience and training on my side. Even before he had the knife pulled halfway back for another stab I reacted. I grabbed his sleeve, lifted it high in the air, stepped under and then whipped it diagonally down across my shoulders. At the same time, I stepped back until my hip hit him at about mid-thigh. When I pivoted on one heel, he stretched out over my shoulder, so when I bent forward and hauled on that hand he left his feet. To assist the launch, I kind of bounced once and then turned full circle to bring him down and around. Since he'd been rude enough to stick a knife in my chest, I helped his momentum by throwing my own weight into the fall. We landed with him on bottom, and my elbow and upper arm across his chest.

He lost more air than I had and lost it a lot quicker. That coupled with the hard cobblestones of the garden path was enough to take him out of the fight for the foreseeable future. I was more thankful than I'd been for anything in a long time. That burst of violent physical activity depleted most of the oxygen still in my system. With my awareness already fading, I fumbled at the guy's pockets until I found what I was looking for. He was a smoker like most of that type. The cigarette just seems to go with the look. What I needed wasn't the tobacco though. I needed the cellophane wrapper.

Clean or not, that cellophane was airtight. I don't worry too much about infection. I do worry about a lung that is getting smaller and smaller as outside air presses it down from a wound. Using the old battlefield technique, I pressed the cellophane down around the wound and held it on three sides. That left the fourth side opened as a kind of one-way seal. When I breathed out, the cellophane closed over the wound. When I breathed in, the air around the outside of the lung pushed out and let the lung re-expand just a little bit more. After several breaths, I could feel my head getting a little clearer.

With luck, now I could get some help. Maybe the cops could come take the little maniac away while I decided whether or not to press charges. On the other hand, I did not want to see any doctors. A paramedic wasn't too bad. I could use some immediate running repairs. Ambulances tend to carry a much better seal than my improvised cellophane valve. They have antibiotics, supplemental oxygen, and maybe a large-bore syringe to go ahead and remove all the excess air in the pleural cavity.

If I could get that much help then I was pretty confident I'd make it. What I made was about three steps. I guess little brother or somebody else was around, because whoever got me this time, hit a grand slam. I don't know if it was the bat again, or a two-by-four, or the bumper of a semi. All I know was it left a very solid sensation in the wake of that very solid sounding "thunk". They say it sounds like a melon getting thumped. To me, it sounded like somebody hit a coconut for left field with an old-fashioned Louisville slugger. This time my coconut sailed out of the ballpark. The last thing I remember was the chilled hard cobblestone under my cheek and a fading view of elder brother McKinnon out cold just a few feet in front of me.

## 6

THE COBBLESTONE WAS STILL cold and hard when I woke up. The wind had picked up sometime in the interim though. It wasn't howling through the trees yet. But the trees themselves were swaying and rustling quite a bit more than before. I tried to push myself off the ground but fell forward after just a few inches. I barely felt the impact on my face. It was nothing compared to the immediate searing bolt of pain that shot through my head like a hammering blow of thunder itself.

Nausea and rising bile curled me up for a long minute. Nothing came up, but it certainly traveled part of the journey. Slowly the tightness in my throat and stomach eased enough for me to get uncurled and drag myself over to a crude concrete bench. With a fit of growing anger in my belly, I pulled myself up and onto the bench. It took some time and concentration but finally, I was on my feet. They weren't very steady but they would carry me around.

I fumbled to find my phone and check the time. It was well after closing time. In fact, people would start getting up and ready for the commute in a couple of short hours. Using the phone for light, I looked around. There was nobody else in the immediate vicinity, so I guess McKinnon's brother or accomplice had helped him up and away after they handled me. They did a grand job of it. I felt thoroughly handled.

That's about when I remembered the stab wound in my chest. The cellophane was caked to the wound with blood. That's probably the main reason I hadn't just slipped away in the night. Exposure is bad enough. Exposure on half a lung is a very bad time indeed. There were several bruises and contusions in addition to the knife wound and the assorted lumps on my skull. I winced as prying fingers proved it was not one lump but two or maybe three. The latest insults to my cranium had missed the first lump by several inches.

I called a taxi and made my way towards the street. It took some effort to get anywhere except on the ground. I fell twice more getting out of the garden. Both times something broke open near the wound and started the whole wheezing and bubbling again. Good thing I heal better than most. By the time I got to the street the bleeding had stopped and I seemed to be operating on somewhere between one and a half and two lungs again.

With the help of a streetlight and a parking meter, I managed to stay on my feet until the taxi got there. I know my bike was just a couple of parking lots over. But it didn't seem prudent to try and drive with a probable concussion and the potential to pass out from oxygen depletion at any random moment. Hel it didn't seem prudent to even try and walk back to the bike.

Fortunately, Austin *is* weird just like the bumper stickers read. I barely got a few rough looks from the driver before he saw the wad of cash. Like I said, I like cash. Most service people like cash too. Cash doesn't always show up on a tax form or any kind of receipt. He never even gave me any lip or complained about the ride not ending in an emergency room. Smart guy, he got a helluva tip.

Staggering towards the bedroom, I stopped for a couple of necessities and hit the head. Even with the blood loss, and being kicked around my back and sides, the old kidneys seemed to be working ok. Just to make sure, I circled back to the fridge and downed a Gatorade then slugged down some ibuprofen before heading back to the bed.

Grimmr joined me with a fairly worried expression on his face for a dog. I noticed even the crow was at the bars on the near end of his aviary as I passed. "What are you looking at, cricket breath?"

The way he cocked his head and turned from side to side, I had the uncanny impression that he was looking at my wounds rather intently for a bird. That was probably my concussion and a little paranoia brought on by the close call. Either way, he didn't add anything to the conversation.

When you're in my shoes a close brush with death makes one think very uneasy thoughts about crows and wolves and vengeful divine figures. Rafe was no Hugin or Munin flying errands for Odin. For one thing, he was about half the size of a normal northern European raven. For another...I knew what the other two looked like. Don't ask. Just believe me when I say, I do *not* plan to see either of them again any time soon. But I promise you that they normally appear quite a bit larger than even a normal European raven.

Grimmr beat me to bed and took up his customary eighty percent of the surface while he watched my antics with a concerned gaze. Instead of dropping in and passing out immediately, I proceeded to wash most of the blood off and clean up everywhere that was beat up with a blessedly warm and soft washrag. Once most of the muck had disappeared from my wounds I got down to the next step.

I filled a small brandy snifter with mead, herbs, and spices then placed it over a tea-light to mull. The next stage was a crucial one. From among the supplies I brought I chose some baby's breath, a bit of antler, and a circle of bark from a willow tree. Focusing on my needs, I quietly began a low growling chant under my breath. The first rune took all of six or seven seconds to sing, the rest took even longer. In all, I prepared three runes, Ansuz, Algiz, and Uruz. As I *galdored* each rune the first time, I "carved" one of each in the bark, the bone, and the air above the bunch of small flowers.

Chanting the next two repetitions of each rune, I dipped one of several goose quills in a special mix of herbs, mead, henna, and a few drops of my blood. As each rune resonated from my gut and vibrated its way into the low growling chant, I drew the corresponding rune across my chest near the wound and the affected lung. When I was done the three runes lay connected but still recognizable as individual components. They were inked in what would have been a henna style "tattoo" that should have lasted for days or weeks. Any normal henna marking can last that long. I had no doubt these would be gone by morning. As a piece of art, it was all straight lines and primitive looking. However, this particular bit of primitive art contained what amounted to a newly created being of magic.

Maybe it was not exactly a "*being*". It was more like a living purpose; an entity of focus given birth by my will, my voice, my breath, and my intent. Those ingredients combined and I suppose gave it not only a purpose but possibly even life on some level. Once I felt that presence though, I put the bark, the bone, and flower in a small cauldron. A bit of mead followed, and then a larger dollop of fairly potent brandy. The brandy I set ablaze and let the flames lick up around the other parts of the working. A feeling of satisfaction came out of thin air and then the presence became a warm and friendly sensation in my skin. That warmth spread with amazing results.

Slowly the swelling and bruising faded until it looked days old instead of hours. The air expanded in my lung and the thin angry mouth of the wound closed into a thin and only annoyed-looking line. In short, I felt several blocks away from death rather than on its front doorstep. That's when I let my coiled tension relax.

As the muscles in my entire body unclenched, I let out a sigh and a groan or two. The henna markings were already fading on my chest. By morning I had no doubt the runes would be gone as the work was completed. Crawling into the bed, I let my mind slip away from the goal of getting home and getting help. Finally, I allowed myself to remember everything that led up to the fight.

Those last moments before the fight were...I don't have the words. There was surprise, and passion, intensity, intimacy, hope, and fear and I don't know what else. I do know that I hadn't expected to feel anything like that. And then to have it all shattered. How could I feel that way about another man's wife?

That thought stunned me worse than the bat to the head did. And the chain of thoughts that followed cut deeper than the knife. I had barely met this girl. We talked a couple of hours, took a walk, and shared one kiss. Okay, it was admittedly one helluva kiss. I can't recall ever having been kissed quite like that. But the emotions that went along with it. Those didn't make any kind of sense. It had been years since I even entertained an idle thought about a woman in any form of long term framework.

Let's face it, I am not a great prospect for commitment and long-term relationships. A man with my kind of worries is not a great choice for settling down behind white picket fences. It wouldn't be fair to the woman. Hel there is a lot about my situation that wouldn't be fair to a woman. So, I didn't deserve her. That doesn't change the fact that I wanted her more than anything I can recall. But she didn't deserve the kind of life I lead...or the albatross I toted around my neck. On the other hand, I thought she probably deserved better than some gangly rage-head riding around in a tour bus.

And if I had my chance he wouldn't be riding around in that bus much longer. I can be a tolerant man. But there's no percentage in letting people take multiple cheap shots at you with barely any consequences. That's why I planned to take the first opportunity and tear him to tiny little...I froze as it dawned on me.

I couldn't kill him. I couldn't do something that might hurt her. I don't know why, but this girl had hit me hard. Even the thought of seeing her hurt and in tears made me want to start tearing down the monsters and making every-thing alright. There was no scenario that made me want to *be* the monster that brought those tears.

Tired, sore, confused, and lonely as I had not been in a painfully long time I settled down and tried to sleep. It was a long time coming. And when it did come it was tattered and chaotic with half-remembered images of dreams. I could recall a raven, a wolf, a much more hostile and mystical version of the little garden I had been in, and runes that went by too quickly to grasp and recall. Finally, I remembered a dream phase in which an attacker shrouded all in black kept slamming something hard and unyielding into my head while repeating... "not for you".

## 7

THE POUNDING in my dreams morphed into a pounding at my door. A bleary look at the clock told me I'd only been in bed about three short hours. It was barely after nine in the morning. The thundering at the door and loud voices, however, showed no signs of abatement. With an effort, I sat up and stuck my sockless feet into combat boots. Without bothering to lace the boots I stood up and retrieved the combat knife. Sheathed, it went inside my waistband in the back. I was still wearing the 501's with a little mud and blood on them. Whoever was at the door didn't sound likely to want to wait while I changed though.

A holster on the back of my nightstand yielded a new revolver I'd had only a few weeks. This one was loaded with three .45 long-colts and two .410 shotgun shells. Each of the shells held a handful of projectiles too large to be called pellets, but really too small to be called bullets. I turned the cylinder until a .45 caliber round would rotate under the hammer when I cocked it or pulled the trigger. With the gun in my right hand behind my back, I opened the door wide enough to see out.

That was my intention. I got a little more than a crack to see out of though. As soon as the door was clear of its frame, I felt it shake with the impact of a good-sized body moving at a fair speed. The opening edge bounced back and took me full in the chest. It might have broken my nose again if I hadn't managed to get my entire head out of the way. As things stood, a door with a zealous young cop behind it was not gentle on the chest. For a minute I worried that there might still be enough damage for something to tear and start the whole bleeding and collapsing bit in my lungs again.

Like I said though, I'm a fast healer. It goes with the job and my last steady employer. I'll explain later. By the time I gathered my senses again, good old, or rather bad, young Officer Chuy was halfway in my house and there was a nice shiny new handgun inches from my nose. I heard him growl something that sounded suspiciously like a Dirty Harry quote. Then in a high pitched voice, I heard him yell, "Gun partner!"

Before that was all the way out of his mouth I'd opened my hand and held the stupid revolver with my thumb and forefinger only. And both of those digits were well away from the trigger.

"Whoa son." Jackson took the words right out of my mouth as he tried to squeeze his bulk through the half-opened door. His left hand reached out and pushed Gomez's hand and pistol down and away from me. His right hand closed over my gun hand and the revolver at the same time. I released it without a trace of hesitation.

As the two stepped into the room, I heard Gomez give an excited little snort. He jerked the knife and scabbard from my belt and I felt his breath behind my ear as he growled, "That what you used tough guy? Don't think cleaning it up is gonna save you either tough guy! We have guys that can pick up a single mote of dust in a conference room. They won't have any trouble finding some blood you missed. You sure as hell left enough at the scene, didn't you?"

That's exactly how the kid talked. It was like they had an elective course in TV cop dialogue in one semester of the academy. While I was still sorting out the random bits of information he'd blurted out so far, he gave me a particularly rude shove with his palm against my previously wounded shoulder. "I think he's trying to flee Jackson. What do you think? Is he evading arrest and trying to escape? Maybe he needs a little manual incentive. Help him calm down eh?"

Jackson's next words went a lot farther than the kid's intensity did when it came to destroying my morning. "The suspect does not seem a likely flight risk officer Gomez. Get his cuffs on while I read him his rights."

I don't like cuffs or chains or any kind of restraint. It's one of the few memories I have of my earlier years. It's not something I like thinking or talking about. I also don't have a lot of control over it. I subconsciously tightened the muscles in my arms and shoulders as Jackson droned out the familiar patter. "You have the right to remain silent. You have...ah hell, Chuy read this guy his rights and get him down for fingerprints and booking. I'll get a ride with one of the other cars after they give the house the once-over."

I was surprised to find that it bothered me to see that look of disgust on Jackson's face. Maybe we'd only met a day or two ago but I had him pegged for one of the good ones. For some strange reason, it seemed to matter what he thought of me. That was probably more surprising than the rude wake-up call at first light.

I blame the surprise and the lack of sleep for the next

several moments. At the back of the house, I heard but did not register someone coming in. Mr. Henderson the landlord was barely audible as he grumbled while letting them in. No doubt he grumbled at them the entire time just like he grumbled at me whether I was asking for some help with maintenance or paying the rent three months in advance. Mr. Henderson is a known grumbler.

No sooner had the door opened though than I heard the rumbling growl. *"GRIMMR, Fridur!"* That's what I started to yell. All I got out was *GRIMMR! FRI-ooooomph"*.

In my sudden haste, I had forgotten the ambitious youngster in charge of me. I was only half cuffed and he probably felt the tightening of my muscles or heard the inhale for my shout. Whichever he sensed was enough. Gomez clubbed me with a nice heavy flashlight. I guess I was lucky that he wasn't still holding the .40 caliber pistol. It was probably even odds whether I'd have been hit or shot.

Needless to say, with his flashlight for a weapon, I was not shot. On the other hand, I now had a beautiful fourth lump to add to my collection. Maybe I was getting used to them. This shot only addled me for a few seconds and I was aware of everything happening around me. I tried to focus on finishing the command. The focus was just out of reach though. I'm pretty sure I was unconscious on my feet and near panic at the thought that they were about to shoot my dog.

The high-pitched tones of surprise and fear from the back of the house told me at least one officer had discovered the source of that very low and rumbling growl. Before the dog leapt, and before the cop shot, we all heard a voice from inside. In fact, we heard a deep voice almost exactly like mine yell. "FRIDUR GRIMMR, FRIDUR!"

Gomez shoved me to the ground and finished slapping

the cuffs on my wrists. His actions were almost frenzied as he scanned wildly around the yard and the windows that opened onto the street. "Who the hell was that?! You didn't say there was anybody else inside!"

Now, what was I going to say to that? I didn't *know* there was anybody else inside? Apparently, someone randomly speaking *Icelandic* was giving my dog a command to "stand down" using a very old word for peace? "Well Chuy, you didn't ask did you?"

I'd rather have my toenails pulled out with rusty pliers than admit that I was just as clueless as the kid. Oddly enough the sarcasm seemed to settle him. He eyeballed my lumps and hefted the flashlight to decide where he wanted to start the next one. He appeared to decide against further mayhem and jerked me to my feet instead. "Who the hell else was inside there Mr. Gustaf?"

I tried to shrug but it isn't as easy as it sounds. I imagine with the cuffs in front you could remain reasonably eloquent with a shrug. With your wrists all but crossed in the handcuffs behind your back though you just get a rather indecipherable motion. "Honestly Officer Gomez, as far as I know, the only other occupants of that house should be a dog and a bird."

That was the precise moment when the bird squawked and said in very passable English. "Watch it dumbass."

"Keeerist Peters, it's just a stupid bird." So apparently two officers had entered from the back; because the guy talking to Peters was not the same voice we'd heard running into Grimmr unexpectedly.

*"Watch it dumbass."* Well, that was a little unusual. Don't get me wrong. There are many documented cases of crows and ravens learning to speak in captivity. Some of those birds have even developed decent vocabularies. However,

none of them that I recalled, had learned to speak whole phrases and mimic dog commands at the same time, more or less overnight. Nor...I winced, had I ever heard of a bird giving the cops a raspberry and laughing with an obvious tone of mockery.

"Okay, it's a huge frickin bird. You go check its cage." That must have been Peters. His voice didn't sound half as high-pitched and comedic when the dog was settled down. Grimmr had trotted out to lie on the porch. His eyes stayed on me and Gomez. That dog truly has some uncanny expressions for a canine. If I didn't know better I'd say he was looking sad and forlorn at the sight of me in handcuffs. At least he wasn't bounding across the yard to remove anybody's hand at the wrist. We learn to count our blessings.

From inside the house, I heard the aviary door open, followed by a hyper-frenzied sound of wings and running men. I made a stupendous effort to keep my expression neutral while squawks, profanities, and assorted crashing furniture echoed from one end of the house to the other. A few seconds later a black and white blur flew out of the open door and up into the sky with a last laughing "Dumbass".

Well, that was one less or one more worry depending on how you looked at it. I didn't have to worry about Rafe starving. He has proven himself a more than capable hunter. I just had to worry about someone taking care of Grimmr. Not to mention the inevitable lawsuits if somebody saw Rafe making off with a kitten or somesuch. He was big for the breed, but I didn't think he could take a child of any size at all. Still...until a couple of minutes earlier I hadn't known he could talk.

"Shit!" Yea the tall blond cop with the waxed moustache was Peters. He stuck his head out of the door to watch the bird flap away and disappear behind a few trees. "Hey Jackson, that gonna require a report?" Officer Jackson came back out of the house looking both thoughtful and annoyed.

"What do you think Officer Peters? Should you file it under resisting arrest or misplaced evidence?" Jackson turned to look at me through thoughtful if neutral eyes. "Yea write it up. We wouldn't want anybody to get in trouble if some disgruntled citizen filed a complaint."

Walking over, he kept that speculative gaze on my expressions. "Dumbass huh? I wonder who taught him that. We'll keep an eye out for your bird Mr. Gustaf. And I personally will take your dog in hand. Just tell the kid...Tell Officer Gomez when and what to feed the mutt. He'll pass the info on. By the way, what was it you and the bird were yelling at the dog, Mr. Gustaf, sounded like Fritter or something?"

"Fridthur would be closer, Officer Jackson. It's Icelandic. It means "peace." All of Grimmr's commands are in old or foreign words. Had a helpful dog trainer teach us the training and we taught the commands ourselves. That cuts down on people confusing the dog with conflicting command words. You don't run into a ton of people around here from say, Reykjavik."

I couldn't find the words to thank Jackson for his offer of personal assistance with my pets. They might just be animals to some people. To some of us, they are all the family we have most of the time. "Don't worry about the bird. Rafe'll take care of himself and either turn up at the shelter or someplace. For that matter, he'd be fine on his own. I'll send someone for the dog as soon as I can make a call."

"Freedthur," His accent was atrocious but I was pretty sure Grimmr would understand. "Got it. That settles him down if he gets miffed eh? Alright, I'll make sure the dog stays here. Don't forget to make your phone call after they book you. From what I've seen, you're going to need a good attorney."

On that ominous note, Gomez got us out of there.

## 8

GOMEZ WAS EITHER COURTEOUS ENOUGH, or rude enough, to leave me alone for the ride to the station. That silence gave me time to plan out the next few steps in this little production. The first thing I needed to do was make that proverbial phone call. When we arrived at the station I was marched towards a small interrogation room. At that point, I balked. "Whoa, Chuy."

The use of his informal name rather than Officer Gomez earned me a dirty look and a little shove. Gomez though was only an inch or two taller than I am and probably tipped the scales at a lean one-sixty or so. His shove produced a grunt, from him not from me.

As for movement, he managed to move my shoulder but not my planted feet. "Officer, I need to make that phone call. I have pets missing and people who are expecting me to fulfill certain responsibilities, and I would like to be represented for any questions you might feel the need to ask."

I'm guessing it was when I "lawyered up" that got his attention. Nobody in the near vicinity looked anything but bored by my responsibilities and pet woes. Some police, however, are all but allergic to the kind of stink that comes from pushing someone who has requested his right to an attorney. I got a phone alright. They pushed me into the interrogation room and produced a phone I could use to call my attorney.

That didn't mean that it was an attorney I called though. When I first came to Austin, it was readily apparent that I might need a few records obfuscated. After some discreet digging at an all-night internet café, I located the right guy for the job. He was universally described as a nutjob and conspiracy theorist with some very stout Net-Cred when it came to hacking through various obstacles. He was also one of the most infamous dropouts from the UT Legal program. "Wild Bill" was the name he used on the forums and websites.

When he first agreed to meet me, I was expecting some eccentric with long hair and a fringed buckskin coat. What I got was a very tall, very lean young man wearing well maintained and pressed "business" casual khakis, a white button-up shirt, and a very subdued navy tie. Even his hair was a conservative and very professional looking style. It had taken perhaps five minutes of conversation to convince me that any disappointment I'd felt in his appearance was wildly out of place.

William "Bill" Wooley, "Wild Bill", had flipped open an attaché and brought out a laptop that looked out of date to me. All of the newest toys seemed to go for slimmer, sleeker, smaller, and more streamlined. This computer had some serious mass to it. Not only that, but it was also a little louder than other laptops. He explained that looks could be misleading. The laptop looked bigger because it *WAS* bigger. It had to be big enough to house all of the extra bells and whistles he'd lovingly crafted into it as well as the expanded cooling system necessary to keep the thing running.

That afternoon cost me a hefty chunk of cash. It was worth every penny. Bill laid a trail of identifications and layers of obstacles that would take your average investigator months and maybe even a few subpoenas to unravel. It was *not*, however, an identity designed to stand up to a serious police investigation.

"Bill, this is Mouse, don't say anything, please. I only have a short while." Really, I had no idea how long I had. That camera in the corner of the ceiling though told me that my privacy in the small room was almost certainly compromised. Since the constabulary had supplied the phone as well I was willing to bet that they were or could be listening in. "I've been implicated in something pretty big here. So, I need you to get some balls rolling. I'll need an attorney. And I need Professor Currie to go to my home and pick up the dog."

I knew that he'd started taking notes as soon as I spoke the first sentence or two. No doubt he'd already leapt to what needed to be done to cover his own trail as well as mine in the earlier work he'd done for me. I just hoped he had time to get it done before we were both very uncomfortably compromised. The fact that I hadn't given him any particulars would tell him that I was probably under surveillance and to proceed with a paranoid sense of discretion.

Bill did squeak in one brief tidbit that might have been interesting in any other setting. "I'm on it, Magnus. Call me when you get more time. I needed to talk to you about a blip in your network."

When the phone call was over I expected Gomez or another officer to come get the phone. Apparently, I was "on ice" though. Nobody came in or so much as stuck a head in the door. True, the long-chained cuffs they had put on me were secured to the table and it would take a lot of effort and probably noise to get free. But I had the impression they wanted to talk to me pretty badly.

I spent the first quarter of an hour going over Wild Bill's comment about my network. The problem was, I don't have a network. There's just the one computer hooked into the router or modem or whatever it's called. He had to mean someone was already picking at my credentials. There wasn't much I could do about that from where I was being held.

I spent another quarter-hour or so reviewing everything I could remember from the crime scene. There had to be some reason they were fixated on me as the perp. I couldn't find a single clue no matter how hard I looked.

Maybe I wasn't thinking on my normal par. I rattled the chains through their eye bolt until I could poke at the new terrain on my head. The lumps felt like a three-dimensional map or maybe a raised chart of the stars. Pretty soon I'd have astrologers trying to read my lumps for the secrets of the cosmos. I'd take any help I could get, even phrenologists and astrologers.

I couldn't find any reason for the increased police suspicion and still they hadn't come to confront me. I did some minimalized exercises to pass the time. The chains and table provided ample resistance to flex and relax muscles that might go to sleep otherwise.

Still, they didn't come in. I spent another quarter-hour reciting the Havamal or words from the wise ones. It's a collection of poetry from Viking age Iceland. The style is unusual, but the content has lots to do with being fore-warned and forearmed for situations unhappily like the one

I was now in. Maybe the book had a clue I was missing. I still hadn't remembered anything useful when the door finally opened.

Jackson stepped in and walked over to drop a folder on the table just like on TV. He collapsed heavily into the chair opposite mine and just stared for a long minute. Finally, the older officer nodded to himself and rose to unplug the wires leading up to that camera. "We're going to talk off the record for a little while Magnus."

I guess I could have breathed a sigh of relief or gotten moist about the corners of my eyes. I did none of the above though. Instead, I nodded once. "Can I have a cigarette then?"

He nodded and produced both cigarettes and a lighter. He even went outside and came back with an ashtray and a battered brown cup that was steaming gently in the air and releasing the unmistakable aroma of the most magical elixir I know. "Cream or sugar? I got both just in case."

When I looked up and nodded, he produced the little paper packets everyone recognizes on sight. Only after I had a lit cig and a draught of coffee did he continue. "I'm going to level with you, Magnus. We have you at the scene of two murders now. The first one you reported. In the second one, you were witnessed having a violent confrontation with the victim. The victim was found several yards from a decent-sized pool of blood that did not match his DNA. I suspect that it will match yours. We haven't located the murder weapon though. I can at least tell you that the blade we confiscated from you was not the murder weapon. Nor were several other such implements we confiscated from your house."

I had to shake my head and squash the surge of anger. They'd gone through my house and stolen my property.

Now I was being held "downtown" on the word of some nebulous witness and a large number of suspicions and theories. If they had a case I'd be down at booking, not in an interrogation room with someone I had actually kind of liked before he started playing *good cop*.

"Who's the witness?" I knew he wasn't going to identify anyone. But I also knew I needed some time to organize my thoughts. As far as I could guess, sometime after I was knocked out, either McKinnon or somebody else had been killed right there in the abandoned garden next to Helstyxx. He was right. The DNA would match mine. I could stall and hope something helpful developed. Stalling would just make me look guiltier though.

"Here." I handed him the cigarette I'd barely started. "That should do for a sample to compare to your blood. Not really a point though. I was there and that's probably my blood. Who got killed though?"

I guess the matter of fact tone took him by surprise. Jackson took the cigarette from me and without blinking an eye ground it out and tossed it into the trash. "Listen, kid, I saw him take a bat to your head. I know you had a shoving match inside the bar. And I know he followed you and the twist outside and got you alone. So, what happened? Did he get rough again and things got out of hand? Give me something to work with here."

As I suspected, he ignored my question about the witness. Let me be straight here. I knew he wasn't leveling with me. He was playing good cop to get a statement. That's his job. I understand. The whole deal with the camera and the helpful tone were tools. That goes without saying, but I think he honestly did want to help me. The problem was, he didn't know enough about what was going on to understand exactly what kind of trouble I could be in. What I needed most of all was to know that Wooley had gotten my records in order.

"Not sure you're going to believe me, Jackson." What the hell, I decided to tell it to him mostly straight. "I had no ill will after the beef in the parking lot or the little testosterone display in the bar. I took my lumps and he took his. Apparently, he wanted to puff up his chest and regain some dignity. I wasn't in the mood."

I took the offer of another cigarette while realizing that this could be another source for the DNA match. Eventually, they were going to match samples anyway. Besides, the cig helped me stay focused. "When I took the girl for a walk I had no idea they were related. Right up until he showed up to play the pissed off husband, I had assumed she was single. He caught us in a fairly innocent little romantic moment. Not like there were clothes strewn all over the garden there. But he reacted like we'd been in the sack together. The blood on the ground is mine. After he ran the girl off he caught me in the head with a padlock-flail. I tossed him down and rung his bell. And then one of his buddies clocked me from behind. Last I saw he was still breathing and just a little glassy-eyed."

I saw Jackson tighten his eyes once or twice. I was betting that something I said rang a bell for him. But in addition to the nod or two, I saw him shake his head once or twice as well. For some reason, he obviously didn't believe my story. Maybe if he talked a little himself I could figure out what was going on.

Before either of us could say another word, the door cracked open to show Gomez and Peters out in the hall. Behind them, I caught a glimpse of uniquely red hair followed by a flash of green eyes. For a single breath, I thought I saw hurt and surprise in her eyes. After that, there was nothing but rage. She came over the top of the shorter Gomez and was barely caught by Peters before she made it into the room. Between hissing and other even more unpleasant sounds, she rolled out a litany of the harsh-sounding Gaelic tongue. I had been right the previous night. I could still identify all of the profanities.

"For the love of ...Gomez get her out of here!" Jackson did not appear to be amused by the interruption. When I ducked a glance that way, his face was turning red first, and then purple. "Officer Peters, please assist my partner in escorting Miss McKinnon out of the office. Make sure she has a ride to anywhere she needs to go. Now gentlemen."

Something about that exchange was trying to catch my attention. I couldn't give it the focus it deserved though. At the moment I was too caught up on the bursting pain in my throat. She looked like she hated me. And it mattered to me a great deal more than I wanted it to. I'd spent years, decades even, limiting my romantic entanglements to casual, light, and usually brief connections. And in the space of a single day that had all changed. It mattered very much that this one seemed to want nothing from me but a slow and painful demise.

"Don't take it so hard kid." Some of my emotions must have been pretty plain to see. "She's upset. She lost a friend and a brother within twenty-four hours of each other. You're the last person she saw with her brother. She saw the beginning of what promised to be a pretty bad brawl. She even admits she lost her temper and went for a long walk herself before going to bed alone at the hotel. So, son, there might be some guilt there as well as the anger at you."

This time the demand for my attention paid off. Her brother? And he had called her Miss McKinnon earlier. Even a widow is usually given the Mrs. honorific. She wasn't married! He'd been her brother! And she thought I'd killed him...

If that thought was enough to deflate me, the next statement from Jackson was enough to eventually leave me completely flat. "Besides we have you on tape. There were only the two of you in that garden."

"Wait, what do you mean?" Despite the fear and confusion his statement evoked, I couldn't focus clearly. My mind kept spinning back to the fact that she wasn't married! All those knots in my gut all night were for nothing. I mean yea there was a problem with the cops and all. But I could clear that up, right? That's when the cop's statement finally dragged me back around.

"What do you mean there were only two of us? He was down, I was down and bleeding from..." Okay, that wasn't going to work. How could I claim a serious knife wound when all I had now was a thin pink scar?

"...from his little ambush with the padlock. So who put me down and out if it wasn't him?" That sounded a little thin even to me but for once Jackson didn't seem on top of the discrepancy.

"I don't know, delayed reaction maybe?" His expression had gone back to professional and neutral. That couldn't be good for me. "That's just your story anyway. It doesn't work for us, Mr. Gustaf."

Back to my surname too, things were definitely taking a turn for the worst. "Mr. Gustaf, I have a counter-theory. You gave me a few clues just now. I was not aware of how you felt about Miss McKinnon until I saw your face. That and your comment about her "husband" gave me a motive for some things that had eluded me. Based on those facts, plus drag marks and a few footprints along with some material from the pieces...from Mr. McKinnon's wounds, here is what I think may have happened."

"You and the kid sister there went for a stroll. Big brother already had it in for you over the earlier confrontations. He catches you two together. Maybe it was as innocent as you'd like me to believe and maybe he saw something a lot different from your description. Doesn't really matter except for the girl if I catch her lying. Well, there were words between the two of them. You both told that the same way. She ran off mad as hell at her brother, and mad at you for seeing her embarrassed like that." His shrug eloquently stated the age-old belief that a man can never really understand how a woman's mind operates.

"McKinnon and you exchange words. He's already mad plus a little protective. You're jealous and maybe a little pissed off too. Just like that, it gets physical. I don't know who took the first swing. That doesn't matter either. I saw you ambushed by the same guy with a baseball bat and three friends. You can't honestly expect me to think he took you down without help and you facing him from the beginning?" He had a point there. How had I let the same guys sneak up and bounce assorted foreign objects off of my head two or three times in the same day?

"After that, I'm guessing you either accidentally hit him too hard, or you went into one of those Scandinavian rages your type seems to be so proud of. Whichever happened, you killed him. We should have a report any minute about the exact cause of death. A tone on his cell phone broke Jackson's attention for a minute. "This may be the report now."

Holding his hand up in a gesture for me to wait, he answered the call. With that same hand, he reached into his jacket and brought out the nub of a pencil and small notebook. "Jackson...Yes sir...with the suspect right now...could you repeat that...Well, what the hell does that mean?... Okay, I'll do some digging...Yes sir. No M.E. report though...Okay, thank you, sir. Please let me know when you can."

He hung up the phone and gave me a suspicious and confused look at the same time. "Not the Medical Examiner, Forensics. Which gives me even more questions? Why did you mutilate the body so bad? What kind of weapon did you use that left traces of petrified wood..." He paused to look at his handy little notebook again. "...and obsidian?"

He looked up with a kind of sick and baffled expression for his last question. "And what did you do with his genitals?"

## 9

My mind was racing with a ton of information and nothing to do with it yet. The genitals bit, while interesting, was just another piece of the puzzle. Something about the obsidian was ringing alarms; the petrified wood was just as intriguing. And that errant thought about how people kept sneaking up on me needed to be hauled out and looked over thoroughly. I'd had an obnoxious young cop get the drop on me, then four biker wannabes in chains and leather snuck up on me, at least once if not twice.

For someone with my range of experiences, that just didn't make sense. I've done recon and been point man in some pretty hairy situations. How am I getting ambushed in empty parking lots? Okay, maybe I'm not in the same peak combat form I had years ago. But there had to be something else at work to keep my senses and reflexes quite *this* dull.

To cover up my thoughts I went back to something else he'd said. "I don't know where you're getting your information. But I was looking right at Seamus when somebody else hit me. Wait, how can you know there were only two of us in there? You aren't telling me there was video surveillance inside the garden itself?"

"Not at all." Jackson's voice didn't betray so much as an ounce of doubt. "First we have the witness that saw you two arguing inside the garden together. Then we have the video evidence that shows you knock him unconscious and drag him out of sight."

He got up as he was speaking and went to cue up a video on the television screen beside the closed-circuit camera. "We have video from Helstyxx parking lot which shows the entire south and west fences. "

The camera briefly showed Maureen and me going into the shadowed interior of the garden. In the image, we could still be seen but only as shadows and dim silhouettes. The camera quality was clearly insufficient to give even minimum detail given the lighting in that area at that time of night. As we watched, Seamus McKinnon could be seen stalking across the parking lot and into the same vague shadows that had all but hidden two of them...of us, his sister, and me.

Mere seconds later, the girl came flying out of the garden in long angry strides. Inside there was a brief pause in activity, and then a flurry of motion. Both silhouettes fell, and then one of them seemed to rise and strike wildly at the other before lurching awkwardly into the brush.

"That's it? That's your video evidence? You can't tell if someone came in from the other side and snuck around behind me or anything. For that matter, the shadow that stood up could have been him or someone else and not me at all. That can't refute my..."

Before I finished, the tape continued and suddenly switched to a different angle, this view clearly showed the entire northern fence and the same shadowed area where the fight took place. "This came from the convenience store security camera. The only border to the garden that we can't see clearly is the front building itself. The store your boss bought has been closed for several months. There was no way up the side, no ladder, protrusions, or handy walkways. There is a tree that might give access, but you would have to take a ladder to get to it. Perhaps someone with the right training and some climbing rope could make it. In these cases, I go with the theory that the simplest explanation is usually the best. There is a sheer bluff that drops off at one side of the building towards the lake below. In front, the only entrance is a double glass door with a chain and lock. That lock is rusted shut and has been for weeks. "

He turned off the video and turned to look me square in the eye just to make sure I was paying attention. "Nobody could get in from the east, and the cameras show every other available approach. We checked the video for twenty-four hours prior to your arrival. There was nobody in that garden but you and McKinnon. We also have you leaving a couple of hours later. It was plenty long enough for say some mutilation and emasculation."

The interrogation went downhill from there. They couldn't break me from the truth no matter how hard they tried. I couldn't think of anything else to convince them either. Finally, they gave up and sent me to a cell until they figured out what to do next.

## 10

I WAS STARTLED awake by a gnarled hand on my shoulder. When I finally got my eyes focused it was only to find the kindly old man I'd spent an hour or two talking with when they first put me in a cell. The old-timer only spoke a few words of English and my Spanish was more Spanglish than Castilian. Somehow, we managed to communicate at least a little for the first part of my imprisonment.

I couldn't really complain or act surprised. Hel, with the video evidence and two witnesses they probably didn't even need my DNA to keep me. I can't say I wouldn't suspect myself if I hadn't been there. In fact, I *DID* suspect myself of something. I wasn't sure what that suspicion amounted to, but I knew for a fact that no chain and combat wearing rock star wannabe should have gotten the drop on me. Not once but twice I had been snuck up on. Actually, if you count my slow reaction time to the cops at my door, that would make three times.

For someone who has seen and done the things I've done in some of the places I've been, that was just unacceptable. I snuck up on people. People did not sneak up on me.

That was the thought in my head when I fell asleep. Now I was waking to old Theo looming over my jailhouse bunk.

Now in my experience, jails, cells, prisons, and dungeons all have certain things in common. They tend to be severe structures made with sturdy but rather daunting amounts of stone and metal. They are often ill-lit, depressing, and somehow cavernous sounding at the same time that they are incredibly close and confining. But the most common trait is that *all* of them without exception are uncomfortable.

That's one of the reasons I was surprised to wake up. I never thought I would go to sleep to begin with. Theo, pronounced Tay-Oh in this instance, stood over me with an odd gleam to his eyes and a curious expression.

When we first met and talked, it had taken some work to get to know my cellmate. Despite the language barrier we managed to tell each other some of what was on our minds. I didn't go into my trouble with the law too much. He had understood that I was brought in over a killing and had even managed to grasp the macabre and bloody manner of the killing. I was surprised that he hadn't avoided me after that. The old man didn't seem to think I was a danger though. Instead, he seemed genuinely interested in the deaths, gore and all. After I ran out of information or at least the language to convey it, he told me some of his story.

Apparently, the poor old fellow was in town looking for a lost relative, someone searching for a cheating husband? A daughter or niece maybe? As I said, we were talking with only my pidgin Spanish in common. Of course, that got me excited and I mentioned the mysterious and exotic widow Brewster. Neither the Brewster name nor Jacqueline got a reaction from the old man though. No, I got the idea the woman he was seeking was much older and maybe even a little eccentric. That was my impression at least. Could be I was wrong. Anyway, he had run afoul of the local law.

Trespassing or breaking and entering? Whatever he'd been caught for had led to a records search and the inevitable lack of documentation. Rather than prosecute him they were planning to turn the poor old fellow over to the border patrol and just send him back across the Rio Grande. He didn't seem that concerned about it, just worried about his relative and whatever trouble she might get into.

The last thing I recalled was an odd look on his face as he mentioned that I looked...sick or tired? Heavy eyed might come closest to what I understood. So that's why it took me by surprise to wake up feeling relatively refreshed and bright-eyed with a kindly old man with feathered gray hair looking down on me. Before we got too tied up with my bad Spanglish, they came and took the old duffer away.

## 11

I WASN'T in the cell alone for long though. Before the clock had moved an hour further I was out of the cage and headed for the interrogation rooms again. I got a little suspicious when we bypassed the rooms with their little cameras though. Those suspicions were laid to rest as soon as I rounded the next corner to find Eachan.

Behind the fashionable professor was a thoroughly stern and professional-looking chap that could only be a barrister or attorney. That sharply dressed man in an immaculate suit and tie was just finishing with the desk Sergeant or Lieutenant or whoever had overseen the paperwork incarcerating me. He never raised his voice even a smidge, but there was little doubt that he was giving quite the lecture. The desk officer was showing a wide range of coloration in his face from pale to red and even purple. It was quite fascinating to watch.

I was called out of my entertainment though by the unmistakable self-satisfied tones of Eachan himself. "I suppose you will not find yourself doubting my prognostications in the future my boy! Scarlet waves and death and destruction was it not? I'd say the pickle you've gotten your-self in fits that prediction to a T my boy. To a T."

If I didn't know the smug bastard better, I'd think he was enjoying my predicament. However, having known the professor for quite some time, I detected a layer of anxiety and uncertainty under his bluster. Men, of course, do not talk about such things. Instead, I offered him my hand and gripped his firmly in return. "Thanks a ton, Prof. But how did you manage to spring me? I don't know what they've told you but it looks pretty grim. Speaking of..."

"Worry not about your slothful hound Magnus. He is currently resting on a very expensive refurbished chaise lounge from a quaint castle near Berwickshire. The dog has no respect for antiquity nor good taste I fear. The chaise came from Scotland's Gothic Revival period. It's rather hideous and gaudy. Grimmr seems to enjoy it though. Personally, I think his addition of red wine mushroom sauce does something for the fabric." As he spoke, Eachan was leading me out of the immediate earshot of any snooping detectives. And detectives by their very nature are always snooping,

"They've actually told me quite a bit, young Master Magnus. I've even seen the video and photos of the crime scene."

At my shocked sideways glance, he nodded. "Yes, connections and money can do some very impressive things. My barrister also represents some highly placed officials in our lovely corrupt state capital. You are by no means "sprung". I have secured some time for you but no more than a day or two. The mechanics are confusing but the legal genius over there assures me that you will be back behind bars within the week barring some sort of miracle. I'm sorry my boy but to be honest I'm amazed to have gotten even this much no matter how much weight I might bring to bear."

My face must have showed some of the confusion and embarrassment I was feeling. With an avuncular chuckle he slipped an arm over my shoulder and clapped the far shoulder blade. "Come now, it's not like I had to sell the ancestral home! I just had to use a few more liquid assets that I am normally comfortable with. I but postponed the purchase of a sailing vessel for the time being to garner the necessary funds. I have it on good authority there are no other offers on her, so I have some time to make up the funds. There might also have been a favor or two called in as well as oh, some salacious rumors that certain officials would rather keep very quiet. The important thing is that I have secured your release amongst the myriad of other entertaining experiences and bits of information accumulated this evening. I suggest we get out of here before someone changes their mind."

In very short order Eachan and I were facing the attorney in the back of the educator's Star Sapphire. "Let me be both brief and frank Mr. Gustaf. My firm was retained to gather information for Doctor MacVurlich. Having done so, my obligation here is complete. Normally we would not do this type of thing however the Doctor is a very good client. Very good indeed."

The lawyer cleared his throat and opened his briefcase to regard notes inside. "In the course of information gathering, I noticed that their video evidence is easily challenged due to blurriness and other factors. These were the basis for my attempt to free you. Frankly, I am confused by the relative ease with which you have been even temporarily released. If I were to hazard a guess, there are people who want you out for their own purposes. Perhaps they hope you will lead them to more evidence to prosecute you. That is beyond the scope of my employment currently. However, I will offer you some advice. Hire as good a lawyer as you can afford. This has the potential to become a national media sensation. Some very good firms will be attracted to that kind of notoriety. If you'd like, I shall produce a list of those most likely to take your case and defend you as well as circumstances permit. I will not, however, be advising that our firm take your case. It may seem harsh to you, but I am uncertain that we could claim a victory here."

At least he had the grace to look back down at his attaché as he so eloquently dismissed my fate. "The evidence is rather overwhelming. I won't ask if you did it. We learned long ago not to trust impassioned speeches of innocence. I can only say that having seen the evidence; I am hard-pressed not to believe your guilt already. However, for a friend of a valued client like the professor we have done as much as I feel is prudent. In point of fact, we passed prudent quite some time hence. If you would like my recommendations for other representation, the Doctor has my contact information."

With a nod of respect to my benefactor, the lawyer exited, and the car got underway. As we drove away I saw him head for the parking garage across the street. I wanted to resent his assessment of my chances. However, even I was a little confused and concerned by the evidence and my half-formed guesses about being ambushed so effectively.

While I sorted through that confusion, I managed to offer my thanks to Eachan. "Professor I don't know how you did this. And I surely don't know how I am going to repay you. I'm just glad Wild Bill got hold of you. I honestly only expected help with the dog, not all of this."

"Was young Master Wooley supposed to be in touch

with me? He never contacted me, Magnus. I got the rune message you left at my home and came right down." For a moment he looked testy, then the old scoundrel gave me a toothy grin that might have belonged on one of his highland raiding forefathers. "It took some interpretation, but I figured out your message. You *will* have to tell me though how you knew I usually attribute the Uruz rune to you. I am quite certain we never discussed it."

That explained the grin. He had broken the code on a runic message and came down to help a friend. The only problem was...I hadn't left any runic messages lately.

Eachan gave his driver directions to my house and assured me that he would watch the dog for a few days while I sorted things out. It was fairly obvious that he thought I was going to go "on the run" as he put it. It was just as obvious that he was delighted to be part of such "irregular" proceedings. I started to deny any such notions. However, after a little more thought I had to agree that it was entirely possible that I might have to dodge the law for a few days while I sorted this mess out.

In many ways, it would be easier to just cut my ties and go start over someplace else. However, I had invested a good deal of time and money in establishing my identity and getting accepted here. That would all be wasted if I ran. And though I didn't want to admit it to myself, there were people here that I would miss if I ran. You don't find people willing to give up a yacht, at least temporarily, to help bail a friend out of jail.

When it came down to it, I enjoyed the guys and the waitresses down at the club too. I had to shake my head and laugh at myself. I knew better. A guy in my shoes should always be ready to run if he had to. But did I really have to run this time? Just as we arrived at the house I remembered the odd thoughts I had about being ambushed and sucker-punched when that was not at all how things normally go for me.

"Eachan could you have your driver wait just a little while? There's something I'd like to talk to you about inside."

"Of course my boy, of course, we probably need to discuss a couple of things before you disappear eh?"

I walked slowly towards the house and ordered my thoughts. As the prof said, time was fairly critical, and I didn't want to waste any of that precious time. On the other hand, I couldn't afford to make many more mistakes. When I heard him come in behind me and close the door, I had already lifted the barely legal shotgun from its concealed panel on the side of a nineteenth-century clock that stands just inside my door. When Eachan turned around he found himself almost nose to nose with the ugly mouth of the twelve-gauge.

"If you don't mind, old boy, don't move too fast or reach for anything. I'd be careful of so much as jumping at your cell phone. You see at this range the lead shot will barely matter to you. The muzzle blast ought to shred skin and muscle before the pellets ever get there. The concussion alone would probably break your neck and pulverize brain matter."

I'm pretty sure I've never seen a better impersonation of a statue. The professor went completely still and turned several shades of grey. It did not, however, last very long. I saw the blue forehead vein start up just as a flush began creeping from his neck upwards. "Urr ye oot yer damned mynd? Ai jist saived yer pumpin' bahookie."

Well, at least I didn't doubt he was Scottish any more.

That convoluted accent and mangled English is almost impossible to duplicate.

"Cha deid cuileag am beul duinte" In English, it goes *Silence is Golden.* In Gaelic, the proverb is *Peace and quiet have immense value.* I could tell the professor caught both meanings well enough. His mouth shut in a very angry looking frown while his eyes flashed dire warnings.

"Sorry about this professor but I had some sudden suspicions. You see, I've been rather slow-witted lately. Haven't noticed people sneaking up on me. Haven't been sharp, on my toes so to speak. I hadn't put it all together until I woke up in the jail cell. Well, my theory is that someone has worked a little magic my way. And I asked myself, who could do that or would have a clue it needed to be done? Who might have some suspicions about my origins or what I'm trained to do and capable of?"

I suddenly craved a cigarette badly. If I was right, this gentleman in front of me was something special. There had been tales for centuries about individuals who could manipulate others' perceptions. Cause fantastic events to occur, steal the very life from an individual. I'd heard of people just dropping dead and others being incinerated to bare bone without so much as leaving a stray scorch mark on the curtains a foot away. Names like Merlin, Taliesin, Baba Yaga, and Medea rang through history. Some of them were even real. People like that could also befuddle the mind enough to say...escape with a prisoner from a jail cell.

I felt the slightest bit of perspiration in my hand as I thought this through. Oddly enough, I noticed that some of the anger had left the professor's face. If anything he looked more interested than incensed. I could also tell that he was fairly bursting with the need to talk and ask his own questions. On the other hand, the stories said some of those wizardly types could kill with just a word or two. Did I dare take that chance? I was struggling with the idea of simply pulling the trigger, when an unexpected sound almost took the choice out of my hands.

"*Dumbass!*" I had forgotten the damned raven.

## 12

WHEN I SLOWLY CRANED MY neck around I saw the bird at the same time that a relieved sigh and sputter of laughter behind me said that Eachan had broken his stasis. From the corner of my eye, I saw something huge and scary coming out of the aviary towards me. I whipped around and lifted the shotgun, but the shadows were too dark for a target. I try not to shoot at shadows. This is probably not a bad thing, as the cream and red fox stalked out of the shadows a good three feet below where my gun barrel was pointed. For once it caught my eyes with its own fairly antagonistic looking glare.

I was still sorting that out when I heard the raven echoing his earlier surprise statement. "Fridthur Dumbass!"

I figured it was time I ignored the antics of pets and got back to the task at hand. Admittedly, my nerves were not half as tight as they'd been just seconds ago. On the other hand, the tightening of Eachan's eyes showed that he noticed the gun still in my hands. The fact that the gun was still aimed more or less in his direction probably sharpened that attention.

"That was a close call Doc. I was already wound up pretty tight. Came close to splattering those highly tuned brains of yours all over the curtains." If the gun hadn't convinced him I was still quite earnest, the tone of my conversation should have.

"As I was saying Professor, something odd has been happening to me lately. It occurred about the same time you came over with a message about the runes and dangerous omens. We haven't really talked about my past though I know you've made some guesses. The truth is that I am or rather was something of a professional soldier. There's more to it than that, but let's keep things simple for now. The point is that as a professional soldier, my senses and instincts are usually as honed and sharp as those educated brains of yours. But I keep getting surprised, ambushed, bushwhacked, and generally snuck up on and abused by people that shouldn't be able to do that so easily." With the gun in my hand, I waved him over to one of the large and comfortable chairs in my living room. Other than a leather couch they are the only place to get comfy in the room. I sat in the other one with the shotgun resting on its arm pointed at Eachan's middle. With the hand that wasn't full of weaponry, I gestured for the scholar to say something.

"Okay, Magnus. I assume that you suspect I may have something to do with these ambushes. But if so, what would be my motivation to get you out of jail? You are in quite the stewpot already. If I bore you ill will I could simply leave you to the mercies of the legal system. With the evidence I've seen, you would be splashed across the headlines of every major news outlet in the civilized world. All it would take is time and I could easily have a ringside seat at the proceedings." Dammit, if he was lying he was better at it than I expected.

"Frankly I have no idea Doc. Truth is I don't *want* it to be you. But it's something that I have to check." Digging into the neckline of my shirt I came out with a simple necklace. Hanging from a leather thong, was a rough hammer of a style popular among new age Germanic heathens. Most of those on the market are similar and patterned after hammers from all over Scandinavia that dated a span of several hundred years. By comparison, mine was as old as the museum pieces the others were copied from.

"We've talked about the old ways Doc. About your beliefs and faith so to speak. Well here's a little bit of lore come to life for you. This is a smaller version of the Oath Hammer that saw Althings in Denmark, Iceland, and Norway back before they were even called by those names. Many an oath has been sworn on it. It has tasted the blood of warriors and kings and more. An oath sworn on such a hammer is not broken lightly. I can't begin to tell you how difficult it was to find and acquire." I leaned over and held the hammer in front of his eyes. This time I was the one who wanted to laugh.

Between fear of the gun, anger at my high-handed methods, an almost religious wonderment, and frankly some discernible greed, the poor scholar had emotions flowing across his face almost too fast to count. Finally, though he nodded as my purpose became clear to him. He leaned forward and took the necklace in both hands and raised it high while he looked me in the eye.

"Magnus Gustaf, I swear on Mjolnir and by all that is dear to me, I have cast no spells, marked no runes, and used no energy to harm, diminish or befuddle you. In fact, I am most assuredly a friend seeking to help you." We each shuddered just for one second from palpable energy as the

Hammer recognized the oath, accepted it, and did nothing to refute that claim.

I sagged in my chair with the release of tension in my shoulders. He would probably never believe how close to the end of his thread he had been. I avoided noticing that his vow was quite specific about being a friend and helping in the present tense. In other words, he was under no obligation to maintain that helpfulness and friendship in the future. Nor was he promising that he had any friendship or assistance in mind before this.

On the other hand, for the moment, and only for the present moment, I could trust him more than almost anyone I could think of. I flipped the safety on and leaned the gun against the wall behind my chair. "Thank you, Professor."

For a very long moment, we both just sat and looked at each other. It had been a very tense moment for each of us in a different way. For the time being, the tension could be felt flowing away and leaving a sense of quiet and calm, and a great many questions.

Some people might wonder how a simple "promise" could go so far in settling our little situation. To understand that, you have to understand a few things about magic and faith. There are plenty of beliefs, guidelines, rules, and rulebooks, that tell one how to do magic.

Many people think you have to be born with a certain gift. Others make deals with various powers or entities. Demons, devils, angels, genies...there are dozens or even hundreds of stories that give you an idea of how to gain power from outside sources.

There are those who claim that knowledge makes a strong practitioner, others claim it takes a supernaturally strong will. For me it's easy. Magic works when I believe it will work. I mean bone-deep belief in it. The runes I use are symbols and names and meanings and much more. When I use them a certain way, it builds my confidence and my belief in what is going to happen. Using the right words with the right intonation, carving the runes themselves just right, focusing my will and my intentions are all part of making myself believe that I can accomplish a minor miracle.

When you add the mystical mass of something like a centuries-old icon, then the energy and faith attached to it become real, dangerous, and trustworthy for lack of a better word. After he spoke his oath, with the hammer in hand, we both felt the equivalent of an old Irish Geasa spell settling in. Eachan could no more break that promise than he could lift that old car outside with his bare hands. If he did manage to break the oath then a curse would kick in and do fairly horrible and unpredictable things until he rectified the breach.

To keep his side of the bargain, the Doctor got right into the problem. "So Magnus, you think someone has "messed with your head" is how I believe they say it these days. I don't suppose you would let me take a look then? Perhaps with a bit of good fortune, we can turn your dilemma to our advantage. "

My first inclination was to deny the offer. Once you've spent a lifetime hiding from unwanted attention, it becomes a hard habit to break. On the other hand, I trusted my defenses to keep the most important bits hidden away. "What do you have in mind Doc?"

"A little simple divination. For this all I would need is a candle, maybe a mirror, and just to be safe some old-fashioned table salt might not be bad. I don't suppose you have a sprig or two of sage lying about as well?" Eachan's smile was smugly satisfied when I quickly gathered all his requests and brought them back on an old tarnished silver tray.

He didn't have to give me as strong an oath as he had. I was just repaying some of that trust by confirming some of his theories about my own level of practice when it came to energy work and old beliefs. Not everyone has sage and salt in small shells or handcrafted candles in a variety of colors and sizes. Or a tarnished silver tray with the runes of the elder futhark inscribed across the top. As a precaution, I had also included a small silver sgian dubh or the historical "sock knife" of a kilt wearing Highlander. I wasn't sure how Eachan worked, but I knew with a little effort I could "cut" a great many spells or energy workings with that simple silver blade.

I have to admit it was rather fascinating to watch someone with a totally different grasp of magick do a "working". He arranged his materials much as I might. If I had not been paying attention I might not have heard the low mumble of incomprehensible words as he chanted or hummed. He also seemed to work from a neo-pagan's perspective when it came to containing circles. The names were not familiar, but I recognized someone "calling the quarters" and assigning watchmen or guests to each of the compass points. When that was done he set up the candle and carved his runes in it.

The candle was blue, depending on his belief, that might represent air, the north, a higher power, even ice or frost or an elemental plane of water. Whatever it represented to him, he carved and whispered his runes into it. He lit it once and then pinched the wick between his fingers to extinguish the flame. Again he repeated that sequence of light and extinguished it. On the third try though, he left the small flame burning. Pouring a bit of wax from the candle onto the tray, he stood the candle up with that melted puddle of support.

With everything else ready, he set the mirror up so that it reflected my image behind the flames for him. As a result, I could look into the mirror and see over his shoulder. For several long breaths, I sat and watched the aging professor mumble and focus until his eyes began scanning left and right across my face. That shifting gaze traveled over my arms and chest and made me wonder if he could see any of the bindings done in my tattoos.

I saw his eyes narrow in concentration as he tried to perceive deeper into whatever working and energy he had identified. That curiosity threatened to occupy my whole attention. The only reason it did *not* occupy me was that I saw a smoky image appear. There was the nebulous outline of a clawed or taloned hand reaching for Eachan from behind. In my runed silver mirror, I could see those talons poised to rake down at the unsuspecting scholar. There was no way to be certain what they were or who they represented, but even the hazy silhouette of that hand sent alarms and chills through my nervous system.

My sudden move must have set the bird off. Out of nowhere, he flew over us both cawing loudly on his erratic path to the aviary. The buffeting winds of those chaotic flapping wings blew the candle out and even lifted it free of its waxy stand to roll around on the tray. A second later, the tray fell onto the floor and spilled the salt right where Eachan had been sitting.

I say he HAD been sitting there because he was no longer at that location in my comfortable chair. Instead, he was several feet away and coming to a rolling stop from where my launched tackle had sent him sprawling. The bird crowed loudly. Eachan barked a nasty and earthy profanity, and the silver tray rang like a bell.

I gasped for air as the unexpected activity stole my breath. I shifted my gaze to Eachan, only to find the scholar between me and the shotgun leaning behind my chair. Clearly, he had no idea of what had been in the mirror other than his divination about enchantments. The look on his face made it plain that he thought I had changed my mind and was attacking him.

I guess the shining silver dagger in my hand probably reinforced that assumption on his part. I had instinctively grabbed the sgian dubh on my way over the table. This time it was my turn to soothe uncertain fears and answer the questions about what had just occurred. "Sorry Doc, I saw something else coming through your sending. It looked like a hostile, so I reacted accordingly."

He hesitated, but eventually, he nodded sharply and then offered me his hand to help him off the floor. That cane he carries is not purely an affectation or eccentricity. The professor's left leg was quite stiff and weak. I had seen him walk with a barely noticeable limp. I'd also seen him shamble around with the cane doing most of the work of supporting him. This time I figured the knee was not going to work well. Foregoing any reservations, I offered him my hand and lifted the grimacing educator off the floor.

En route back to the comfort of his chair, he asked me the first question that probably came to mind, "What exactly did you see that made it seem like a grand idea to tackle an aging cripple as if we were on the rugby field?"

"It was claws on a hand Doc, almost like it was made of smoke but more solid seeming somehow, I saw it over your shoulder and when it started to move for you I tried to get you out of the way. Sorry if I surprised you..." I shrugged and helped him get seated before finding his cane for him.

"Claws you say? Out of smoke? Are you sure you weren't just being paranoi..." The sudden pause in his interrogation snapped my head around. I instantly saw what had caught his attention. There on the floor was the silver tray, and in a perfect arc along its edge, were four faintly smoking crescent holes. One side of the candle was scorched completely black, and the salt had fallen in a rough scattered line between the tray and the chair where the prof had been sitting. A wide band of that salt was also gray and scorched looking. In fact, it looked about the width of a forearm; say a forearm coming down with claws to rake at an unsuspecting rune caster.

## 13

BOTH OF US stared at the scorched salt for a long moment. Eachan half-fell into the chair we righted for him. Lifting the silver knobbed walking stick he always seemed to have, he gently stirred the blackened crystals and then pushed them aside to peer at the unmarked wooden floor beneath.

"Well my friend, that is not something you see every day." The professor opted to try and keep things light. "In view of recent developments, I must withdraw the crass sarcasm in my previous question. In its place let me offer my fervent thanks. I do not think I would like to know firsthand what such a working would have as its purpose. The scorch marks, controlled and contained as they were, affected only the salt that disrupted the energy attack. You will notice that not even a faint discoloration appears on the hardwood. That indicates that all of the energy was channeled into an attack and once the "line" so to speak was broken, all of the energy was consumed by the salt."

If I had to guess, I'd say Eachan fell into the role of educator any time he was unsure of how to handle or respond to someone or some event. Now he was in lecturing mode until his nerves settled enough to slip out of the façade. "The salt is a common protection in many cultures and paths. Fortunately, we seem to be up against a practitioner who is as disrupted by sodium as I myself might be."

This time his face grew thoughtful and then developed into a rather disturbingly cunning look with at least some malice. "Magnus grab something you can smell distinctly, aftershave, incense, spices, something with a potent aroma. And please, *hurry*"

By the time I was a few steps out of the room, the professor was gathering items out of the mess that had tumbled from the table. When I returned, he was already scratching new runes in the stub of the old candle. "Now get anything you might need to defend yourself against that attacker."

Reacting to the haste and intensity of his voice, I went to retrieve the Kabar knife and my semi-automatic from the drawer. That is when I recalled that the police still had both items in their possession. That left me with few alternatives. If I had a couple of hours I might have retrieved a small but fairly impressive arsenal. Something told me that the professor could not wait that long though. I considered the. shotgun, but that was much too conspicuous even for the streets of Austin.

Look, the lone star state is known for its Wild West attitudes and gun-friendly culture. But Austin is more like San Francisco than it is like a lot of other Texas towns. Hippies and new agers gather in parks along the river and vie for space with drummers and gentle friends of the "green movement". Keep Austin Weird is a mantra adopted by the community as a whole and it says quite a bit about that community. They are weird, proud of it, and predominantly peaceful idealists. There are still people walking the streets of the city that remember a sniper shooting down from a tower into the college campus. They don't like guns in Austin as much as other parts of the state.

The shotgun was out. I had a couple of cubby holes that law enforcement might have missed. I shoved a corner of my bed aside and searched for the little compartment hidden in that leg. All I had in that one was another of the quirky revolvers and a sheath knife. The next nearest gun was blocks away in a storage unit. For now, it looked like I would probably have to rely on minimal gear along with wits and that odd mix of martial and occult backgrounds I could claim. Fair enough. I'd survived some pretty nasty situations with no more backup.

I handed Eachan the cologne that some well-meaning flight attendant had gifted me for Yule. It was too sweet, a little bit spicy, and nothing that I would be caught dead wearing. In fact, the only time it came out was when the young lady called and told me she had some free time between flights. On the other hand, it was a very distinctive aroma. Eachan took it with a nod of satisfaction.

"Excellent, it's not a popular brand so you won't be misled by some fraternity brother on the prowl." Eachan carefully sprayed some of the questionable cologne on a small pile of the blackened salt he had gathered and put it in one of my small offering bowls. The bowl rested once more on the silver platter and was surrounded again by even more candles which were all lit except for the one nearest where everything had spilled moments ago.

"Okay Magnus, when I cast the spell, and then release the circle around it, you will be able to smell the residual energies from this attack. The effect will have a very limited range and duration. We must hope that the attacker was within the city and near enough for you to reach in less than an hour. By the same token, I cannot come with you since my game leg would only slow you down. Are you ready?"

At my nod, he lit the last candle and growled no more than two or three words that I could not hear quite well enough to understand. At the last utterance, the candle flames bent down as if being pulled into the circle. The tops of all four candle flames seemed to lick at the smoke-blackened salt before snapping upright. As soon as he saw the burning wicks stand straight again, the professor clapped a hand and all four candles simultaneously went out. There wasn't even a spark or smoldering ember. "Go, lad. And good hunting."

## 14

IT TOOK LESS than a minute to discover certain limitations of a scent-based spell. Eachan had told me I'd have to walk but I was barely listening. Consequently, I managed to get the Enfield fired up and down to the end of the driveway before I lost the scent. It is also worth noting that Enfield motorcycles do not have a handy gear for reverse. Walking the bike backward took longer than I felt like wasting but it was necessary to regain my trail. After that, it was a matter of going slow and paying attention to the nuance of the scent growing stronger or weaker. Basically, I was playing a nose-based version of "hot or cold". In relatively little time, I realized that the trail was going to take me across the street and through several yards and at least one solid building. In other words, I wasn't taking a ride to follow that scent.

I made a mental note to discuss better tracking spells with the professor. On the other hand, I wasn't sure how he managed even as much as the scent thing. Before the previous half-hour, I would have told anyone who asked that sea salt was one of the most effective things I knew of to stop or shield from spell energy. Yet he had used the *salt itself* to focus his ritual. As far as I knew that was impossible. Which goes to show exactly how much I knew about other beliefs and energy workers.

The problem lies in the sheer individuality of practitioners today. A thousand years ago there might be a single shaman or priest capable of working with magic in each village or maybe even less than each village. In some areas, wise women or seers or a shaman might have a circuit of several villages and towns. When they came to town those who needed healing or divination, or a particularly potent prayer, would trot down and make their requests then pay the seers, in something like chickens. See? I told you there was a time you could get almost anything with enough chickens.

Today though there were so *many* people. To make things worse, a fair number of them viewed things in their own individual manner. Instead of the traditional apprentice and master relationship, modern "witches" often bought their grimoires and books of shadows in large chain stores. Without a guiding hand or firm cuff to the head, they developed their own beliefs and their own quirkiness with magick. I could no more have cast the spell Eachan had than he could survive some of the things that wouldn't *quite* kill me.

The thought of being mostly killed again after the episode with the deflated lung was enough to spur some focused frenzy. Turning off the motorcycle I kicked the stand down and got off. A quick grab secured my duffel stuffed with my hastily assembled stash of defensive and offensive options. I was limited to more or less legal toys. There was just a touch too much "official" interest for me to take a lot of risks. I had a license for the handgun. The knife they'd missed was sheathed and secured inside the duffel so that too was legal. Of course, it wouldn't stop some cops from digging through stuff and detaining me while the tracking spell dissipated and finally vanished.

The scent led me down a couple of alleys and every time I had to detour it took a few minutes to find the trail again. I thought for a moment it was going to take me across the lake itself. That would have been as impressive as the salt had been. As a rule, large bodies of water ground and wash away magick just as salt or sage often do. In the case of water, I'd always thought of it as a cleansing barrier between mother earth and the rest of us.

In my mind, humankind are children of mother earth. Most of us are tied to her for everything from everyday needs to deeper more spiritual or occult pursuits. Water washes that connection away and breaks our contact with the mother and the source of magick. I've known some followers of sky pantheons that might make a liar of me. On the other hand, since I believed the water would stop magick, it usually did. This time it didn't have the chance.

I had been walking or jogging off and on for close to half an hour when I started to suspect where I was headed. With every block, the conviction grew until I stopped with the lights of the club just around the corner. At first, I started to blindly run down the alley and go through the back door. My little session with the police videos drew me up short. The last thing I needed was to be spotted on more video going into what might turn into a paranormal slugfest. If I hadn't been in such a hurry I might have thought of this possibility. But I hadn't been sure enough of Eachan's spell to chance delays while I made my own runic preparations.

Crossing the street for a better angle, I realized that the trail did not actually go to the nightclub itself. It seemed to miss the corner of the building by a few yards from where I was standing. In fact...it led straight to the garden where I had been attacked and the other gent had been bloodily dispatched. Beyond that, it would indeed cross the water. Not only did I firmly believe the spell couldn't do that; I was all but certain that the strength of the scented trail had led me to its goal. Somewhere in that garden was the source of the spell that attacked Eachan.

Sitting on a bench down the street, I looked over the situation carefully. Just as the videos showed, there were only a few ways to access that garden. From my bench I could watch about ninety percent of the available approaches. There was a little shadow at either side that was out of sight. As I recalled from our stroll, there was no place inside the walls to climb either in or out at those points. One side had some fairly thick rose bushes, and the other was a koi pond with no koi and a lot of algae or other scummy pond growth. I didn't expect anyone to get through those obstacles unmarked.

I was pretty sure I could remove the video camera problem. That would do nothing to help me with the patrol car and police officers I watched cruise up and park. Maybe they were just on a break. Or maybe they were staking out the bar and the garden to see who "returned to the scene". They were in my way whatever their purpose might be. Back behind the tattoo shop was an old-fashioned fire escape. Just like the ones you see in all of those movies from the northeast. Usually, they host gunfights, or chases, or romantic Romeo and Juliet scenes. In this instance, the escape gave me a rusty path up the building. From that vantage, I would be able to see even better. Not only the approaches but into the garden itself. An added advantage was that with the approaching sunset, there would be ample shadow up there for hiding an aged and suspicious ex-mercenary.

When dusk was just falling I made my move from the bench down the alley. Going up the iron steps was not the most silent thing I'd ever done. I doubted anyone would hear me above the metal music below or the vibrating needles of the tattoo artists. Once up top I quickly got a couple of goodies out of the duffel and got to work. In minutes I had a completely legal "plinking" rifle assembled along with an inexpensive low-light scope. The gun was powered by compressed air and fired nothing more than small pellets. They'd come a long way with such guns since Ralph had asked for his Daisy Red Rider from Santa. The newer models looked just as inoffensive as old BB guns. On the other hand, I could kill anything up to small game with it.

When I say low-light, it's not the same as the "night scopes" you see in movies. Low light scopes can be powered or simply well-made telescope sights that gather ambient light. In full darkness, they would be useless. However, in a city the size of Austin, there is very rarely full darkness. Perched in my chosen shadow, I aimed the scope down and watched as the officers took off their caps and shook hands with someone. A few seconds of tinkering cleared up the image and I saw the cops driving away as a vague figure disappeared behind the fence and into the garden. They didn't go far, just around the corner to park at a drive-in burger joint. That should give me a quarter-hour or more to investigate. If I was lucky it might take longer. If I was *very* lucky, I could be inside and gone before they got back.

That brought up another worry. Wasn't that a crime scene? Was there another cop staked out inside the garden now? Who else would they have allowed in? The worst part was I couldn't wait much longer. Already the low light scope was vague. Give it a couple of hours more and all I could identify would be silhouettes. Blowing out my frustration with a deep sigh I shifted the scope. The first shot cracked the lens of the back-door camera at the club. Subsequent shots disabled the convenience store camera and a couple of other cameras that hinted at having the proper angle.

When I was sure that my approach would be safe from filming this time, I aimed the scope back down at the garden. Early evening wrapped the entire abandoned store and gardens in shadow. At least it seemed that way at first. Looking through the scope, I could see movement in those shadows, but you couldn't even see a decent silhouette in the gathering darkness. After a few moments, there was a flash in my lens. Blinking away the surprise and sudden blindness kept me briefly distracted. When the spots and flashes went away, I could see the waver of a small light down below the fence line. From my elevated position, the light was small but clear. Down at ground level, the most anyone might see was a vague glow from within the fenced area.

There was still the odd movement or two, along with the flickering light. Was it more cops? Or was Eachan's attacker down there preparing another strike? Try as I might, I kept returning to the only foolproof solution I could think of. Somehow, I had to get into that garden and get my eyes on whoever and whatever was inside. I couldn't just fire blindly down at murky shadows. What if it was some honest local policeman? Besides, it's just not professional to shoot without identifying your target. Even in the chaos of battle I liked to pick out my targets and make sure I was shooting at foes and not friends or allies. In a small more or less unoccupied garden inside the city limits, I had no excuse at all.

The rifle broke down as easily as it went together. I made my way down the building and through the alley. With luck I could approach the garden from behind the club; get into one of those areas near but not quite opposite the koi ponds and make my way over. From my recon, I knew there were plenty of trees in that sector of the garden. Most of them were willows or other less than sturdy little saplings. However, there was one scrub oak tree growing close enough to the wall that with some moderate luck and agility I could get over the fence and into the foliage with a very small window to be observed.

The whole approach was almost ruined as the backdoor of Helstyxx opened and splashed light and sounds all around me. The first instinct to freeze worked in my favor. A quick movement will draw attention almost every time. In contrast, it takes minimal camouflage to remain unnoticed in a dark alley with flashing neons overhead, as long as you are lucky enough to freeze out of the brightest of glares.

When the door shut, the strobing and pulsing lights from the floor show disappeared to leave me blinking away the after image. By the time I'd cleared my eyes, the bar back was already tossing the clinking and clanking bag of empties into the dumpster. That bag was followed by two more just as large and just as heavy with empty beer bottles and other detritus from a night of reveling gothic youths. This must have been a new kid. I didn't recognize him when he turned and went back in without bothering to look up and see me only half concealed by shadow. Only when the door had shut away the metal music again did I let out the breath I'd held for the last several weeks it seemed.

## 15

---

TAKING my cue from the Havamal or words of the All-father, *Wary I bid you be, but not too wary and quarrelsome. With ale be the most wary, With another's woman as well.* I took my hand away from the holstered sidearm. I wiped a suddenly moist palm against my pants, then hefted the duffel and continued towards the gardens ahead.

My agility wasn't quite up to the task of getting quickly and quietly into the oak tree. Luck made up for that. I was barely over the fence and was reaching for the closest oak branch when the top bar of the fence shifted beneath my feet. Without having a good grip on the branch, I fell awkwardly towards the tree, and the cactus and mesquite planted around it. There was a moment when I had the choice between lunging for my grip and turning to avoid the branches and leaves on my way down. I barely made the choice before gravity brought me down twisting frantically to avoid the dry and crackling branches. I managed to avoid contact except for one forearm that caught on a jutting piece of oak.

That's where my luck kicked in. Despite losing my

balance and falling, I missed the stream that curled towards the Koi pond. Instead, I landed in soft, recently turned dirt. So rather than a thrashing crashing tumble, I came to mother earth with barely a thud and a stifled hiss to contain the profanities that wanted to come rolling out. Once more I rabbited, freezing in the darker shadow of the oak, while my eyes and ears adjusted to the garden shut away from the bustle and boil of Austin proper by its metal fence shrouded in creeping plants.

The first thing I noticed was the flicker of light ahead. It didn't look like a policeman's flashlight as much as it looked like a small flame or fire. The next thing to grab my attention was a low feminine voice chanting too quietly to comprehend from where I knelt. Before I started to move closer, the hair along my nape lifted. Even without opening any magical senses as some wizards and shamanistic types can, I was able to feel a gathering of forces. A darkness seemed to be coiling inward and gathering strength around me in that garden. More imagined than not, a foul rotting stench suggested itself to my imagination. The branches around me seemed to shake themselves as if waking up or trying to convey some message. Those small omens and messages filtered themselves into my thoughts, but I was already moving as the urgency built.

There was no way to know if the covert policeman had been dealt with by whatever witch was operating here. He might be hiding and waiting to figure out what exactly was going on, or his body might be lying in the shadows within yards of me. I willed away that image and crept close enough to distinguish some more details in that dim light.

It wasn't one flame, but several small candles lit and arranged around the spot where I had fought Seamus. To be precise, several of them were arranged in an arc near the puddle of blood from my previously perforated lung. This close I could also tell that volume was not the only issue with my chant comprehension. She was singing so softly to make understanding her hard enough, but she had to complicate it by singing in what sounded like a foreign language from the little I could hear.

The candlelight itself wasn't sufficient to make out much detail. The stain from my blood was just a dark spot on the paving stones. It was a darker gray than the path. Not blood red or even black. If I didn't know what it was, I might have missed it in the wan light of the candles. Similarly, the feminine figure was just the curved and soft looking silhouette that might have been pleasant and inviting under other circumstances. With all but the last candle visibly lit though, it didn't seem like a good time to linger and think about pleasant curves. For all I knew her spell might be well on its way with the lighting of that final candle.

In that instant, I understood a couple of mistakes I had made. From my perspective at the house, those curved claws had been poised to rake at Eachan. The professor had his back to the projection or attack or whatever it was. But now I was willing to bet that had he been watching; those claws would have been poised to strike at me rather than him.

The presence of the caster so near my own blood was coincidence enough to warrant that concern. You've probably heard of using hair or fingernail clippings for voodoo or other esoteric rituals. The truth is that short of a victim's physical proximity, their blood is the best way to break through defenses and ensure the effects of energy attacks. If I had been the target rather than Eachan, then it would account for this location as the origin of that attack. They had a large dose of "psychic" or emotional energy from the fight, and a ready supply of blood that would have lost its connection in just another day at the most. Sunlight has its way of washing the "magic" out of certain connections and materials. Just as thresholds wear out those same things.

There is a reason that vampires and other creatures are leery of entering homes. Many people think it has to do with the whole invitation business. That *does* help to a degree because it makes the space beyond the door more "open" to the space outside. It makes it available to more people if they are allowed inside. But the majority of that drain on creatures sustained or empowered by magic, is the transition between spaces. Transitions themselves wear at abstract connections like magic and spirituality. Don't believe me? Walk outside from a church in session. You can almost feel the burden of that ritualistic space as it lifts off of your shoulders.

By the same token, you can walk into certain parties that have been carefully planned or filled with people who expect to enjoy a loud and rowdy time. Just by passing that threshold, you lose some of your connection to the exterior "you" that was not necessarily in a frame of mind for chaos and mayhem and fun.

And to stretch the "threshold" further, there is a threshold between day and night. At dawn, the world passes from the domain of darkness and creatures of the night. At dusk, it passes from the industry and purpose of daylight back into the realm of darkness and sometimes fell creatures. Even the most mundane person fears the dark at some point in their lives. The transition between those worlds of light and darkness is its own threshold and reacts to magic accordingly. After a few sunrises and sunsets, my blood would be useless as a spell focus. That of course, was if I did not just hose the area down with saltwater or a sage smudge.

Those thoughts flickered swiftly through my mind. They had no time to do more than flicker though. I started moving as soon as I saw the tapered candle dip towards its unlit mate. The last candle in the ritual waited for that light and judging from the oppressive and malignant feel of the shadows around me, that spell was cocked and aimed.

The chanter heard me coming and spun to face me with the lit taper in her hand. There was a gleam of eyes reflecting the firelight from inside a deep cloak and cowl all in cobalt velvet. Another gleam was the naked knife blade rising in her other hand at my approach.

Okay, I might not know her language. It's possible that she had some major advantage when it came to spells and magic. I was, however, willing to bet that she couldn't teach me any surprise lessons with clean steel. I felt the familiar wolf grin shaping my features as I stepped in and circled just out of reach of that knife.

At least she wasn't chanting any more. In fact, she was moving almost completely silently. The dark blue robe covered her from head to toe. There was a wide opening in the cowl, but it was deep enough to hide her features in our less than ideal lighting. We circled silently and slowly at first. Something kept tugging at my attention, but I refused to take notice for the time being. For this moment in time, my focus was on the girl and the knife while that little voice should have been minding its business and watching our surroundings.

I wasn't keeping my eyes locked on her face nor the blade itself. I watched the middle of her chest. The chest and line of the shoulders tell you where a thrust or slash is coming. The position of the feet and how their weight lies over them tell you which direction a foe might step or leap. While I was keeping track of the knife and the feet, I spent much more time watching that chest and shoulder line. That's how I slowly came to understand that my little voice was trying to point out that there appeared to be nothing underneath that robe but some very intriguing femaleness. What can I say? My little voice can be something of a whoremonger.

The sway and lift of breast told me that she wasn't wearing anything to restrain that precise part of her anatomy. A long gliding step to the side also bared an inordinate amount of bare leg to about mid-thigh. That did not surprise me. A good percentage of modern pagans subscribe to the kind of magazine that talks about moon rituals and the power of going "skyclad" or for our purposes...nude. It was apparent that this young lady was only a step or two away from that skyclad state.

No, that didn't surprise me. What caught me unawares was the color of that thigh. I guess my subconscious had been working overtime while I was busy being oblivious. Somewhere in my mind two and two had reached four and subconsciously I had expected the girl facing me to have smokey chocolate skin and smoldering umber eyes. This was *not*, however, a smoky brown thigh. It was the color of sweet country cream and sprinkled with freckles.

While I was dealing with that moment of confusion, she thrust or feinted or at least made a sharp move towards me with the knife-hand. Instinct took over. I pivoted sideways to the attack and stepped into it. This girl was tall and athletic. She responded by trying to sweep backhanded at me with the blade. That was almost perfect. It allowed me to get my arm under and then around hers. At the same time, I stepped back into the spin so that both of our arms were rigidly horizontal to our left, while my chest was pressed against her back.

I tried to snake my right arm around to restrain her further. This girl was having none of that though. Since she was, in fact, a few inches taller than me, it was no hard effort to get her heel up between my legs behind her. I had been expecting such a move though. In modern America, women are taught that an attack to the groin will disable, dismay, or at least discomfort any male encountered. I caught the backward kick on my thigh and used the momentum of our spin to pin that calf between my legs. Once I had her leg immobilized I could hang on and move her around at will.

That was my intention at least. Maybe she hadn't read all of the current books on how women are supposed to fight. Instead of completing the kick upwards and into my delicate nether stones, she drove the leg further back. In the process, she shifted our weight until I was poised precariously above her leg anchored between my own shorter limbs. As she drove back she had been turning sideways. I saw what was coming. In my mind, there were several responses.

The first two tactics would have ended in her badly wounded, perhaps even shot and mortally wounded. The next handful of approaches would have ended with the girl spit on her own knife. I just wasn't entirely sure that was what I wanted.

Before I finished making up my mind, she snapped her body into position. With my weight poised over her hip, her forearm under my bicep, and curling to pull me forward, she had me in an almost perfect position for a step back hip toss. It looked like Judo maybe. Or I guess it could have been Hapkido. Judging from the "energy" tingles I was feeling it was probably the latter.

She had me in position and started the roll that would launch me over her hip, followed by her own weight slamming me down to double the impact. The problem was, the same height that had given her the advantage in a backward groin kick, gave me the advantage when it came to our centers of gravity. Her second issue was that she had probably rarely fought anyone with the muscle density I had. Spreading my legs put my weight lower onto her pivot leg. At the same time, it lowered my center of gravity even more. To further negate her maneuver, I took a deep breath and locked my spine.

She strained and huffed and hauled at my arm. We both knew that the initiative was no longer on her side though. Straining, I pulled her back against me. With her leg trapped under my weight, she was forced to arch her back which reduced her leverage even more. On the other hand, I could neither shift my own weight, nor could I release her left hand which held the knife. A shift of my balance would end with her regaining the upper hand and tossing me to the ground in a manner I imagined would be as painful as it was humiliating. Releasing her hand would no doubt earn me several stab wounds in need of stitching and antibiotics.

Locked in this stasis, we strained against each other. I felt her breath rasping raggedly from her back against my chest. Underneath that ragged gasping for air, I could feel her heartbeat racing. My hand, locked around her knife wrist, could feel her pulse racing there as well. Between my legs, I could feel the shift and play of her thigh muscles. It was distracting as hell. When her hood fell halfway back it exacerbated the distraction. Her scent washed over me from under the fallen hood. It was heather and soap and vanilla and so many subtle fragrances that I lost myself for a moment in the heady aroma. The next thing I knew my mouth was on her neck.

I felt the surge of outrage along her spine. It spurred a new flurry of exertion as she writhed and tried to break my hold. That lasted for all of a second or two. Just as suddenly as I had found her neck, she melted into the thought. A sound that was as much moan as growl came from where the hood had fallen further back. Turning her head even more, she broke the contact of my mouth on her neck. Before I was too disappointed though, she replaced her neck with her scorching lips.

The warm soft demand of her kiss, the cinnamon, vanilla, heather, and spice smell of her, even the physical contest itself added to the heat of the moment. I tasted her tongue and felt her hand unlock from mine. Instead, it arched over our shoulders. With her fingers locked into the short nap of my hair, she pulled me into the kiss and growling and moaning louder into my lips. I felt the energy shift.

Both of us went from wary and cautious, to heedless and desperate. In a flash, she turned in my arms. I let go of her hand as the knife clattered down behind us.

"Dammit, why are you here? And what are you doing to me? Are ye using magic on m' desires?" Her question came out in segments separated by gasping breaths and long torturous kisses.

Without considering the consequences, I let my hands shift down to the waist-high openings at either side of her robe. With my hands separating the sides of the slits, more and more of her flesh was exposed to the greedy touch of my exploring hands. Her skin was velvet and fire and desire made flesh under my fingers. She hooked one leg around mine and let her bare foot curl against my calf and pull me tighter against her.

"That was my question." I guess my own response was a little broken and breathy as well. On the other hand, this was one time I found the aftermath even more intense than the battle itself. "I came here to stop you from recasting a spell at me or my friend...whichever was targeted. But why are you attacking either one of us?"

She didn't seem to mind my hands against her under the robe. At least it seemed that way from the way she pulled one of my hands even higher under the cloth and arched away from me. Between the moonlight and the candles, I could look down to see the gently mounded curve of her belly, the swell of hip that narrowed into a high waist and fit but feminine torso. The oblique muscles at the side of her abdomen slanted up to support those very intriguing breasts that had first clued me into what she lacked in the way of undergarments. Under her hand, mine curled over one soft but firm breast. At my touch, the center of that delightful softness swelled and pressed insistently into my palm.

"AH!" She gulped in a deep breath before answering. "No spells. Candles"

Her mouth closed on mine again and for several breath-taking moments, neither of us spoke. For my part, I didn't even think about speaking. I was too attentive to the feel, the smell, and the taste of my Maureen. For that moment she was irrefutably mine. I could feel the melding of us as clearly as if it had been written across the stars. Then her mouth was off of mine, so she could continue. "Candles for Seamus."

Saying his name seemed to at least partially shake her loose of whatever was engulfing us both. "Candles for my brother that YOU killed."

Yea, the moment definitely seemed to be deteriorating.

"So are you here for me now? Or do you mean to get another band member? Perhaps our little brother?" I felt her muscles tighten but that was not as important as it might seem. I looked back at my foggy memories of the last few minutes. Had I imagined that dark and malignant energy when I came over the wall?

A quick glance around me showed that the shadows *still* seemed darker and more menacing than they ought to. The light of candles made the immediate area around us warm and welcoming. Beyond the small circle illuminated by flickering candlelight, the trees and the shadows themselves seemed to be stalking back and forth just out of clear view. Again I heard that rattling, as if the branches were long talons sharpening themselves against each other.

"Maureen! No time!" My voice was sharp, focused, not panicked but sharper and higher pitched than normal. "Are you a witch or not!?"

She never got to answer. The tree branch caught her almost precisely the way it had caught me when her brother died. There was a nauseating dropped-melon sound as the wood impacted her head. If she hadn't already been in my arms, I don't think I could have caught her in time. She fell as if someone had cut her puppet strings. Nerveless and boneless, she collapsed, and I barely managed to lower her to the walkway.

## 16

It is almost never a good idea to have your arms full of even a very attractive girl at the precise moment you meet a monster out of legends. I let part of my mind shut itself away from the rest. That part of my thoughts was clear of worry or anxiety or almost any kind of emotion. It was a trick I had learned over the course of many battles. Isolate the "scout" in your head. Let your mind work free of distraction. I guess some people would call it your subconscious. All I know is that I can segment my awareness in extreme instances.

Right that moment, the isolated portion of my senses was drinking in the images and sounds around us. It would come up with some thoughts and plans and let the rest of my head know what it had come up with. If it managed to come up with anything worthwhile at least.

While that was happening, I was assessing the damage to the girl in my arms. Her breathing was shallow and irregular, her pulse thready but there. Instead of a knot and contusion, she had a very LARGE goose egg that had split down its length. It was a good thing the blood was not gushing but instead pulsed out in a slow trickle along with her sluggish heartbeat. At least she was breathing and her heart was beating. That would have to do for the moment. I couldn't help her until I dealt with the thing my isolated attention was starting to gibber about.

Before I could pinpoint the exact source of the sounds and movement in the trees, that source took care of that problem for me. One minute there were menacing trees and undergrowth in front of me. And in the next, there was another woman. She was tan with green eyes and hair that ranged from honey blond to nut brown. The sight of her was enough to incite a holy man to unholy thoughts. Oh, and of course she was as naked as a newborn babe.

She didn't walk towards me. At least I never could recall her crossing the distance. There's a very vague memory of her undulating forward on hips that worked with different components and specifications than normal women possess. The shift of her shoulders with each liquid stride did some very distracting things to the bare and flawless upper torso she aimed at me like weapons. If they were weapons then they were loaded and primed to fire.

Like I said, I don't recall her crossing the entire distance. She was stepping out of the shadows with that wanton and seductive stride, and then she was at my side helping me lower the unconscious girl to the ground. "There we go pretty man. We put her down unharmed and then we have business you and I, no?"

The heat of her hand on my upper arm threatened to drive memory and thought alike from my head. My heart was pounding out a rhythm or a drum message maybe. The message was enthusiastic and friendly towards the woman with her delightful muscle shifting to peek and hide again in the shadows from the flickering candles. "So my pretty

pretty, we are finally alone. The last time we were alone I could not indulge myself. There was a job to do, no?"

Beneath the silken touch of her hand on my skin, there was an odd feeling as if the silken skin covered rock hard muscle or maybe coarse sinew. For some reason though, that seemed right and quite the way all women should feel. Again that segmented part of my head was screaming a denial. It can be a very annoying crusher of fun and entertainment though. I decided to ignore it. In the meantime, this newcomer with the sultry crooning voice and the silken tresses had circled behind me from the left to the right. As a result, it was my right arm she reached for possessively. "Step back into the trees with me pretty boy."

Her hand on my arm was insistent, but it was not aggressive or violent. If anything, it seemed to hint at unrestrained passion. Or maybe it was barely restrained passion. Whatever her own emotions were, she was fanning my desires into flames of arousal and possessiveness and other fiery and not particularly endearing directions. So, when she made her next comment it seemed only proper and logical. "You want me, do you not, my pretty? Come to me and feel the heat, the passion, and the price of sating yourself."

I could feel the compulsion trying to shut down any resistance. She had strong magic. It wanted to keep me dull and complacent, like the cows walking through the door of the slaughterhouse. A smell of damp earth and raw meat came to me along with a heady aroma of perfumes and smoke, wine and good whiskey, vanilla, cinnamon, and chocolate all warred in a confusing tangle of half-real smells. There are many names for it. Clairvoyance, divination, the Sight, or Aura reading probably fits in the category.

For me, it's not really a sight or view. I sometimes get smells. Sometimes if it's strong enough I'll get a taste in the back of my palate. As she started to draw me to the ground beside her, the rune inside my left earring flared almost as bright as the flickering candles. I smelled a scent that reminded me of campfires, and mountains, and somehow it reminded me of thanksgiving?

I never saw the strike coming. But I knew from the tightening of her hand on my wrist what was about to happen. My defensively raised knee burned like fire and that line of flame and pain shot from the knee up to mid-hip. I saw the surprise in her own eyes as my free hand came up to smash into her throat. Men typically go for the knockout punch by striking the point of the chin and driving an opponent's jawbone back into the ganglia of nerves at the back of the jaw. This tends to leave the target of such a blow dazed, if not completely unconscious.

That's not a bad disable. But just below that target is the throat itself. And at a particular part of the throat, rings of cartilage are protected by a single bone called the hyaloid. It is small and light and easy to break. Normally a punch or side of the hand to that location doesn't simply render an opponent unconscious; it leaves them panicked and struggling for breath in an airway that won't maintain its shape. It swells from the abuse which further closes the passage until little or no air can get in. A foe doesn't simply go to sleep and wake up with a headache. Without competent medical help, they go to sleep and just don't wake up.

The blow to her throat ended in a snap and crunch, just as expected if there's decent damage to bone and enough cartilage. She, however, did not fold over and start gasping for air. There was the shock I expected. Her eyes flared in confusion and astonishment. It's a good bet that she had used that sexual whammy on dozens if not hundreds of victims. It had always worked for her before. Then again this was probably the first time she had faced somebody who expected some mental manipulation and had a defense readily at hand.

I let the wolf-smile steal over my face. "Surprise, tree bitch."

You would think that given enough time, I might have learned never to gloat until they start to decompose. And even then, you have to make sure that decomposition isn't just a phase certain creatures are going through. I mean, a vampire? Already decomposing from what I hear. Zombies? Decomposing is what they do best. There are others. But you get the idea. This one wasn't decomposing or even on the path towards such a condition. I saw the shock and confusion change. Just my luck it didn't change to pain and unreasoning terror. Nope, she got angry.

There was an actual gleam of flame in her eyes as she reacted to my attempt to kill her. Her kick caught me square in the chest. I felt at least one rib snap and it felt like my sternum snapped in two. I knew that the latter was only an impression or sensation though. Her kick had been strong enough to break a rib or two. My sternum, however, felt fine. Or rather it would be fine once the muscle spasms let me catch my breath. For the moment my entire chest felt on fire and that same burning sensation seemed to be spreading to my head and from there to every other part of my body. Her eyes also burned with a clear flickering flame. In the semi-darkness, it looked as if she had candles for pupils, or perhaps she was just remembering one of those kinds of events that really stick with you. If it was an event, it was probably one of her least favorite memories. Her keening wail rooted me in place just as I managed to regain my stance after that stunning kick. The heat of her rage and pain was palpable. The raw emotion stripped away at my protections and left me gasping for breath myself.

"Burn faithless wretch!" The flames in her eyes seemed to leap across the space between us. The next thing I knew I was slapping at the sparks and licking flames that sprang from all over my clothing. In seconds her keening and furious gaze had me reeling, disoriented, all but paralyzed, and slightly ablaze. If nothing else, the witch knew how to make an impression.

There was a jolt that vibrated into the muscles of my stomach. That jolt was followed by a nauseating sound as of leather or skin parting to reveal what was beneath. Fortunately for me, it *was* leather and not skin. Even more fortuitously, what it revealed was the polymer plate of a protective vest under my leather coat.

She paused long enough for a look of shock to show on her face. By then I was already moving. Just a few steps away was the old koi fish pond. Now scum covered and a little unpleasant to smell, it was nonetheless at least half full of water. I felt clawed fingers rake at my back and rip away the rear plate as well as most of the ballistic material that held it all together. At the moment, the crackling flames eating at my clothes and flesh were a larger priority.

When I came out of the water a little bit of scum or algae or fish crap, something like that, came with me. The flames were out though and the water helped clear my thoughts. I might have slowed down the sexual charms, but this creature knew her business. The fear and paralysis were real and powerful magic of the mind. I didn't have time to reflect on that though. The bitch was changing.

As she stepped into the moonlight, the delightful package of feminine flesh shifted and changed. Pale skin darkened and grew ridges. The rest of her body changed to match the nine-inch long talons she had grown to rake my armored vest apart. At the tip of each long wooden looking spike of her fingers, a greenish tinted sap or liquid shone.

I abruptly remembered the fiery pain from her first attack when I'd blocked what I thought was a punch to the groin. Looking down, I saw the raw flesh and radiating redness from a wicked slash that went in a few inches above my knee and ripped down to raggedly exit almost at the joint itself. No wonder I'd felt that burn. If I had to hazard a guess, she'd injected a hefty dose of that green toxin into the wound.

I heard her throaty and raw laugh while I gaped at the wound. "Yes, pretty man, I hit you with the sap. Right now it probably burns. In just a few seconds or maybe minutes..."

She cocked her head and looked me over again. With the pants leg shredded and my jacket and shirt likewise in tatters, she could now see quite a bit more of my frame than most people ever get to glimpse. The heavy slabs of muscle festooned with a number of tattoos drew her eyes. "Yes, I'd say you can fight it a few minutes, child of the north. The big ones always take a little longer. Are you going to fight me too? That makes it faster but it's so much more fun than just waiting. A good fight is almost as intoxicating as when I take apart all the lovely pieces."

Reaching down, I hefted the front plate of my vest and spun it around. What should have been shoulder straps would make a decent set of grips wrapped around my left forearm. With the makeshift shield locked in place, I reached over to the field pack dangling by one shoulder strap. From an outside loop I drew the old OD green, army issue "E-tool" short for entrenching tool. It had been made decades ago as a one-piece survival tool. Depending on how you tightened the lug it was a hammer, club, axe, shovel, or even a pickaxe. I spun the lug a couple of times and got the blade at just the angle I wanted for my hand ax. "Well then, tree bitch, let's have some fun."

She was already running at me with her fierce anger hissing and whistling between green and brown lips. For my part, I came off the ground like a runner from the blocks. In the instant of drawing the makeshift axe in my hand, I'd also stepped onto firmer ground. This gave me the footing I needed to meet her charge with a counter charge of my own. Her wooden claws raked the air as I twisted my face just out of reach. That gave me the perfect view of two of those fingers flying off to plop into the pond. I hadn't been sure the axe would be effective. It too had a few surprises though, like the anodized coating that contained a fair mix of silver, or the runes carved into both blade and handle.

Her backhand swing lifted me off my feet and dropped me back to a knee several feet away. I stayed in that position with one leg bent back beneath me and my shield propped up in front. Without moving I took in her furious rage as well as a hint of shock and fear when she saw the wound from the axe. This time her voice was as venomous as her fingers when she snarled. "So! You want to make yourself a hero? Like one of the old Vikings in your stories maybe? You only have a few minutes before the sap puts you to sleep. Do you think you can fill those shoes, child?"

With a grin, I ripped the shirt off to reveal not only more of the muscle she had already noted. It showed all of the tattoos placed over a period of decades. It also revealed a whole bevy of scars and burns, including the raw red scar of the spear thrust that had taken part of a lung and ripped my heart in half about a thousand years ago. "If I still had the shoes, I'm pretty sure they'd fit."

She was still wide-eyed and slack-jawed when I sprang

and swung the axe again. This time there was more resistance. It didn't quite remove her other hand at the wrist. But that hand dangled from a strip of bark or leaf I guess. A long vein of darker and harder wood stuck out of the partially severed arm. It dripped a similar green sap or oil and I watched as the bone or branch writhed and lengthened looking for its dangling counterpart.

Another incredibly fast backhand blow rocked me. This one didn't drive me to my knees. It did ring my bell for a good few seconds. When I shook my head to clear it, I saw my foe bent over the woman who had come to mean so much to me. My heart jumped up and tried to come out with my horrified yell. Instead, the yell choked past it and left my heart in my throat. I saw those three remaining spiked and poisonous talons poised over Maureen's throat.

They didn't plunge down and I decided maybe she was supposed to be a hostage now.

The next words spoken confused that issue. "No! She is not part of the bargain! I cull the faithless men! Not helpless wives and daughters!"

The eyes were not seeing me, nor were they seeing the girl in front of her. Instead, this tree creature was gazing up as if looking at someone perched somewhere between her eyes and the moon. "NO, I say again! She is not my prey!"

This time I could almost hear and understand a murmuring voice. It seemed to be carried on the wind itself. I couldn't tell exactly which direction it came from nor could I understand even a single word. I knew it was a feminine voice, but then it became even less understandable as the odd argument between tree creature and nebulous voice switched to what sounded like Portuguese.

Now I could catch a few words from the tree, but none at all from the other voice. I wanted to edge closer and finish it.

At the same time, I wanted to get as much information as possible. It seemed unlikely that the woods woman was also the spell caster that had brought me here. Maybe if I waited I could get a clue about whom or what else was involved.

I didn't get the chance though. Screaming in a piercing note that silenced the sounds of the night and even some of the city sounds around us, the creature reached down and instead of slashing the pale girl, gripped her by the hair and slung her bodily to land in the pond with a dull splash that sent muck and swampy water geysering. I understood enough of what she said. It amounted to, "No I will not. We will let fate take its course and decide."

Before the echoes of that scream had faded, the now tall and gangly looking woman was running towards the shadows among the trees in the middle of the lot. There was very little in this world that I wanted more than to chase her down and hack that unnatural brown flesh into kindling sized pieces. But the one thing I could not ignore was the fate of that unconscious girl in a few inches of water.

When I got to the pond she was barely submerged, but barely is enough when it comes to breathing water. I tossed the makeshift shield over by my pack and bent to lift the girl. Despite her height and muscle tone, she was no real burden. Then again, I was also more than a little charged with adrenalin. Any fight will get your heart beating and adrenaline pumping. Toss in some pre-fight passion, and a supernatural foe, well those adrenal glands get a real work-out. And that was not a good thing for me.

From the conversations and odd phrases, I thought I knew something about what I was dealing with. This creature was a tool of vengeance. She wanted her "faithless" victims paralyzed or disoriented. But she wouldn't want to deprive them of the fear or the pain of her vengeance. She would want them aware, terrified, and in agony as she exacted her payment. So it seemed that if I could stay awake, there was a better than even chance that I could get the girl to the hospital and fade away in the confusion.

True the venom hadn't managed to put me down, yet. Part of being a more or less dead warrior is that toxins and such don't have quite the impact they might. On the other hand, we can't ignore these things indefinitely. Once the girl was safe, I dropped my bag beside her and dug in it to find one of the herbal pastes I'd made for infections and such. With any luck it would help keep the sap from taking its toll. I also had the sneaking suspicion that the venom was not made to kill. I doubted it was even made to knock me unconscious or deprive me of my senses.

Yep. That was a good plan. I plastered Maureen's head wound first, mostly as a precaution. After that, it was only a few minutes' work to tend to my own wounds with the salve. I had just finished and put the jar back in the bag when I heard the familiar little metallic snick of my revolver being cocked. And then Maureen shot me.

## 17

I UNDERSTAND ALMOST everyone has their own belief in what happens in the afterlife. There's Nirvana, Heaven, Elysium, and many more. Those are the more positive outcomes. There are numerous neutral and negative outcomes as well. I don't know a lot about most of them. However, I am pretty sure that very few people expect to wake up to a full and fruitful day of torture after being shot. Of course, this wasn't the first day. I'm not sure what day it was. They tended to blend into one long, delirious, gut-wrenching battle of sadistic pain in direct competition with a weak but determined will.

Each morning was the same. I woke to find myself already at the feast table. My old brothers would stomp in and settle around the table to hurl good-natured insults at each other and hilarious dire warnings at me. They altered the warnings with suggestions to my captor and his assistants. The Ravens were bad enough. They were much more creative than the wolves. But neither furred or feathered torturer held a candle to the Valkyrie Kara, or Kara the

Stormy. She possessed dark hair that was rare amongst us, and eyes of a tumultuous grey and blue mixture. But that wasn't why she was Stormy. No Kara had an almost limitless capacity for vengeful violence.

She was also my "handler" for several centuries. You might say she took it personally that I evaded her and everyone else from my old life. She took it very personally indeed. Most days she didn't get her chance until later. Old one-eye would give her a shot at me during the feast after everyone fought and trained and had a full day of typical Viking "stuff".

By then the wolves both had a bite or two. The ravens usually took an eye. Just one. They liked me to be able to see what was coming. They'd take bits of lip or ear but never the tongue. I needed the tongue to beg for mercy. That was, after all, the point. That was the one thing I concentrated on every day. I was determined, utterly committed, to not give them the satisfaction of a sob or plea for mercy. If I held on long enough or managed to make one of them mad enough, then I'd either pass out from the trauma or simply keel over to start reaching room temperature.

Death was a boon in that it meant the end of the pain and degradation. For that day. That after all is the lot of Einherjar. Training, fighting, or simply engaging in typical acts of random bravado and stupidity often ending in a fatality. Valkyries always awakened their chargers after any fatality. If they didn't perform adequately, they might awake the next morning, weeks, or even years later to start all over. If they performed admirably they would wake for the feast and have a raucous joyful evening of good-natured banter and random violence along with a little testosterone-fueled sexual tension as the supernaturally lovely warrior-maidens circulated amongst them.

For the past few centuries, there were even a few Amazonian female types sitting at the table. Of course, the all-father had not gained enough enlightenment to have male Valkyrie at the table. I heard somewhere that Freyja had designated a few men as choosers but so far, they weren't admitted to Valhalla itself. If I was particularly hardy or my tormentors particularly lax in their job, I might still be up by the time the others arrived to feast. That was the hardest part in some ways. My brothers had a fairly rough sense of humor. Each and every one of them seemed to take pure joy in describing my plight in ever more graphic and degrading terms. That was worse than when they shouted encouragement and suggestions for my further humiliation and mutilation.

That was when Kara was usually given her time to play. She was particularly fond of doing moderately nightmarish things to my groin. She also had a few lifetimes of knowledge of anatomy and combat techniques including up to date training on pressure points and such. This, of course, made her highly efficient if she kept control of that tumultuous tempest of a temper. That was my usual ploy. Since they left me my voice, I did my best to nudge her over that line. It hurt like the fires of creation itself, but it was usually over in mere minutes if I could spark that rage.

That was the first thing in my thoughts this morning. Like I said, I didn't know how many mornings I'd been tied to the same chair down the high table and opposite the All-father. He had a good view of the proceedings from above me and a few scant feet away. I did not like the opposite view as much as he seemed to relish the entertainment my tortures provided. I tended to keep my head down and shoulders slack as if asleep. That's probably why I didn't notice the difference at first.

Normally, the stomping of hundreds of boots at a time is accompanied by various semi-bestial growls, grumbles, yawning, and ribald commentary. This morning, however, there were fewer boots crunching and no other sounds at all. I should have guessed what was up given that information. I'll blame anxiety and preoccupation for my failure to notice right away.

When the oddity caught my attention, I cautiously looked up. Instead of sitting and gloating from the high-seat, old Ygg of the single eye was walking around the table pausing to murmur to one or two of the seated warriors. Here and there he gave his blessing. Behind him, a trio of the Valkyrie was doing much the same thing. To my almost palpable relief, Kara was one of them. She was not stopping to talk to whole tables of men like the other two. I recognized them, but could not recall their names.

Each Valkyrie was in the "official" uniform. All leather and gleaming metal with furs and sharp steel. Their hair was rich, thick, and luxurious. Even without a hint of a breeze, it looked like their tresses were a split second from flowing on the wind while light isolated and highlighted the perfection of their features. They almost always looked that way for a team about to go on a mission. Or for one coming back from a particularly grueling assignment.

Those "choosers" walked among their men and refilled their cups with mead, coffee, or any of several other beverages depending on the man, his culture, temporal origin, and personal tastes. Kara waited impatiently behind them. It didn't take much imagination to see that she was on the verge of toe-tapping and scowling. That would not be appropriate though when in formal mode. Like the others, she was dressed as the very image of a Valkyrie. Instead of silver and golden light from no origin though, she radiated a cold blue aura with random flashes of silver and grey.

Finally, the stormy chooser could pass her two sisters where they stopped to laugh seductively with their teams. Instead of going to a table of her own men though, Kara strode briskly to the head table and stepped up to one Einherjar sitting by himself. With a growl that sounded almost as angry as it did wanting, she curved herself into his lap and wrapped her arms around his neck to draw him into a kiss that was feral and heated and completely engrossing for the recipient. I remember feeling one or two of those myself. Before I escaped, before I was lost on a mission and stayed off their radar for decades.

When Kara extricated herself from the arms of a very glassy-eyed and even hungrier looking warrior, her eyes lighted on me. A cruel and amused smile curved her lips even more. With a much more seductive purr, she reignited the heat and hunger of her soldier with another even more feral joining of lips and arms. Perhaps he was already pretty far under. I don't think he ever noticed that her eyes stayed open and locked on mine. Nor did he react when she spoke to me rather than the man wrapped around her. "Remember when it was you in my arms? Even in my bed? Remember when you felt the scorching kisses of the tempest and the passion of the storm? But now you only get the uncertainty, the fear, the pain."

Again, she bent to her task of driving all thought from her man and reinforcing his orders for the upcoming task. This time she did close her eyes and gave him all her atten-tion. But her eyes were on mine again when she rose and tapped him on the shoulder. He rose with a surge of power and purpose. That's when I saw the odd uniform. If I had not been free of her spells for recent years, I'd have been mystified. My own lifetime made me more familiar with Ring Byrnies and leather armor. But those unattended recent years gave me insight. I recognized a suicide vest when I saw one. I also saw that this Einherjar had darker skin and a darker beard than any I had served with.

So, old One-eye was promoting current chaos and mayhem? Or maybe he was just getting paid to help one side or the other. It didn't really matter, but it did reinforce my belief that if I got out, I'd do almost anything to avoid coming back. The choosers and their boss had their own goals and beliefs. Those didn't always make me comfortable. I liked the fight. I enjoyed the heat of battle and testing my strength against other men of war. But I did not like war as it was waged these days. Too much collateral damage. Too much destruction and dishonor. And too many times I think I'd probably been fighting on the wrong side of conflicts.

At least the other teams were wearing normal combat uniforms of one sort or another. A few dozen had on their typical camouflage BDU's. Another dozen or two wore commando-style black sweaters with black combat pants and boots. Their weapons were smaller, more portable, and all looked thoroughly trained with the suppressed firearms and short vicious looking blades and even tomahawks. Yeah, they were going to go play special forces someplace. In some ways, they were even better than traditional spec ops teams. Einherjar knew they'd wake up to feast whether they lived or died. They fought without fear though they also fought smart. At least they did if they were "programmed" for a sense of survival.

I hadn't been paying attention. Before I recognized that she moved. Kara's lips were soft and seductive against my ear. "Don't be jealous,love. He's not as special to me as you are. I must go to watch over my man. But I didn't want you to think I'd forgotten you. And we'll have some nice quality time tomorrow while these and the others are here to watch and cheer me on. For now, though...a little reminder."

The icy burn of preternaturally sharp steel told me she'd actually started my day with the way she usually ended it. I felt hot wetness spreading along my breeches. From past experience though, I knew better than to look down. If I kept my eyes away from the damage sometimes I could pretend I didn't know. She wasn't done though. Still, with her lips caressing my ear she reached into a belt pouch and drew out a tightly closed jar which she opened to upend over my now ripped and blood-soaked breeches. "I got you some pets. They're called Bullet Ants. They make the bite of fire ants feel like a gentle kiss. Enjoy."

She was right. I'd never felt anything like it. Even hot steel in my guts seemed a pale sensation compared to whatever in Hel those little buggers had in their bite. And all of them seemed drawn to the deep cuts on my thighs and groin. The first scream came out before I could even think about choking it off. That drew a laugh from Kara and a frown and less than happy grunt from the All-father. "Dammit girl, you've deprived me of my challenge."

He walked over in firm strides that seemed to shake the room. That stern old man with the hair brushed over one eye and shoulders like a weightlifter strode with the bearing of kings and warriors. Strength still radiated from him as well as cold certainty in his place in the world (or worlds as the case may be). When he came to tower over me, I had lost my sanity. I'm quite certain all he saw was the wild sightless gaze of an animal in pain and fear. "Dammit. We'll start again when he wakes up. Hugin! "

I never saw the Raven take wing from the back of the All-father's high wooden seat. Normally I'm sure his rending claws and beak would have made me want to scream in pain and terror. This time I barely noticed as his beak popped my eyeball like a grape. And it was almost a relief when those raking talons and beak tore into my brain and brought relief and rest.

## 18

DAYLIGHT WAS COLORING some really cheap hotel blinds when I blinked the morning crust out of my eyes. I blinked like that maybe a half dozen times before memories of Valkyrie and ants and ravens came crashing back. Before I caught myself, I was scrambling atop the mattress to get my back firmly to a headboard that banged and echoed off the thin wall behind me. The pain of that movement took my breath away and reminded me of the end of that nightmare. But this was not the same. There was no longhouse hall. No wolves or ravens and nobody waiting to torment me. My heart was still racing and breath rasping out in raw burning gasps as I looked around to figure out exactly where I was.

From the thin and topographical feel of the mattress, I was in something less than a four-star hostelry. The carpet was a grey-brown where the worn sections didn't show through, or various stains did not cover its threadbare glory. The walls were presumably white, though a thin varnish of cigarette smoke and untouched dust made that a hazardous guess. Even the thick blocky television would have been more at home on the set of Magnum or Miami Vice. You don't see box-shaped TV's anymore. These days they are all streamlined thin beasts with high definition and so many thousand pixels per centimeter or so.

The net effect was of a cheap motel room from an eighties or nineties era detective show. Atop the miniature cultivated lands of the mattress, I tried to roll over but was brought up short by a recurrence of the pain that had been smothered in my terror from the dream. Don't get me wrong. Pain and I were old friends and occasionally more than friends. We'd had some pretty intense flings from time to time. However, it had been quite some time since I *woke up* in pain.

First off, I had more actual battlefield medical experience than most doctors would ever see. That meant I could repair quite a bit of the damage I encountered from time to time. Secondly, I rarely went to sleep with wounds that would bother me the next day. It took more than a casual trauma to put me or one of my brothers down. For the past few years, I was always coherent enough to put together one of those healing rune binds before letting exhaustion or agony or trauma send me to oblivion. Thus, I almost always woke up on the road to recovery and needing only minor pain relief to ignore anything I'd suffered in recent memory.

This was not the case when I woke up in a cheap motel near Round Rock. My chest and neck were screaming at me and it felt like several fiery claws were digging into the muscles atop my shoulder. I would have expected my leg to be the worst after dealing with the green ichor or venom of whatever she had injected me with. The terrifying fact was that I couldn't feel that leg at all. When I gave an experimental wiggle, I couldn't even feel my toes and that was worse than any pain or fear so far.

I can recover from most wounds given enough time. It was a perk of my previous work for Kara and One-eye. We were tougher than most people we encountered. Infections and poisons took longer but they could still finish us eventually. It was the same with blood loss, food poisoning, shock, and most injuries. But limbs don't grow back without divine assistance. Nerve damage was almost always a major issue. We could take a good hit to the head, but actual brain trauma was tricky. It might recover as quickly as a scratch elsewhere, or it might leave one of us shattered and incapable of normal function. The same could be said for spinal injury.

I had reason to know that last bit myself. I have decent memories of my first couple of decades. Other than that though I have very spotty memories of Valhalla and our assignments from that eldritch place. Maybe that was from the injuries that left me in a MASH field tent in Vietnam. That's a story for a different time though. The important part was, if I lost the leg it meant I was a cripple until something killed me. That's if there still *was* a leg under those cheap thin blankets.

I wanted a very large straight scotch, preferably a double. Two or three would be even better. Hovelish motels, however, are not known for hospitality bars or room service. As a result, I had no choice but to take a handful of slow deep breaths, bolster my courage, and flip the blanket aside. Almost immediately my probing hand encountered heavy gauze soaked with something that smelled bitter and antiseptic.

Whoever had done the first aid was much more enthusiastic than they were skilled. Bandages went almost from hip to mid-calf. I guess they might have opened the wound to drain some of the poison out. That was not very likely though. Like I said, my brothers and I handle such injuries a whole lot better than most people. What was more likely, was that somebody with better intentions than training had used too many bandages and tied them too tight. That would explain the loss of sensation at least.

I glanced around the room and spotted the contents of my pockets on the dresser. The tattered field pack was right by the bed and within easy reach. I tugged that pack up beside me in the bed and dug through it until I came up with a little pocket knife with a locking three or four-inch blade. It took several minutes, and I managed to cut myself no less than four times but eventually, the bandages were off and I could see the wound packed with some sort of yellowish pungent paste.

A couple of odd little incisions confirmed my assumption. The wound had been drained. Whatever the yellow powder was, it had done a good job. There was very little in the way of swelling and none of the expected angry red lines of poison. The numbness was all from the bandages. They were tight enough to work as a tourniquet. The whole leg started to burn and throb as blood started pumping into it again. At least it looked like I didn't have to worry about being a cripple.

With that worry out of the way, I used the same knife to get the thick pad of bandages off my chest and neck. The entire region had probably been swollen when I was bandaged by my unseen benefactor(s). Now it was bruised looking with a handful of ugly punctures. From the look of it, she'd found my quirky little revolver and hit me with one of the .410 shotgun rounds. It looked like I caught four or maybe five of the small caliber pellets in my neck and shoulder. Two pellets above my collarbone were probably cut out.

The other three had carved bloody furrows in the meat atop my shoulder and at the side of my neck.

Once more, the attention looked thorough but somewhat rough. They'd dug the shot out and packed the resulting wounds with some gauze treated in the same powder as my leg. Whatever that stuff was it seemed leaps and bounds ahead of the modern AMA's solution to infection and toxicity. I used a bag of leftover tape and gauze to put much lighter pads over my chest and shoulder. The neck wound took some further work.

I would have loved hiding the bandage and the wound with some makeup or maybe with a high-necked shirt. Too bad the only shirt around was a plain grey sweatshirt from some thrift shop. It was in a bag along with similarly worn grey sweatpants, socks, and gym shoes just a size or two too large. At the very bottom of that bag was another smaller brown paper sack. That one held the most prized object in the entire room. A bottle of good Irish whiskey sat unopened and beckoning with its smoky amber curative powers.

I showered and dressed with only a little bit of assistance from the amber bottle. Sitting on the creaking and uncomfortable bed, I tried to plan out my next move. Nobody came back to check on me. I searched the entire room without finding a note or a clue about who got me here and tended to the first aid. Maureen wasn't laying around anywhere wounded alongside me. In short, I got shot, had what I was hoping were just some horrendous nightmares, and woke up clueless *and* without the girl. Not my best morning.

Okay, I needed some priorities. In my search, I discovered that the gun and sheath-knife were gone as well as my e-tool. The only thing close to a weapon I had was an inoffensively small pocket knife. Considering the entertainment schedule from the previous evening, weapons were a priority. Thanks to my new attire I could go out in the street and start looking to re-arm.

That brought up another priority. Somewhere a fair supply of my blood was saturating clothes, jackets, and such. There were things a good practitioner might be able to accomplish with that blood as a focus or link. It seemed kind of important to find the bloody items and make sure they weren't a threat.

It might be nice to know what happened to the girl too. I was pretty sure she'd been conscious and with little more to worry about than a headache. She'd been at least healthy enough to pump one into me from my own revolver. Unless the nature witch or tree creature or some still unknown threat had popped up, she should still be okay.

And *then* there was whatever that thing was. I needed some answers and I needed some defenses. I might have some clues about what I was up against now. But then again so did she. There weren't a lot of folks running around who could do the things she'd seen from me. Truth be told, it was kind of stupid for me to let that cat out of the bag. Sometimes the old urges and instincts came back though.

When I was just old enough to be counted a man, I went on my first raid across the seas. That first raid was westward. We struck those Irish villages on their northeast coast, and then circled back to winter with the Scots. Back then it was hard to tell if the settlers of Scotland were closer to being Celts, or closer to being Norse. The ports and hospitality of the Scots were well known and well worth the prices they charged for a little layover between sailing seasons. The hospitality of those lovely Scots women was just as well known. And it was just as worth the effort to win them.

In those days, there were a handful of ways to earn the approval of the women, or for that matter, the older men in your clan or hold. Shipbuilders were always respected. Skalds with their stories and songs to while away the winter hours were popular as well. There were Shaman, priests, fat merchants with their rich clothes and trinkets.

But every boy dreamed of becoming a warrior. We could gain treasure, lands, goods, weapons, and followers on a successful voyage. The better a ship's warriors, the better their chances of returning home with a load of goods, coin, and a few choice slaves.

You could gain renown from feats of strength, acts of bravery, and oddly enough, a good boast or insult could gain you recognition and approval. Good insults were told with relish as were the better boasts. Now make no mistake. An empty braggart was scorned and ridiculed. A good boast was more of a chance to state what difficult task you would achieve. But woeful was the lad that made a boast and then failed dismally. Or even worse off was the youngling who made his claims then never even fought for them. Old men would remind a youngster of that failing for years.

It was in our blood then. When facing a fearsome enemy, you made your boast and you got the job done. Well, I'd talked the talk. Now it was up to me to get the job done. Running this creature off for one evening wasn't enough. Nor did I think she would be *allowed* to drop the fight. Unless I was dealing with some sort of schizophrenic personality with delusions, she had someone else pulling her strings. Someone with enough power over the tree to force her against her will. But not someone with complete control.

I had to think that it went against "orders" to toss Maureen into the water. Oh, sure she could have drowned.

Not good odds though. The cold and wet could have snapped her out of the daze pretty fast. Maybe that's what the tree-she's plan had been. It was fairly apparent that she'd been arguing about the fate of the Irish lass. Now whether her debate opponent was someone with power over her or just a voice in her own head didn't really matter. But it seemed important that my foe was not of a single mind.

In my opinion, however, getting more info about the enemy was a top priority whether she was multiple entities working as one or a single fruit loop tree witch with a few personality issues. Let's be honest, how many things like that were likely to be floating around in a garden shop in the middle of Austin, Texas?

I'd never gotten into the whole cell phone obsession. Don't get me wrong. I have one and it's a pretty handy little toy. However, when you grow up having to wait for a chance to walk or take a horse or sail a boat to deliver a message, well, cell phones just didn't always spring to mind. True to form, I didn't have one on me and couldn't remember the last time I saw it.

The cheap black hotel phone beckoned. I rolled over and read the instructions in a torn and dirty label alongside the number pad of the archaic beast and then dialed nine to get out. Apparently, there had been some anxiety on the other end. The rich Scottish accent came through before the first ring tone was over. Of course, the voice showed no anxiety. In fact, it sounded more like a business receptionist or maybe a desk clerk at a hotel. "Professor Currie's Residence. How may I help you?"

I knew from the voice that it was ole Doc Curry himself and not some well-paid butler or gentleman's gentleman. "I need your help Eachan. Need a ride and some research and the faster the better."

"Of course, my boy!" The relief in his tone was subtle but still gratifying. The old bookworm sounded genuinely concerned for my wellbeing. "I'm quite content to hear you're alive. Do I need the lawyer again?"

"Nope, just get your elegantly clad ass to..." I had to look at the dingy yellow laminated advertisement for the hotel and its services. "Oh Hel, really? The Tumble Inn on Riverside just east of 35."

The Riverside address was on the paper but I had already noticed the steady swish of high-speed traffic and could see the sign for a well-known burlesque club as well as a billiards hall that told me where I was. It was hard to fathom that here, a block or two from the interstate, was a little "barrio" of sorts. Lower-income families lived in a jumble of smaller houses. Sometimes there were even two or three families in a house the size of what would pass for a gardener's shed further south where the wealthier folk lived across the river. The hard part to fathom was that just a block or two the other side of the strip club and pool hall, the houses, and property value went up dramatically. For someone who grew up where farmsteads and villages and towns were all usually a good day's ride apart, such a drastic change in living conditions in such a short area was mind-boggling.

I didn't let it boggle my mind for long though. There was too much to be done. Apparently, Eachan agreed with me. "On my way my boy. Meet me outside in half an hour. You know how traffic can be."

By the light coming in through the window it was already noon or close to it. I needed to get moving. The old scholar was right though, Austin's roads were laid out for far fewer people than lived in the area now. Traffic would make his half-hour estimate optimistic at best. "Thanks, Doc. I don't know how I'll repay you but I definitely owe you after yesterday, and now, today."

## 19

IT DIDN'T TAKE HALF an hour. Eachan showed up in almost exactly one hour. By then I had breakfast at the Waffle Shack next to the hotel. Their coffee wasn't as good as the Doc's. On the other hand, it was the best big breakfast I could find for under ten bucks. I was still lingering over a cup of the sacred Joe when Eachan appeared in his venerable and ever so elegant automobile. The metal monster eased into the parking lot and then circled like some prehistoric shark until he found the parking place he wanted. The driver parked just a door down from the room I had so recently vacated. I nodded to myself thoughtfully and tossed a few extra dollars on the countertop to pay for any syrup stains or coffee rings. Nobody paid much attention as I left.

I was halfway to Eachan's car when the patrol car pulled into the parking lot. I tried to tell myself that it was just a coincidence. Maybe someone passed a bad check or trashed a motel room. Hel, maybe they were just here to roust the hookers that accumulate in cheap hotels like this one. None of those arguments held up though when the car turned right at me and flashed the cherry bar just once to let me know they were serious. I considered running. I also considered the fact that there wasn't any place *to* run. The drab wings of the motel extended for dozens of yards on each side of me. There was one alcove, but I had no idea where it went. And if I ran, well I might as well sign a guilty plea on the spot.

So, instead of bolting for some nebulous hiding place, I carefully held my hands away from my body and any imagined source of a concealed weapon. It was a somewhat demeaning posture since there is no way to pretend you're not holding your arms out away from your body. No real casual posture accommodates that particular stance. Eachan's car door opened and I could all but see him stalking forward to confront the local police with his cane like a cattle prod. The old fellow was sharper than I gave him credit for. Instead of marching over to make a scene, he limped a little more than usual and walked over towards the soda and ice machine along the front wall of the rooms.

He was still fumbling for change when Jackson got out of his squad car and started towards me without so much as a nightstick or flashlight in his hands. Maybe his posture wasn't threatening but there was a definite note of intimidation in the voice he directed at Eachan without so much as a glance. "Hey, money bags. Why don't you delay ruining your palate with a coke and come join us for a little conversation?"

My thoughts towards Eachan were a little less than charitable as well. For one thing, how the hell did he know which motel room was mine? Over a dozen doors were facing that parking lot so why park just next to mine? It was a stretch of coincidence if nothing else. Then there was the even more suspicious timing of his arrival within minutes of the cops. A less suspicious man than I might think that all three coincidences were related and anything *but* accidental. Maybe good ole Eachan was the bait to draw me out for Jackson. If so, it had worked.

Truth be told, most men were less suspicious than I. It's what had kept me out of cells, or government research labs, or the unsavory attentions of some pretty powerful beings. So it should be understandable when I gave Eachan a hard look and a couple of rather harsh slang words before accusing him. "Thirty minutes eh? Must have taken the other hour to arrange for the cops to show up. I mean you already knew which room I was in didn't you? I suppose you and the girl were in it together."

If I expected a look of guilt or even embarrassment the professor disappointed me. His initial reaction was simple astonishment. That quickly turned into something a little more intense. It was an emotion that left his face a blend of purples and reds. It also left him in a very precise and erect posture. He stood with his feet about shoulder-width. His hands rested atop the cane which stood exactly along the midline of his body as he looked at me with a stern and rather cold gaze. "That is twice my boy that I have gone to some trouble to assist you. It is also the second time that you have lambasted me with baseless accusations. I would vehemently suggest that you abruptly and very sincerely find a means to apologize."

While I was still digesting his attitude and trying to come to some conclusions, Jackson interrupted us. "Yeah about that Doctor Currie. How *did* you know which room was his if he didn't tell you?"

"Officer...Jackson, is it? Yes well, I am afraid I am disinclined to answer that question. In fact, I am disinclined to answer most questions. I'm afraid my acquaintance here has made me rather irritable. If you are not going to arrest me for something then I believe I'll just be on my way. If on the other hand, you do plan to arrest me then I should need to call my attorney." I could tell from his tone that it might be some time before he forgave me for this one. Honestly, if he was being truthful, then I would probably feel the same.

It appeared that Sergeant Jackson was less impressed with the old man's righteous indignation than I was. "Right, we'll skip that question for now. I have other questions. Like what does a wealthy and respected college professor get out of paying high powered attorneys to bail out a bartender? Or how about, why would the victim of a terrorist bombing hang around with someone like Mouse here? I mean he's a fun guy I suppose, but there's that fingerprint that links him to a cold case murder in Boston. And that victim in Boston turns out to have ties to the same IRA cell that took credit for blowing some people up in Ireland. People like a young Eachan Currie and his entire family."

I guess that explained the prof's cane and limp. It also caused me no end of embarrassment. For one thing, I had no idea the guy I aced in Boston had ties to the IRA. For me, it was a quick pay-for-revenge beating that went wrong when the idiot pulled a gun. I hadn't even known I'd broken his neck until the newspaper came out the next day. I was still trying to think of a clever deception when the cop continued.

"As for you Magnus, why is it that the fingerprint belongs to a Magnus who is near, as I can figure, sixty some odd years old?" This time it was my turn to stand still as a deer in the headlights under the policeman's scrutiny. "I also find it curious that the guy killed was under contract from his ex-wife for whoring around and beating her ass as well as carving up her face. Kind of like the dead guy that was screwing around on his wife with your boss."

I never got to talk to Eachan. Apparently, the old boy was quicker of wit than I credited him. "As I said officer, I am not comfortable answering questions without my attorney. If I need to call him let me know. Otherwise, I have engagements with people less skeptical of my innocence and goodwill than this current company. Here's a little light reading for you, in between interrogations, Magnus." With a withering look of disdain, he dug into an inner pocket and dropped a fat brown envelope on the pavement between us.

His limp was much less noticeable as the fashionable educator returned to his car. He gave an inaudible set of instructions to whoever was at the wheel and slid into the back himself. The driver of the heavy old machine looked vaguely attractive and younger than the vehicle itself. Probably a research assistant or college intern making some extra cash or extra credit on their grades. I barely got a glance as the vehicle moved predatorily out of the parking lot and into traffic on the access road. The automobile looked not only pretentious but large and possibly hungry. Probably headed out to eat a smaller Japanese import or something.

"So, I guess that leaves you and me Mouse. Why don't we duck into your room and have a talk? There are things I need to know and things you probably ought to know. Bring the envelope." Turning his back as if he could hold me in place by force of will alone, Jackson got in the car and drove the cruiser off to the side of the building out of sight from the highway. I had the door open and was sitting at the beat-up little table by the window when he came in.

I gestured to the small bucket of ice and the half-empty bottle of whiskey while he sat down opposite me. He helped himself to a drink despite being on duty. Only after a strong jolt and a glance around did he speak. "Nice decor. They going for early French ghetto?"

"Could be. I was guessing, Cheap one-night stand." It was hard to remain casual while my thoughts were digging through plans and contingencies. There was also a portion of my attention trying to guess at what all the police knew already. It's a lot easier to sell a deception if you can sneak in some small truths that they already know. It's even better if they think you are unaware of the knowledge they have. "So, what did the prof ask for turning me over? Thirty pieces of silver sounds a little biblical for him. Maybe a plea on something you found on him while you were digging on me? And where'd you get my fingerprint?"

"Hmm? Oh, process of elimination. We had the prints of both victims and their sister offered hers. We just processed the crime scene and sent off the prints unaccounted for. I got back a result with the same name as one of the suspects and Denmark suddenly smells a little fishy. I just got that info today. Of course, the age thing is a little off. But government workers have been known to fuck up a train wreck. A typo on your birth date seems a safe bet eh?" He reached for the envelope between us and started to open it. I guess I probably could have stopped him. I'd already looked though. It was just some information about old German wives' tales and myths.

He skimmed a few pages while I went out to get more ice and then refilled our drinks. "You really on duty or want another?"

"Another what?" He pushed the glass towards me and continued to read.

By the time he'd finished skimming, we'd both almost finished our second drinks. He shoved the papers back in the envelope and handed it to me. "Been off duty since about half an hour before I got here. That's a small bottle. Let's go someplace with a better selection and bigger supply."

With my previous ride long gone and presumably still furiously angry with me, I wasn't spoiled for choices. I got in the front seat beside him. In retrospect, it was probably better than being shoved in the back seat. I was still trying to decide what all to say. Apparently, he was content with his thoughts as well. Even the police radio was considerately silent for a few minutes as we drove. I did catch him glancing sideways at me a couple of times in the car and then again as we walked into a bar and pool hall that was all but empty this early in the afternoon. Still, nothing was said until we sat down.

"Interesting character, your Professor friend." He gestured in the general direction of the brown envelope in my hand. "He really buy that superstitious crap? Some forest woman from the old country chopping up men who trespass in their woods?"

I caught myself shrugging rather than voicing what might be a lie. "He teaches that kind of thing. Germanic history, language, myth...all that stuff. Hard to say what he believes though."

"I guess I can see a connection. *If* your boss didn't chop up the first victim and you didn't butcher the second one as a cover-up. Then maybe his machete pissed off the German wood nymph or whatever the hell she is." He was interrupted by the waitress dropping off two glasses. His was another glass of some name brand whiskey. I hadn't recognized the brand though. I went with a tequila sunrise under the premise that drinking orange juice right after you wake up was just a healthy addition to breakfast. The tequila was not part of my equation. Or maybe it was an antibiotic.

Between the fish crap, algae, and tree sap, I probably needed some internal alcohol to fight infection.

He gave my glass a look combined of pain and disgust. "I don't know how the hell you drink that. If any of the other cops see this they'll think I got a new boyfriend. Hell, it oughta have a pink lace umbrella sticking out of it."

He lifted his glass and took a long drink which was presumably made of manhood and Chuck Norris sweat. "Tell me about Boston."

"You want the current info or something from the revolutionary period? My American History ain't great but it's better than my knowledge of the contemporary northeast."

"Look, Gustaf, I'm being polite here. Came to talk off duty. Gave you a ride. Having drinks and being civil. So....Do NOT fuck around with me. Tell me about Boston." I had to admit. His tough cop routine was pretty good. I couldn't remember the last time I saw better.

"Off duty and off the record eh?" I took a refreshing draught of my "orange juice". He was already suspicious and had the fingerprint. Maybe admitting a little of what he already knew would get me some wiggle room.

"Ok I killed the guy accidentally. Heat of the moment, fog of war, whatever you wanna call it. His old lady hired me to teach him what it felt like to get knocked around. She didn't tell me he had a gun. He got one shot into my, ahem, hip area. And I hit him with one of the best shots I ever threw. He went over a concrete wall in the garage where we were having our discussion. Wasn't much of a fall but he lost his gun into the drain. Looked pretty well worked over and I was hurting like hell from a bullet in the...umm rear hip area. I left him there and went to a guy who would patch you up off the record. So, I got the bullet out, got disinfected, stitched and shot up with antibiotics. The next day our little spat was in the headlines and the suspected terrorist with IRA connections was dead." I left out the payment. He didn't need to know about the friendly little intimate bonus she gave me. I didn't think he needed to start thinking of me as some mercenary or vigilante either. Maybe he'd buy that I was just a concerned friend of the abused wife.

"That checks with what I have on file." He pulled out his little notepad and golf pencil and made a few scrawled notes. "It fits most of what the ex-wife reported to the Baawst'n cops. She gave a pretty good description of the jealous boyfriend who killed her ex too. Brutal thug with tattoos on his upper arms and chest and other interesting areas. Kinda medium short guy with lots of muscles and a crew cut. The unfeeling criminal killed her estranged true love and then fled like a coward. You could tell it was true love because she was still his beneficiary. Good thing she had all that insurance money to help her through the grief."

He put the notebook away and looked at me with a sly smile making little evil-looking slits of his eyes. "Of course, now I owe some good civil servant an apology. That crime scene thumbprint was from about thirty-five years ago. You look really good for someone in his sixties. Looked really good last night when you were scrapping with that weird bitch in the cosplay outfit too. Young and fit. Agile even. What bugs me is how bloody and messed up you were as well as shot up. But you ain't even limping between the car and here. Why do you think that is?"

Damn. He was good. I thought I was playing his assumptions and all the time he was playing mine. I took another drink. Part of me wanted to ask him some questions about what all he witnessed. The worst part was, I didn't have a clue he'd been around. The priority was to ease at least some of his suspicions though. "You saw that huh? Better think this one through Jackson. You probably shouldn't ask for answers you're not going to be comfortable with."

Surprisingly enough, officer Jackson didn't get angry. If anything, he looked amused. "Son, I've been married twice and divorced twice. Buried one of my kids while he was in junior high and watched another one get through college on the money his fiancée made working a brass pole. My daughter was in and out of rehab and therapy until she got a little straightened out and became one of the drug counselors herself. And that's just family. It don't count the blood I've spilled and seen spilled or all of the mothers asking *"Why???"* Ain't alot of questions or answers that make me real uncomfortable. Why aren't you showing a bunch of scars and busted bones when you were last night?"

I toyed with the idea of telling him the whole truth for a minute. Well more like a second. A very brief second. "Would you believe it was all just acting and makeup? The cosplay chick and I were working on some stuff for the next convention."

Jackson tossed a weird knot of half a dozen sticks on the table. It took a minute for me to realize it looked somewhat like a hand. A hand made of knotted and cracking wood. He then did a credible Spock impersonation with one eyebrow and kinda half growled. "I said Don't Fuck with me."

He wasn't giving me a lot of wiggle room here. Maybe *this* time just a shaving or two of the whole unbelievable truth would do what the last attempt could not. "Ok. If you really think you're ready. It was magick. Eachan knows some old-world spells. He also uses some non-AMA approved herbology and maybe even some alchemy. He was keeping an eye out while I looked for more clues at the crime scene so to speak. And then I ran into something really weird. I don't know what that thing was any more than you do Jacks."

"Joseph" He grunted an interruption. "Or when I'm on duty stick with Officer Jackson. Don't call me Jax or Jackie or any of the other cute shit you can think of. When we're sitting around knocking back some booze...even girly orange juice drinks, call me Joe or Joseph."

"Joe Jackson? Really? Like shoeless Joe?"

He shrugged and took another hit of whiskey. "My dad liked baseball. My mom liked reminding daddy that he married a black woman. Joe Jackson did it for both of them. We ain't talking about me though. So, you ran into something weird, got your ass kicked by...a forest woman, wasn't that what the envelope said? And then what?"

"The Prof must have dragged me out of there. I figure the hotel was in his name and he patched up the worst of my injuries. He probably did some of his energy work along with some poultices and herbs. Then reconsidered this morning and led you to me rather than risk being an accomplice. Maybe he even decided I really was the murderer and he was doing the right thing." I decided not to say anything about the girl, for now.

Jackson nodded a couple of times and raised a finger in a circular motion for the server to "circle the wagons" or bring another round. "That sounds crazy as hell. It also sounds like it may have a few glimmers of truth in it. I can only think of one other umm...cop, that might believe you. Got a nephew, works for one of the federal level spook shops. He's always reading crap like this envelope."

He fished in his wallet and tossed some money on the table for when the drinks got there. "Other than that...it's pretty much bullshit. Next round's on you. Now tell me about the gunshot and the girl."

Dammit, what did this bastard *not* know? I sighed and slumped back in the chair a little bit. I mean yea, she shot me and I should probably be mad. I mean who goes shooting someone after what we'd just shared? Or maybe she didn't feel any of it at all and was just keeping me distracted while the big bad bushwhacker got in place. Either way, I didn't want to see her caught up in trouble. If she was innocent I wanted it to stay that way. And if she set me up I wanted to deal with it myself.

"Look, nobody is hurt except for the weird tree bitch, right? Just forget the gunshot. I don't even have the gun anymore. Lost it back somewhere along the way. As for the girl. I figure she was doing the same thing I was. After all, it was her brother that got slashed up the second time. She was looking for clues. She saw me where she thought I killed her brother. Instinct probably kicked in and she grabbed the first weapon at hand. I got grazed but no harm done. She probably dropped the gun and ran before the prof got there and hauled me out. And then good ole Eachan sold me to the cops." I'm pretty sure the bartender across the room could have heard the bitterness in my voice. I thought I'd gotten a read on Eachan. And he'd broken a promise that most practitioners of *any* system would have blanched at. How the Hel did he do that and not suffer any kind of retribution? I was baffled.

"So the old man was watching over you. The girl panicked and ran. Then the prof hauled you out, patched you up, and paid your passage down the river. And nobody but the superstitious old college Wiccan or bruja or what-ever has any ideas about what attacked you? That's a pretty big tale. And boy does it make you look stupid." He started twitching around the shoulders. The shakes got bigger and spread to his ample middle. That was about the time I noticed he was laughing so hard the tears were already forming in the corners of his eyes.

"She panicked and he sold you out!" He laughed some more. "Man, that's awesome. That's fuckin rich is what that is."

He took the glass from the waitress who was smiling a little uncertainly at the big cop with tears running down his cheeks. "Thanks, sugar. Bring us another round on my friend here in about five minutes."

He watched her walk away with an appraising expression while his hilarity slowed down to controllable levels. "That young lady has a very fine stride and a great ass."

He set the whiskey carefully on its faded paper coaster and looked at me like he was ready to bust out laughing again. "That treacherous old man showed up at the station first thing this morning to pump me for info. He stonewalled hard when I asked what he could tell me or where you were. I even showed him what the cells looked like and told him I could put him away for abetting the flight of a suspect. He blew me off and left about two minutes ahead of me after answering what I'm guessing was your phone call. I held him up a little longer, but he finally stormed off flinging threats about lawyers and lawsuits and lost badges."

"As for the panicky young lady? I saw her put a shot into you. Then she started to leave. I could see her expression pretty well when I was sneaking up just in case she wanted to shoot cops as well as bartenders. She looked mad, and confused, and frustrated, and maybe a little sad or startled. Finally, though, she threw your pistol down by the water and bent down to pick you up. She was carrying you with an arm over her shoulders when I popped up and took the other side. The room is in her name. The poultices were hers too. She even let me watch her do some weird chanting and crap after I got back from buying her candles and stuff out of the spice aisle at the grocery store. Then a little after, before midnight, she sent me back out for the clothes. When I got back to the room she was gone and you were sleeping like a helpless baby." Now he'd stopped nodding and was shaking his head with a clear look of disapproval.

He reached down and put a brown wrapped package in front of me. "That's your pistol. I fetched it and cleaned it up. Might have washed away some blood off the ground and some chalk markings around those candles. In my report, it says something about suspected kids messing around the murder scene. Not your name. Not her name. And I sure as hell didn't write any report about a big assed tree bitch coming to life and half killing my suspect from another crime."

I sat there without a word. I thought about the professor stomping off with his wounded pride. And I thought about how sure the tree woman was about her venom. I looked at the faint fading scars on my arms which weren't even sore anymore after the poultices and everything else. "Well shit. I think I owe some people some apologies."

## 20

BETWEEN AT LEAST two days of excitement and a variety of abuses inflicted on my battered old body, sleep was a much more valuable commodity than I am accustomed to. Who knows? Maybe the alcohol brunch contributed to that drowsiness as well. Whatever the cause, I slept a good chunk of the day away. When I woke, I was almost immediately certain that there was no time for something like a regular job. For the first time in months, I called to let Roy know I wouldn't make it in for a scheduled shift.

At least it was a weeknight. Typically, those are slow enough that the college kids and barbacks can keep the servers from having to kill someone. People never believe me, but I've seen plenty of waitresses hurt someone in the process of putting down a fight. The female of most species generally seems deadlier than the male in my experience.

The phone rang a half-dozen times and then the canned message for the bar came on. That in itself was unusual. Normally a call to Roy's office never got to the machine. If he wasn't right there he forwarded the phone to the front where people would be getting ready for the busier evening hours. He had a lot on his mind though. It's not every day you get accused of killing your secret girlfriend's nomadic lover.

I left my message and made a mental note to call later and confirm with a living person that I wouldn't be in. After that, it was time to make the first of my apologies. Fortunately, I'm pretty good with numbers and I'd made sure to memorize the one that had been scrawled in a fit of anger on my hand just a couple of nights past. I dialed it and waited only to get a mechanical female voice telling me to leave a number. What the hel? Two numbers in a row at a time when both should have been available? Maybe I'd missed some catastrophe on the news.

On the off chance that my phone was cursed, I put it away and took a quick shower. As I passed the birdcage, I noticed that the bird was back inside merrily annihilating a phone book. Moving slowly to avoid spooking the little shit, I managed to get the door closed again with Rafe properly on the inside. I felt a little guilty. In all of the excitement, I'd forgotten all about my poor pets. Well, that could be remedied. Rafe was set for food and water for the time being. When I'd settled everything else down I'd see about doing some more research and getting him a suitable treat. The dog I could check on at my next stop.

Still in the long thick bathrobe, I started the coffee pot with a little of the Professor's left-over blend. There was smoked salmon in the fridge and probably time enough so that I could toss a couple of eggs in to boil. Add in a pan-toasted bagel and voila, a meal for the ages. After I ate, coffeed up, and drank a glass of cranberry juice the whole body started to feel more animated.

Hey, I'm not a scientist or anything. I mean there were indications that my metabolism wasn't any kind of normal.

That doesn't mean that blood sugar and caffeine can't have their own impacts on my system. For that matter, I didn't even have much of a hangover after a morning full of whiskey and tequila.

I got into a kind of velvety soft green collarless shirt with a button neck. The catalog called it a Henley neckline I believe. Jeans without any tears or blood or sap or mud on them were next along with my alternate pair of polished Army Jump boots. With the shirttail down I could clip the short-barreled Taurus revolver and holster on my belt at the right hip. I figured with the kind of trouble I was already in a weapons charge was unlikely to break the camel's back. Besides, the quick clip holster could come off and be tossed into a dumpster or even the lake in a split second. With my teeth brushed and no real need to make a production of my short hair, I took a look in the mirror.

There were few signs of the beatings I had. No bags under the eyes or pallor to the skin. In fact, I looked absolutely bright-eyed and bushy-tailed. Maybe a hat? Eachan would probably be susceptible to the old "hat in hand" apology and humility routine. Too bad I wasn't still beat and bloody. In fact, I felt pretty damned good.

That probably should have been a clue. I'd have been better off crawling back into bed for another twelve hours or so.

When I knocked at Eachan's door, an intercom came to life beside me. The voice came out in the rich tones of what was probably the professor's native Scottish accent. "Mac-Vurlich aka Currie residence. Who might be on my stoop?"

I'd screwed up earlier. Probably best to admit it right away. "Some teenagers left a flaming sack of shit on your porch. I think you're supposed to come stomp it out."

The intercom went off without a word. I waited for

several minutes. I was about to give up when the door finally opened to reveal the old man. He was dressed in an anachronistic hodgepodge of fashions. His pants were...breeches? Whatever you wanted to call them they were loose at the thigh and tight at the knee where they ended tucked into high hard boots that a cavalry officer might have worn a couple of hundred years ago. Above the breeches, he had a paisley vest in fall colors atop a tawny poet's shirt with billowing linen sleeves. The heavy .455 Webley revolver in his hand was only a few decades old by contrast with the rest of the fashion statement.

I noticed the gun first and tried to analyze its meaning. Just the fact of its presence was enough to make me think. That Webley was a tried and trusted bit of British history. It had served admirably through two world wars and was still an intimidating piece of hand artillery. It fired bullets roughly the size of gumballs and it fired them with an authoritative amount of power.

The angle of the weapon was little help. While he hadn't precisely pointed it at me, the barrel was unnervingly close to my leg. When it comes down to it, a .455 caliber bullet tearing through your femoral artery is about as deadly as one in your chest. It would leave a hole about the size of my thumb in the front of my leg. Most of the back of that thigh would be a gory mess though and likely sport some bits of bone amongst the mangled meat and pool of blood.

Without changing the direction of the weapon, he looked me over and finally replied to my earlier statement. "There must have been several miscreants to pile this big a sack of shite in my entry."

Yup, should have gone with the hat. "Professor, I am most sincerely and humbly sorry for the stupid ass I made of myself not once but twice since this all started. I have no excuse or explanation except to say I'm a paranoid jackass who doesn't know who he can trust and who he can't. If you'd allow me I'd very much like to come in and thank you for all of your help. There might be some groveling as well. And after suitable abasement and humiliation maybe we can talk about that envelope you gave me."

He paused and then lowered the hammer of the Webley. It didn't have to be cocked. A cocked revolver though was quicker and just a tad more accurate. Not that accuracy was an issue at two feet. I made a conscious effort to be still.

"If there's going to be abasement and groveling I might need a glass of cognac while I enjoy the show." He turned from the door and went down a high-ceilinged entry into a very large two-story foyer I guess you'd call it. A hand-carved wooden railing ran along the curved sweep of stairs that started at the right wall and deposited climbers near the middle of the opposite side of the room. Halls led from the circular room in four directions. We were in the southern hall. The northern entrance led to a large dining room while the east and west halls each had a door into what were presumably large rooms on either side of each hall.

The floor appeared to be Italian marble. I got a glimpse of heavy oak or teak tables bearing floral arrangements and sculptures as we made our way into the east hall and into a study that seemed to border the dining room. Eachan poured himself a stiff drink out of one of several carafes and limped over to the chaise lounge. With his wounded leg elevated he swirled the reddish amber liquid in the glass then pointed it at the table of carafes. "Help yourself to a drink. It limbers the knees for proper subjugation."

I wasn't sure which part he was kidding about. The self-abasement or the drink. I decided to take a chance and mixed myself soda water with just a little whiskey for color. Joining him across the room, I opted out of going to my knees and sat in a sinfully comfortable leather chair wide enough for the front line of the Longhorns football team. Leaning forward with the untouched drink between my hands I put as much earnest sincerity as I could in my voice.

"Honestly Eachan I am as sorry as I can be. There was no excuse for calling you out like that. You've done nothing but help me. I'm just paranoid as hel about this whole thing. Somehow people are jerking me along like some damned puppet and I don't like it. The coincidence of your parking right at my door made me think you had followed me. Then the cops come in right behind you. I assumed you led them there." I took a drink of the weak whiskey mix to settle my nerves.

"I know now that my assumption was a lie. Jackson told me about your trip to the police today and then he explained a few other things that I was mistaken about. Basically, his story makes almost everything I thought I knew just so much smoke and self-delusion."

At the professor's nod and easing of the furrowed brow and disapproving frown, I began to relax. His next words gave me some hope that I hadn't irreparably damaged our friendship. "You're an idiot as well as a jackass. My arrival at your door was no coincidence. I told you I had tacked a little tracking component onto the spell to nose out our attacker. When I got close enough to you there was still enough of the energy left to tug me right to your door. I'm surprised it didn't lead me to the diner where you had breakfast."

Shit, I hadn't even thought about the tracking spell. Now that he mentioned it though, I'd caught a few faint whiffs of that cologne when I woke up. Between everything else, I'd just not put the two together. Maybe I ought to trust people more.

In for a pfennig in for a pound. I told him the whole story from the minute I got to the crime scene until he showed up at the hotel. I even gave him what Jackson had added to my story. When that was done I fished the brown envelope out and tossed it back to its original author. "So what's that about?"

His expression went from interest and engagement to icy disapproval in an instant. He probably didn't like my cavalier attitude about his research. "Goodness my dear boy. I had no idea you were illiterate." It appeared that a miffed Eachan came along with a healthy dose of sarcasm.

"I assure you though that I didn't type all of that for my personal amusement...or even copy and paste a good chunk of it. You were supposed to read the material."

He opened the envelope and peered inside while I answered. "I'm sorry doc. I genuinely appreciate the effort. Jackson had to be dissuaded from adding more charges to my rap sheet though. And then, of course, to find out that the slow-moving old cop was stringing me along kind of distracted me."

He lifted his gaze from the envelope as I continued. "Between all of that and being beaten, stabbed, poisoned, and shot in the last couple of days I didn't get around to reading the whole thesis. I did skim it, however, before the inquisition. But maybe you can explain some more about these Elle-maids. They aren't exactly like the stories my old gran used to tell me."

I leaned back and made myself comfortable. Mostly I hoped that the doc was as interested in lecturing as he was in being angry with me.

## 21

THE INSTINCTIVE NEED TO tutor the unschooled won the round. "Hulder, Forest wives, Ulda or Skogsra they're all a kind of wild woman. There are several versions including your Ella-maids. In most, she appears as a lovely young woman. Sometimes supernaturally seductive and sometimes innocently and deceptively defenseless looking, they usually appear to men alone in the woods. In many stories, they are not particularly fond of men. They curse men. Haunt them. Spirit lone lumbermen away to their hidden lairs. In the most extreme instance, they kill intruders rather messily."

This last brought a thoughtful nod out of me as the light came on. "Yea a messy death fits alright. But these folks don't normally work in alleys, do they?"

"Alleys? No. But wild growth areas seem sacred to them. If the area were disturbed by say renovation, or someone with a machete, or even painfully loud and disturbing music? In such an instance I think a Hulder might react negatively and quite lethally."

It probably should have bothered a reasonable person

that we were sitting and talking calmly and rationally about a centuries-old suspect. Then again I had some special circumstances to make me a little more receptive. This kind of study was truly the old professor's lifework was it not? Still, the alley thing bugged me. "So after all this time, with the lake over there and some park-like trees, this Hulder wife gets mad and starts chopping people up over some metal music?"

The smile that curved Eachan's lips was smug if it was anything. "Did I mention that the old garden shop was run by a German couple named Gruber? They weren't good fifth or sixth generation Texans from Braunfels or anything either. The two of them moved to the area straight from rural Deutschland. I only know because I recognized her name when I was doing my research. She wrote some pamphlets about elves and faery folk and old myths and herbs and such. Probably a quarter of my notes on the Hulder were from her work."

"What if this Hulder wasn't newly angry. What if it was just newly unrestrained? Perhaps Mrs. Gruber was some sort of Hexe witch from the old country and brought along a little companion. Or maybe she just found one already here. When the old lady dies, the leash comes off. And right after that, some oaf with big plans starts chopping up her weeds and bushes. When she watches the oaf leave, he goes across the street, so she waits for the right time to engage in proper skullduggery. The night is when it's dark and harder for people to say what they've seen. She sniffs and sneaks around the building where her victim is. And then alone in the alley, a door opens and the horrible cacophony from inside angers her further. Here's one of the miserable creatures threatening the sanctity of her small wild space with its sharp blades and violent noise. I believe we know the outcome of such a meeting."

Something about his premise bugged me. But I couldn't put a finger on it. Was it because the thing had almost attacked the girl? Was a fractured personality part of the normal Hulder makeup? There was just too much I didn't know. And still that nagging feeling kept popping up.

It made sense though. The whole damned scenario made sense despite my reservations. And who was I to toss stones at European myth? "Okay, it fits Doc. You've got me mostly convinced. So, we've got a starting place. I need to know more though. What can this thing do? What are its abilities? More importantly, are there any weaknesses I can exploit?"

It took a couple of hours but I compiled enough notes that I might have a chance at getting this thing resolved. I doubt many people would take a supernatural threat from a centuries-old myth seriously. Then again, I ain't most people. I happen to *be* a supernatural being from centuries-old myths. I could make myself believe in Ella-maids. The worst part of the research was that everybody had a different version of the witchy woods-women.

The Dutch were the ones that originated the Hulder tag. The Swedes had a version or two. Germans, Danes, as well the Irish and Scots had their version of the old superstitions. There were even similar stories from Central and South America. Unfortunately, no two of them seemed alike enough to draw firm conclusions. It was a good bet that they didn't like men. It was a better bet that they *did* like trees. It also seemed apparent that they liked fire even less than men. That might explain why the creature had used flames once I got her good and annoyed. We tend to want to do the things that horrify us to people who really make us mad.

Unfortunately, flamethrowers were in short supply on the open market. I probably didn't have time to try and contact any arms dealers either. There were things I could do though. Give me a couple of days and I could whip up some homemade napalm. There were runes I could add to a blade or two as well. And of course, there *were* people who might be able to get me a flamethrower, or at least a good chainsaw. While I was considering various forms of mayhem, my phone rang.

A very large part of me wanted to ignore the device. Sometimes new technology fascinated me. Sometimes it left me bewildered, frustrated, or just plain pissed off. The mobile phone fell into both categories. On one hand, it was fascinating that such a compact piece of electronics could duplicate a dozen different machines from just a decade or two ago. Hel, I remember the first computer I ever saw. It filled half a room. Compared to a modern telephone the old IBM 360 computer was an idiot cousin from the shadowy back corner of Arkansas' infamous Inbred Woods.

On the other hand, people used this modern miracle for a variety of purposes that went from painfully trivial to openly self-destructive. Some part of me hated the sense of being monitored more than everything else combined. I've spent decades trying to fly under the radar. Patterns are hard to break. If I hadn't left messages with a couple of people, I probably wouldn't have answered. Turns out it was neither of them.

"Magnoose, wot the hell. I been tryin' to call Walter Roy all day. He don't answer me so I catch a ride to the bar. He ain't there. Those cops come back or somethin?" I winced as usual when she made my name rhyme with "Moose". Her accent seemed the least of my current worries though. There was real fear in her voice. She was worried about the wrong people picking him up but at least she was in the right ballpark. I'd finally figured out that niggling little feeling that started bugging me during Eachan's lecture. If the loud music and crowds were enough to set off a murderous, German, serial killing wild woman of the woods, what was she going to think of someone chopping up her garden and talking about turning it into a parking lot?

"Quick Connie. Go ask whoever is at the bar when was the last time anyone heard from the boss. Do it now and get right back to me!" At first, I started to run out of the door to my bike and head to the bar myself. That wasn't going to help though. Instead, it was time to think. What do the paratroopers say? Slow is smooth and smooth is fast. Time to slow down and get smooth.

I covered the cell-phone with my hand and spoke aside to Eachan. "Timetable just changed. Mr. Roy isn't around. I forgot about his plan to demolish the old garden and shop for his own uses. What are the chances this Hulder thing grabbed him?"

Connie's voice pulled me back to the phone. "There's a barback here. He said the cleaning company got pissed and left a note on the door. The doors were unlocked, and the office was all wrecked. They clean it up a little bit but they say they don't get paid to throw out furniture and stuff."

"Okay. Connie, you gotta tell the head bartender he's in charge tonight. Tell him Mr. Roy left a message with you. Everything has to seem as normal as possible. If somebody is watching they don't need to know we're onto them." I knew she wanted me to take the time to explain everything and console her. I didn't have that kind of time though. "Look, Connie, you've got this. Walter needs you and he trusts you. Just keep the place running. Bodie has the door. Vic has the bar. You run the servers. Everybody knows their job and you just let them do it. Just like the boss called in sick or something."

I hung up and turned to Eachan. As soon as he saw me close the phone he started his spiel. "Okay, everything she's done violent so far has been done at night. Perhaps she grabbed Mr. Roy last night. If that's the case, then it's very unlikely that you can help him now. If, however, she got him in the early hours of this morning, then perhaps it's not too late. If she had meant to simply kill him then the cleaning crew would have found a corpse in that dismantled office space. That seems to indicate that the creature has another use for your employer.

"Perhaps she means to draw out his death. On the other hand, if your rendition of your own encounter is accurate then she may be a practitioner of some sort. Perhaps she is even a creature of some faith. In many cultures, larger spells and sacred rituals often centered around sacrifice. If Walter Roy is not yet deceased, then I would estimate that he has no more than two days to live." As he spoke Eachan was limping around his room without the aid of his cane. Perhaps he needed both hands free. The cane remained leaning against his chair as he lurched around gathering books and a few other items from shelves and drawers within the study.

It took me three tries to get his attention. On the third and loudest repetition of his name, the Scottish scholar turned towards me. "Eachan, why two more days?"

"In three days it will be May 1st. May Day is its own holiday. In Germany however, there is another holiday the night before May Day. It is called Walpurgis by some. By others, it is called Hexennacht, or witches night. It is a time of celebration by many pagans and is considered a time of power much like the Wiccan Lughnasa or the winter equinox for many faiths. If a creature and follower of old ways were to make the proper sacrifice on Hexennacht, such a ritual might be considerably more powerful and effective than other less significant dates." Eachan finished his lecture as he was closing a large leather satchel full of various materials and writings.

"I suppose you need to go to your place and make your preparations. I propose that you gather whatever you need and return here. I have a fully prepared and shielded sanctum within which we can work unheard and unharmed to prepare some counters for the abilities you might encounter when next you face the creature." He didn't show me the door so much as wave vaguely towards the hall that would eventually take me outside. "Be back here before nightfall. The creature might make another attempt on one of us. Best to be prepared."

I noticed that he did not go towards any of the other halls in his spacious mini-mansion. Instead, he grabbed his cane and headed for a doorway at the end of the hall. It had the ornate and heavy look of an exterior door rather than an interior one. Knowing how Eachan traveled and dressed, I was willing to guess that he might have tea patios and English Rose gardens or even a large hedge maze. Someday I'd have to find out where a college teacher got that kind of cash.

## 22

Typical Austin traffic took my mind off the professor's financial successes in mere moments. Drivers in Austin are an odd mix. In many cities, everyone drives aggressively. An abrupt lane change, or the perception of cutting someone off; either one can lead to an episode of near homicidal road rage in most cities. Sometimes it even crosses the line from near homicidal to actual murder. That rarely occurs in Austin.

Maybe it's the abundance of, shall we call them, recreational herbalists? Whatever the cause, the end result was a populace that seemed a better fit for California than the wild and raucous state of Texas. Keep Austin Weird bumper stickers were everywhere. Tattoos, piercings, and ear gauges abounded. In fact, a good portion of the populace would probably have been quite content sharing tents and various pharmaceuticals in rainy old Woodstock.

As a result, you were more likely to get a smile and a friendly wave than anger and obscene gestures while making a lane change. The problem wasn't the drivers. The problem was that the architects of Austin's street and highway system may have retired back when the horseless carriage was a fad that everyone expected to go away. Instead of a few thousand horsemen and the occasional cattle drive, Austin held close to a million permanent residents. The sporadic trail herds were replaced with tens of thousands of college students and government employees in the state capital of one of the biggest states in the good old USA.

It took close to an hour to navigate the highways without major risk of life, limb, and sanity. I finally made it home mid-afternoon. Sitting in my driveway was a familiar police cruiser. Jackson leaned on the front quarter panel with his arms crossed and watched me pull in to turn off the bike and drop the kickstand. Sharp on the final stuttering echoes of the motorcycle engine, I heard the ratchet sound of a pump-action shotgun.

When I turned, Jackson was still leaning nonchalantly against the car. His expression was both tired and maybe a touch embarrassed. Off to one side and behind good ole Joe Jackson, the ugly snout of a shotgun peered at me over the top of the squad car.

"Mr. Gustaf, please put your hands on top of your head with your fingers laced together." Jackson's voice was as weary as his expression. Other than weariness though it held no emotion at all.

"If you are armed it would be advisable to tell me where the weapon is. My partner has you covered as you can see. Any resistance at all will result in the use of deadly force." In slow deliberate motions, the cop I thought was becoming a friend, unsnapped the case holding his cuffs.

Then he read me my rights in the same flat monotone. "You have the right to remain silent. You have the right to refuse to answer any questions. Anything you do say may be used against you. Do you understand this right?"

Jackson waited for my nod and continued waiting until I grunted a "yes".

"You have the right to an attorney before answering questions. You have the right to consult an attorney during questioning. If you cannot afford an attorney one will be appointed to you before any questioning if you wish. Do you understand these rights?"

This time I answered promptly with a frustrated, "Yea I got it." I did *not* have time for this shit. Walter was missing. In all likelihood, he was a potential victim waiting for my swashbuckling hero routine. It's difficult to pull off derring-do from a jail cell.

"If you choose to answer questions without a legal representative you may stop the questioning and request an attorney at any point. Do you understand?" Again, he got his affirmative.

"Knowing and understanding these rights as I have explained them, do you choose at this time to answer questions or make any statement?"

This time he didn't get the nod and agreement. "Officer Jackson, it is going to be difficult to make a statement when I don't know what the hell is going on or what your charges are."

From across the roof of the cop car I heard officer Chuy's familiar voice. With what I was beginning to consider his typical amount of rancor he spat at me. "Watch your mouth goon. You'd be splattered across that concrete if we didn't need to know stuff. So, drop the bullshit act. You answer pretty, and Jackson and I won't take turns giving you a memory massage with our Maglites."

"Just move slow and easy Mr. Gustaf. Don't give anyone

any reason to get shot here. Chuy, you take a deep breath and ease off the trigger while I cuff him. Magnus, you've seen it on TV if you haven't done it before. Move up to the car until I tell you to stop. Leave your hands on your head and stop now. Lean forward with both hands on the hood." At that point, he stopped me. I was well aware that it would take a very strenuous move to keep from falling if I shifted weight from my hands on the hood.

Chuy had moved around the car to be behind me and to the side. With the shotgun a very real and threatening presence, I didn't move so much as a follicle of hair. Jackson pulled one hand back behind me and wrapped the steel cuff around it. With one hand steadying my weight he pulled the other hand back as well and secured the two together with a loop of chain through my belt loop. It wouldn't stop me if I wanted to rip my hands free. But what was I going to do with them chained together?

"Jackson...can you cut through the shit now. What's this all about? I thought we talked about this stuff th..." That's all I got out before the hand at my back shoved me like a train wreck into the side of the car.

"Shut up skell. You're under arrest for suspicion of kidnapping, abduction, murder, resisting arrest, littering, and fucking jaywalking." He rapped me against the car again and then unceremoniously opened the door and shoved me in back. "You say a word, one fucking word, between here and the holding cell and I'll make sure your dentist has enough work to last him a lifetime. You got it? Don't talk! Just nod." I'd never heard that particular note in the older cop's voice. I'd prefer never hearing it again.

The silent ride across town gave me time to think. The first thing that seemed to require some thought were those charges. Abduction and suspicion of murder didn't sound very promising. Walter Roy was missing. Did the charges mean they'd found the body? If he was dead then Eachan and I had miscalculated badly. If he wasn't dead, then we didn't have time for me to be locked up for days or weeks.

I try to look for the silver lining. I mean I watch for the shadows but there's usually some upside to a situation. I didn't see any upside or even a hint of silver in the shadows around me in the back of that car.

The silence continued when we got to the station. Chuy locked the shotgun back into the bar between the driver and passenger seat. Jackson grabbed me by the upper arm and jerked me out of the car to propel me towards the plain steel door behind the building. Once inside and without anybody watching he steered me away from the main hall and the security cameras there. "Look, keep quiet and try not to step on your own dick, we're gonna ask you some questions. You've been read your rights so you know what that means."

When the door opened behind us, Jackson gave me another much less forceful shove than the previous few pushes. "Chuy get the door ahead. We'll put him in the interrogation room and get this started. Who knows? Maybe we can find the victim alive instead of dead."

The younger officer managed to shove me sideways with his shoulder as he passed. Once the door was open he took up station in the corner under the video camera. Jackson unhooked one of my wrists and put a cuff with a slightly longer chain on. The longer chain ran through a steel ring atop the table and closed in another cuff around my opposite wrist. With his own handcuffs removed from the perpetrator, otherwise known as Magnus, Jackson tucked them back into his belt and sat down across from me.

"Okay, Gustaf. I'm going to tell you a few things I know. When I'm done you're going to fill in the blanks. Chuy is just going to sit quietly in the corner to back up a poor old man if you decide to break through the table and come take my lunch money." The older cop shifted to get slightly more comfortable then crossed his arms before speaking again.

"We know you had a beef with a guy that ended up dead. We know the dead guy had a friend sleeping with your boss's twist. The friend ended up dead too. At the scene of the second crime, the victim's sister was allowed into the property to light a candle for her brother. We talked to the patrolmen she spoke with. We also know there were reports of a disturbance and even possible gunshots in that garden. Nobody saw anything though." I blinked at the first discrepancy between our new conversation and the one just a few hours prior.

"That's also the last time anyone saw the girl." This time I didn't blink. I may be slow but if you buy me a vowel I can catch the rest of the clue. For some reason, Jackson didn't want his partner to know about the talk we had at drinkfast. Or maybe he didn't want it on security cameras.

"If you don't have an alibi for last night then things are going to start looking pretty grim for you. So, Mr. Gustaf, do you have an alibi?" This time I didn't have a hint of what he wanted. But maybe I could switch things up and find out a little more...

One of the runes I'd drawn with the henna ink was designed to help with stealth. It was a binding of the rune Ansuz and Isa. The original intent had been to freeze or lock down the sounds I made. Ansuz is the rune of communication and Isa is the rune of stagnation and ice. It was possible that I could tweak the magick of that rune briefly. The effect would be fleeting but it might give me enough time...

Gathering my focus was hard in the cold grey room with everything pressing in around me. The palpable hostility of the younger cop was a distraction at least. At most he was pushing an energetic barrier to foil anything I might try. It's a good thing he wasn't well trained or particularly strong-willed.

I gave a mental shove to clear the angry red waves of energy and grunted the name of the two runes I was invoking. At the same time, I put every ounce of my concentration and energy into sending those runes out as an invisible barrier to sight and sound. If I did it just right, his sight and hearing would simply freeze for a few brief minutes. Time would still pass but ole Chuy should be effectively isolated and ignorant of the passage.

A quick intake of breath was necessary after the mental and vocal effort of the casting. After that, I had just minutes, maybe even seconds. "Joseph the girl has been taken and so has Roy. I have to get out of here and help them. We've got seconds to get this handled."

The cop's head snapped towards the corner where his oblivious partner stood as if carved from the ice I had used to compel him. "No time Jackson. He isn't aware of any of this for now. So talk to me. How the Hel do I get out of here? Then tell me what you can to help find the girl."

A sharp slap of sound behind me drew my attention to the mirror on the wall. *Son of a bitch. Mags old man you've seen the damned TV shows enough. Two-way mirror? And you just used magick and stated it out loud. Well Magnus, if we're lucky it'll be a loony bin. Otherwise, we're probably headed for a prison psychiatrist.*

The sound either coincided with or caused the end of my spell on the irritating young cop. He kind of shook himself and looked around suspiciously before resuming his scowling surveillance. "C'mon Jackson. Just slap the confession out of this jerk and we can throw him in a cell. I got no use for scum that kills people and kidnaps girls."

The door of the interrogation room opened to reveal not another uniformed officer, but a man only slightly older than Chuy himself. "That will be all Officer Gomez. Please go check the surveillance camera for this room and bring me the disc."

When Gomez started to object, this newcomer gave him a much sterner look than his age would have suggested. "I need that disc *now* Gomez. Jackson and I can handle one perp handcuffed to the steel table that is, in turn, bolted to the floor don't you think?"

The set of his shoulders and sharp stride were indicative of exactly how little Chuy enjoyed the command or the task. I could only imagine how he would react to what he was going to find on that surveillance video. Denial followed by anger maybe? People often object to the use of magick. Modern types think anything that defies Bill Nye or doesn't come from the Pope is blasphemous evil devil's-work. The crucifix and Saint Michael's medallion he wore made me think that Officer Gomez was likely a good catholic boy and might be less than enthused about my heathen spell work.

"Don't worry about the disc." The newcomer waved for my attention and produced a large metal ring. "Somebody seems to have left a large stereo magnet by the computer monitoring this room. I'm betting it doesn't work very well now."

As if spurred by his words, the door reopened to show a very red-faced Gomez. "The damned computer won't boot up. I'll take the media stick down to the computer geeks. You want any other backup while I'm gone?"

"That's fine, officer. Get the video copied and bring us a laptop to view it on." New Guy spoke over his shoulder without taking his eyes off me. If I cared to guess, I'd say his expression was a combination of impatience, excitement, and possibly a shade of triumph or maybe self-vindication.

This time when the door shut, Jackson allowed his tough-guy demeanor to crack. "You want the cuffs on him or off Drew?"

"Let's leave them on for the moment. We don't need to strain Officer Gomez's sense of propriety any more than we already have. Chances are it will take him a while to find a laptop. Then there will be a further delay while he figures out why the media stick he's carrying is empty." Almost as an afterthought "Drew" pulled an identical media device from his pocket and dropped it considerately in the middle of the large round magnet he had previously produced from another pocket.

"Hello, Mr. Gustaf. My name is Andrew Dixon. I'm not going to tell you what agency I work for. Just assume it is what you mercenaries call an alphabet agency. You will note that the eager and quite inflamed Officer Gomez responded promptly to my suggestions. That should indicate the amount of clout I might wield either for or against you today."

He drew a chair from the corner and sat at the side of the table diagonally across from me. When I said he wasn't uniformed that was probably a mistake. The assurance and self-confidence were part of his uniform as much as the clothes themselves.

The suit was most likely a good deal less expensive than something Eachan might wear. That made it only five or six times as pricey as the best suit I kept for my own formal use.

It was dark charcoal with a barely visible lighter grey pinstripe. The shirt was a light blue twill. His decorative pocket kerchief was maroon to match a tie in stripes of the same color and grey. To finish the look, his jet-black hair was slicked back sharply. It was also a length that I'm betting bordered on too long for his job description.

With his folded hands resting atop crossed and fashionably clad knees, the "suit" eyeballed me as intently as I was looking at him. "You, Mr. Gustaf, are a long-anticipated and most incredible find."

He nodded to himself while I opted to remain silent and try to project curious confusion. "Yes, by the way, may I call you Magnus, or do you prefer Mouse?"

"I was just getting used to perp and skell Mr. Dixon." Okay, so remaining silent isn't always my strong point. The guy was obviously trying to put me at ease for some reason. I just had to figure out if he was looking for a confession or had triggered on something he saw from behind the glass.

"I think I'll stick with Magnus." If he was irritated by my bout of wit it didn't show. "You see Magnus, I've been doing research into things my colleagues consider wild goose chases. It started as a hobby. During my legal service, however, it has expanded. There are things out there that skeptics and naysayers can't explain. Crimes that don't fit any profile or pattern of evidence. People who do things that seem impossible. All of these things occur despite seeming to be impossible. The fact that they occur at a much greater rate than most people would believe is what I find fascinating." He nodded and leaned forward and shifted his hands to the tabletop.

"Would it surprise you that I had a couple of technicians in the other room? Oh, most people would not call them technicians but I do. I consider their work out of the mainstream but still quite valid. I wonder if you've ever had people like that about when you perform your little tricks?" He didn't even wait for me to answer a positive or negative either one.

"Of course you haven't. Looking at your files, I'd say that you've done a very good job at flying with a very low profile, wouldn't you?" The file he was handed by Jackson was much thicker than anything I'd seen the cop working with before.

"It took some time. I had round the clock security people working on some of it. But it was your own man that was the most useful. Don't blame Mr. Wooley. He had little choice but to cooperate. Poor Wild Bill discovered that some of his less...savory...operations were not as undetectable as he expected. Honestly, they were quite impressively hidden. But my people have access to better computers than the best Bill managed to put together. I try not to pry into where their technological advances come from down in the cyber departments. Rumors of alien assistance are probably a joke... I hope."

Opening the heavy binder full of documents, Dixon continued in a flat voice as he glanced through the paperwork. "Frankly, I doubt we'd have got you without his help. You gave us a very small window here since the first blip on my radar. I also have little doubt that you might mysteriously disappear once the current situation is resolved."

A glance at the clock brought a very low voiced but quite unpleasant and earthy phrase out of the federal suit. "Very well, I just wanted you to know that you are not as low under the radar as you once were. I've got an eye on you, Mr. Gustaf. Eventually, I want to find out who and what you are. For the moment though we don't have time. I'll get you out of this interrogation. I'll even help handle whatever charges are currently against you. In return...I hope you'll share your story with me at your convenience. I have no doubt it will be fascinating. In the meantime, I'll intercept Officer Gomez. You'll have two or three days to clear things up. After that, I doubt I can hold back the local authorities. Good luck Mr. Gustaf."

I was beyond confused. My worst fears had materialized. A government agent who knew much too much for my comfort had witnessed me using magick and heard me discuss it. And now he was leaving and nobody was talking about hooking me up to a bunch of laboratory equipment in a secure facility someplace.

At the door, he paused and turned back. "Maybe I should have said...Good hunting Mr. Gustaf. And Officer Jackson? Please tell Aunt Dot that I got the graduation announcement. Cousin Jerry will get a fat check since I have no idea what else he might like. Good day gentlemen."

I don't know what buttons were pushed or favors were called in but I was out of the pokey and back on the street in ten minutes. Outside the same solid steel door, Jackson handed me back the gun from my belt and then offered a large duffel bag that must have come from an army surplus store. "Sorry for the pushing and shoving earlier Mags. I had to make it look good for Chuy. I had to give the story to my nephew Drew as well. He can pull strings I can't."

Jackson cleared his throat and dropped his voice to a whisper. "He's also on the level about his hobby. What I gave him was the window dressing. He dug everything else up with your buddy locked away for the day or two. I won't say he's always a nice kid. But damn he can get results. He won't turn you in either. He was already telling me about plans to use you to get a handle on other things from the wild side. Nothing official about any of it. Just a kid's obsession with too much Tolkien or Brothers Grimm when he was a kid. The bag's a gift from both of us for the trouble of dragging you down. He's also giving your hacker buddy some new toys for the trouble. I have to get back in now and do some paperwork or Chuy will have em on my ass like ticks on a coonhound. Like Drew said...Good hunting Magnus."

## 23

IT'S PROBABLY a good thing that taxis are almost as common as bail bondsmen around the jail. I made it back to the house before dark. One peek inside the duffel bag in the back of the cab made me zip it shut in a hurry. I didn't need to be arrested for attempting to rob a taxi on top of everything else. There wasn't enough time to spend any more in interrogation rooms. If Eachan was right, we had two days to get this taken care of.

On the other hand, if the Hulder had two victims instead of one, tomorrow might be too late for either Roy or Maureen. For that reason, I didn't dawdle. Once the cabby was paid and tipped, I made a beeline for the door. When it opened in front of me, I almost dove out of the light. Only the glimpse of Eachan's distinct cane and paisley vest prevented me from making a spectacle for the neighbors. With the appearance of police vehicles two days back to back, I had no doubt the neighborhood busybodies were glued to windows whenever a passing car or motorcycle neared my house.

"I came over when you didn't come right back!" Eachan

spoke with a mix of relief and admonishment. "Did you have a hot date or something else more important to do than save your boss and end a supernatural threat? Maybe your dry cleaning was ready?"

"Sorry. I stopped to use your restroom and got lost. Fortunately, a British explorer found me and brought me back to civilization. Or maybe I got to go hold hands with the police and a spook for the afternoon and they pinned me down about not being exactly a mundane every day John Doe. Sorry, my procrastinating with the po-po inconvenienced you. Oh! Speaking of inconvenience, Walter Roy isn't the only one missing. So is Maureen." The words came out in a rush as I pushed past the professor and led the way to the small table we'd used for the tracking spell.

"We don't have a focus for the tracker this time. But if we're right about this Hulder creature then I'm gambling on her keeping the captives in her garden sanctum. You get to work here. I'll feed the bird..." I didn't get to finish the sentence as several stone-weight of exuberant dog hit me from the side and knocked me sprawling.

Maybe I should feel guilty about not worrying too much about the dog. He'd been in good hands though. Eachan's place was in a walled community with private security. I'd also heard him mention his security systems. That doesn't even take his spiritual or less mundane abilities into consideration. I hadn't been looking for them but it wouldn't surprise me if he had some sort of triggered wards surrounding his home. If he had aggressive or automatic wards in place, my own defenses would have given me a warning. There's a reason I have several different earrings. Wards that might sense or attack my aura of magick would normally cause the amber earring with Ansuz and Algiz to alarm. To me, it would be a sizzling kind of hiss. To anyone else, it would be inaudible. It did not, however, sound an alarm of warning before a stoutly muscled yellow fur bomb ambushed me.

Despite the hurry, I wasn't going to ignore my buddy after he'd been evicted from his own home for days. Even Eachan in his hurry-up mode knew better than to interrupt. He waited with only a few impatient taps of the foot until Grimmr caught me in the wind with a Kodiak sized paw. Well, maybe it wasn't Kodiak sized. It was sufficient to drive most of the air from my lungs though. That was enough to end the rompage. I called him into the kitchen and poured a hefty bowl for the beast. I gave him a ruffle of his ears on the way back to my room and the duffel.

Out of my bag of gifts, I pulled out a purely lovely toy that was reminiscent of something I'd carried in my own time. I'd seen one in a catalog before but never held it. The blade was known as a tomahawk MK some number or other. I could remember using much cruder versions of the implement as far back as my early teen years. More recently, we'd been given a few in a unit of mercs I worked with briefly in the middle east. This was like the high tech grand-child of those weapons.

It was matte black with a small but serviceable flat axe blade on one side and a short wedge-shaped spike on the back. Instead of a hardwood handle, this one sported a metal rod engineered with a beehive reinforcement inside. The whole thing was streamlined and designed with every-thing from high carbon steel to a slip-resistant tear-resistant super grip polymer handle. I liked it almost as much as the heavy crude axe I'd carried on a longship for my first trip to France. Of course, back before France, I hadn't known some of the tricks I know now.

One spare bedroom I kept up for guests. The other one,

however, was a combination workroom, library, and museum of sorts. I carried the duffel into that room while I hefted the new tomahawk in my right hand and gave it a few short test chops. The balance was good and the weight was just enough to make it nasty without making it tiresome and awkward.

With the duffel propped in a chair, I pulled my work stool over and dug some tools and materials out of desk drawers. In what was half a work of artisanship, and half a form of ritual, I etched and Galdored runes into the flat black steel.

Galdoring is an old skill. Those who worked with Runes as more than an alphabet or a divination tool would often Galdor them. Galdor is a deep-seated sound that comes from around your root chakra. Each rune has its own identity, its own spheres of influence. And each rune has its own sound as defined by the perceptions of the practitioner. When I rown a rune or Galdor it, I've been told it sounds like a Klingon version of Tibetan throat singing.

In this instance, I chanted each rune in a long droning note for as long as my breath held, then I repeated the process as I etched the runes deeper and wider on the metal haft. When I was finished there were close to a dozen runes. Some were linked into more complex rune binds, some were solo runes with very loose enchantments. Each of them was a slumbering entity to be awakened when the weapon was used a certain way.

I won't try and tell you every rune or combination I used. Tyr was there as the rune of victory, so was Kenaz; the rune of knowledge and the fires of creativity. There were others as well. Once the etching was done, I used the small spring-assisted knife clipped to my belt to draw blood from one of several scars still visible on my forearms.

The drop of blood went into a mixture of silver, ash, ground bone, and crushed seashell. The silver was potent in many beliefs, it also came from the earth and added that element to my working. Ashes from an air fern gave me both fire and air as well as a plant component to work with. Ground bone invoked my ancestors. Finally, the fine bits of abalone shell added the water element. They also gave glints of rainbow-like reflections within the runes. Those glints of color really shone within the flat black of the metal. Hel, it was pretty as well as functional. Imagine that.

Of course, that meant I'd have to keep the handle concealed until actual conflict occurred. It would be a shame to waste a bunch of skulking with some pretty twinkles of light giving me away at the wrong time.

Once the tomahawk was done, I took the remaining mix of ingredients and added a pinch or two to my henna. A few more drops of blood went in to maintain my connection and root the runes to my internal battery so to speak. After that, I don't know how many minutes or hours it took to add more layers of protection and enhancement to my more permanent ink.

When I was done, the trance-like state of focus slowly receded. It did not fully leave me though. Even in the darkened room, I could see better. Some of that came from runes to enhance my senses. Some of it was the result of hours of meditative focus and the amount of energy I had channeled and stored in and around my personal space.

There were a handful of trinkets and objects from my collection strewn about the worktable. Each had added some to the gestalt of energies in my enchantments. Each had left its flavor to my aura and perceptions. And each was depleted to the last dregs. They could and would be recharged. Only my death or capture would prevent me from restoring the energies in those artifacts.

Even if I did die, most of my belongings would go to Eachan. I have no doubt he'd take good care of some surprising toys I would leave behind. I took the time to type a short note and sign it to be given to Bill Wooley. He'd be able to get the proper documents dated, signed and notarized to carry out my wishes.

How could I trust him after the feds got all of my data from him? It was easy. He was a businessman and a computer nerd. Nobody expected him to stand up to interrogation or even intimidation by the feds. He reacted as could be expected. Besides, I sent Eachan a note to tell him where some gold Krugerrands were to pay for the papers from Bill. With the two of them dependent on each other, I was pretty confident my last-minute will would work out as planned.

He also had instructions about what to do with my remains if necessary. Not that I expected such a need. If I died, there was little doubt that Kara would get what was left. That's when the real fun would begin. I mean who doesn't look forward to an unknown length of torture and debasement at the hands of a supernatural psychopathic mistress of mayhem, magick, and sadism?

I considered a much different note for Maureen. Considered it and discarded it. I mean, let's face it. I'm not some moonstruck teenager. This was not my high school sweetheart or spouse. She was a lovely lady I'd met in passing. We shared some covert glances and flirtations, one walk in the dark, some very hands-on fun in a garden, and one murder plus a mutual assault. Come to think of it, I'd seen relationships founded on less, but what could I mean to her at this point? She even half believed I'd killed her brother.

No, that was no basis for some pitiful last-minute death's bed declaration of love and devotion. I added a line to Eachan's note, "Keep half of the goodies in my grandfather clock. Use the rest of them to send a shop full of flowers to Maureen and help her get home or resettled if she needs it." With that done, I dug some old coins and a small stack of the South African gold Krugerrands out of a hidden spot. Nobody needs to know where or what else was in there. The packet of valuables went behind the face of the battered old Grandfather clock in my entry.

That took care of my last wishes pretty much. I figured the Prof would take care of Rafe and Grimmr the best he knew how. Chances were he knew better than I would how to deal with bequeathed pets in current society. My damned dog would probably live the rest of his life eating haute cuisine on satin cushions if I didn't make it through the night.

I finally went back to see how Eachan was doing with his preparations. When I got there, he was sitting amid a pile of his own relevant trinkets and candles. There were scrawled papers he'd used for this circle or that circle while he worked his particular style of magick. I could tell that other than runes and basics like candles and daggers, our styles did not have a great deal in common.

He leaned back in the most comfortable chair I had. The one that cost about as much as one of Eachan's throw pillows. "Well, my boy. I've done some digging and prodding with divination. It is my forte so to speak. I can tell you that the site of your recent conflicts is steeped in ritualistic energy. Even through a distance viewing, it is apparent that someone has done bindings of a sort within that garden for...well, longer than either of us has been alive.

Leaning forward he drew a rough outline of the garden

and then a much more ragged circle around it. "I also can sense a great deal of energy *beneath* the business. I would speculate that you might find a large basement or possibly some form of excavation. It too has been a focus of energy. Oddly, the energy beneath has a very different flavor. It still feels like a binding or possibly a summoning done year after year for a very long time. They are much older indeed than the other energies I encountered. In fact, I suspect they were in use pre-Columbian. Quite a fascinating thought eh m'boy?"

He pointed to a laptop computer he'd plugged in to pursue his curiosity no doubt. "Were you aware, Magnus, that we are within a few scant miles of one of the more significant archaeological and anthropological sites in North America?" Picking through several web pages that he had marked, he continued with the animation one only finds from educators discussing a topic of special interest.

"Just outside of Austin and Round Rock, actually closer to the suburbs, an excavation in the seventies and eighties discovered an intact burial site with a complete human skeleton rumored to be ten to thirteen thousand years old. Do you see m'boy?? That cave or excavation might be over ten thousand years old! With ritual energy built in it through millennia of periodic habitation. The Leander Lady as our exhumed burial site was named, might have known of the cave and considered it sacred. It's absolutely fascinating."

Eachan pointed to his stiff and awkward leg that I now knew was the product of a terrorist bombing. "I do wish I was capable of going with you. If you find the time, please search for the source of that older energy Magnus. And do try to avoid destroying anything down there. The whole site may be a priceless window into dim parts of history we know so little about. In the meantime. I shall work from here to lock down hostile energies where I can. Here take this amulet. It's a simple silver triskelion but I've put my own divinatory and protective enchantments on it."

The gesture touched me. I had just expected information from the old man. When I tried to put it on however, there was an odd buzz and the chain lifted from my chest like hair affected by static electricity. In seconds the heat radiating from the amulet became painful. In that brief instant, I once more considered whether the learned scholar and professor was truly an ally or just a cunning foe. All of the previous accusations and results, however, made me stop before uttering another offensive statement at the man who had helped me all along with no real incentive other than professional curiosity.

That didn't mean I could keep wearing a charm that was now audible even a few feet away as well as hot enough to bring a flush to my chest. "Ouch. That's not going to work Eachan. I appreciate it though."

When I offered the gift back he made a pushing gesture. "No, my boy. Just keep it. Perhaps you will find another use. If nothing else put it where I can access it as a focus for my own viewing purposes. If I have any chance at all I will try and shut down any hostile divinations attempting to spy upon you."

That just about wrapped up preparations. I tossed a couple of my own packages into the duffel and started out to the bike.

"Take the car, Magnus. I have a driver who will drop you off and disappear. He will, of course, see nothing and remember nothing. I'm told the lad has a promising political career ahead...if he does not fail one of my classes." I had never noticed how sharp and unsettling Professor Currie's smile could become. It was positively vulpine in a predatory and amused manner.

I might have politely declined his offer. But the truth was, riding in the back gave me a chance to finish some of my surprises. It also allowed me to try calling Walter Roy and Maureen alike and anew. There was no surprise when Walter's phone went unanswered. This time, however, Maureen's phone did not ring at all. It went straight to voice message. Which probably just meant her battery had given out between her capture and now. That's what I kept telling myself. I didn't want to think it might have been destroyed.

## 24

WITH THE POINTLESS phone calls out of the way, I pulled out my duffel and began getting ready. One of the other gifts from my new federal friends and the local police, was a swat issue protective vest. This one had no markings on it though. No badges or numbers or big letters spelling SWAT. Just a flat back vest with some high-tech plate front and back. An integrated PALS system let me attach a soft molle holster for my short .45/410 revolver. There was also a military-style first aid kit to add. There were a few more pouches but they weren't particularly useful in this situation. I stuck with the holstered weapon, med gear, and a flashlight as well as the tomahawk through a loop at my waist.

Before I put on the vest, I draped a sleeveless shirt of chain links over my black sweater. A hood of the same chain and a soft liner went over my head. Then came the plate vest and molle gear. And finally, all of it was covered by an oversized hoodie. The net effect of all that was to make me look even wider and thicker than my normally abnormal appearance. A few inches shorter and I could have passed for one of the dwarves in that Tolkien movie. It would have been a skater dwarf in his hoodie. Or perhaps a gang dwarf?

I tossed the duffel back into the car and watched it drive off after dropping me a couple of blocks away from my goal. I might as well have saved time and driven straight to the decaying garden. There was still yellow police tape around the entrance through the broken fence, but no police were visible. All the visible security cameras were pointing away from the entrance as well. I wondered if that was for my anonymity or a precaution of the thing waiting inside.

After a few seconds, I shrugged. It didn't matter who had turned the cameras. It just mattered that they were turned if they'd been repaired at all. I watched the entryway for movement. There was none. No lights or candle flames flickered. No eerie shadows coiled around inside. After an hour, it looked to me as if the place was as dead and still as a grave.

Fair enough. The prisoners were probably inside. They might even be in the odd cave that Eachan had "sensed". Then again there was no reason to make too easy a target of myself. Going through that hole in the fence would leave me exposed with the lights of distant businesses behind me. Maybe I didn't have to worry about a sniper, but I also had no idea what other surprises this creature had.

Preternatural toughness and some sort of venom were bad enough. The flames I'd felt might be real or illusory. Either way, they indicated that the Hulder was adept with some form of magick or hypnosis. I was optimistic that my runic defenses could counter those. The problem was, I had no idea what else she might have in store for me.

With yet another eloquent shrug, I unleashed my own little surprise. Instead of going through the fence, I took a dozen or so quick but nearly silent strides and triggered one of the runes on my calves. I felt a surge of wild heat as Uruz made my leg muscles spasm in a ridiculous burst of strength. It worked perfectly. I had no doubt that the henna was faded to near-invisibility as the rune used all of the energy stored in it to send me lofting into the tree branches of the sturdy old oak near the pond.

The enchantments for stealth kept my impact from being heard more than a few feet away. The sway of the branches might have given me away except that there was a nice sporadic breeze blowing. Chances were that any such movement would be taken for the wind. Crouched in the joint of the tree's main branches I sat and waited again. Again nothing happened. Nothing moved. No creature larger than a cricket made any sound. It was as if time had stopped except for the breeze, and my shadowy presence in the tree.

After a few more minutes of tension and straining senses, I lowered myself to arm's length and dropped the last foot or two to the ground. Around the back of the tree, the grass was thick and soft with a few weeds. Nearer the pond would be harder going. Even with enchantments, I might make enough noise to be heard.

I started around the old oak with the one hand ready to draw the tomahawk at a moment's notice. The strain of watching and not finding any expected attacker or victims was beginning to fray my nerves.

Every sense was on high alert and every muscle and sinew taut with explosive energy. Enough so that I involuntarily jumped and thumped my head on the overhanging branch when a feminine voice hissed from the other side of the fence. The force of the impact was enough to ring my bell. I sat down abruptly though I assume silently.

"PSST" there went the hiss again...or maybe I'd punctured my head and some of the air was leaking out? No. I wasn't an airhead. I was a fathead. It must have been lard leaking out and hissing.

"PSSSSSST! Magnus!" My thoughts tried to circle back into a recognizable pattern. I was pretty sure that the fat in my head wouldn't know my name. That meant somebody else was hissing in the still and empty darkness.

"Can't be empty darkness if someone else is hissing in it, can it?" See? I could make sense if I needed to. Although it didn't make much sense to sit around in the dark mumbling to myself either.

"Magnussss help me over the fence!" Despite the urgency, it was still a hissed whisper. In fact, it was barely loud enough for me to recognize the voice.

"Maureen? Dammit, I'm saving you. You're supposed to be in the fence or maybe in the cave not outside hissing! So be quiet or you'll wake up the guards before I can get you out of the tower...or cave." Wait another minute, knights and princesses in towers were after my time anyway.

I sat down and cradled my head as another hiss...this time of exasperation, cut through the shadows. A few scrambling and scraping noises came from the fence and then she was there beside me.

Maureen produced a small vial that glowed faintly like something in a blacklight. With that in hand, she peered close to my head and checked the lump I could feel expanding. Maybe the fat needed another way out? "Och, you've rapped your pate on that old grandfather oak, Mouse. You'll be right in a minute or two. Now, what was all that about a tower and a cave?"

"Shh. Just...be quiet a minute. Let me get my fat together. I mean my head. Let me get my head on straight." As incredible as it sounds, the girl did just that. I leaned against the knotted trunk of the tree and felt the lump again myself. It was tender and would make wearing a motorcycle helmet a problem in a day or two. That's what I get for letting my armored hood down to scout around. I flipped the chainmail and cloth back over my head.

"Okay, there's supposedly a cave or cavern or something under this garden or grove. Of course, *supposedly* there's also a fair Irish princess captured in said cave. But here you are ruining an amazing rescue. Next thing I know, Walter will show up with his machete to chop through the brush here." It occurred to me that I was wasting a lot of time grumbling. It also occurred to me that a self-inflicted wound was apparently not covered by the runes when I'd formed the protections in my mind. Something to think about next time I guess.

I wasn't quite embarrassed enough to refuse the hand up when Maureen offered it. I was a little more irritated when she chimed in with more useful information. My damsel in no particular distress was starting to cut into my heroic rescuer mode. "Hmm. I remember thinking that the pond I was thrown in felt...weird. Like maybe a fake pond and not very stable underneath? There was also a weird feeling rock under all the scum. Let's go back and look."

I might have argued with her. I'd have been arguing with her backside if I had. Without waiting for my consent, agreement, or even an opinion she was off to investigate her hunch. I had little choice except to follow her. Or try and come up with a clever insight of my own. Too bad I refused to find any clever insights.

When I got there, I could see that the moon had taken its time but now had broken through the thin clouds overhead. In the wan silver light, I got a glimpse at my maiden for the first time since she shot me. She wasn't dressed for the same kind of business as she had been last time.

There was no revealing and minimally protective hooded robe this time. Instead, she had on thick leathers of the type professional motorcyclists wear. Judging from the way the skin-tight material moved along her distracting contour of the thigh, the padded areas were filled with something more protective than just padding. There appeared to be some type of hard surface inside those pads at thigh and hip. Presumably, the pattern continued in the protected areas of the upper leathers. The entire suit was made in a green so dark it appeared almost black within the dark of night.

She wore a leather jacket over the top of the suit that would have been more appropriate in a Harley commercial. The main difference being that hers had more chains and spikes and all of the said metal work was finished in a dull grey or black that barely reflected the wan moonlight.

"Probably *"Bard"* would be more appropriate than *Princess*," she said as she bent over to reach under the nose-wrinkling pond scum. "We do go back to Conn of the hundred battles but I've always felt more drawn to the O'Daly period of family history."

It took me a minute to understand she was referencing back to my comment about fair Irish Maidens. "Bards? Like minstrels and troubadours are more interesting than an Irish king?"

"You're not serious, are you? A king was a king. But a bard could reach the exalted rank of celebrity, entertainer, educator, and historian all rolled up into one. The training was fierce. And much of it done with nary a piece of paper to write on. An Ollam, or the epitome of a bard recognized as such by his bardic peers, was one of the most honorable and noteworthy positions in all of Ireland....wait, I think I have it." She gave a wrench at something in the pond. I couldn't help but notice how the tight leathers displayed an impressive level of fitness in her lean muscled thighs. My attention was drawn from those thighs and a mental image of other attached anatomy when a sucking sound heralded the success of her efforts.

## 25

IN SHORT ORDER, the entire pond drained down to reveal an old handwheel atop a hatch like you see in old submarine movies. Maureen had managed to crank the wheel enough and lever it up a crack so that the water in this shallow part of the pond drained away. When she opened it and started in, I reached out to grab her arm. "Look, so you're not a damsel in distress. If you don't mind though I think I'll go down first. After all, my male ego could conceivably take permanent damage if you keep hogging all of the macho parts."

With a smile, she stepped back. When she turned, I could tell she also had some gear but not anything as military sleek as my tactical stuff. Hers appeared to be an old haversack of some sort slung diagonally across her torso. In the dark, I had missed it. Now though I saw her dig into it and pull out a few unidentifiable items. Time was pressing. I decided to ask what she had at a later time and place.

Once the hatch was up descent was easy as pie. The first few feet were a vertical ladder. After that my boots hit a slick but navigable stone ledge. Within a handful of yards, there was another drop of only inches to the next ledge. In a series of wide gentle tiers, the steps reached down into a cave that widened in front of us. Even my enhanced eyesight was taking a few minutes to adjust to the darkness.

Maureen had the answer to that too. Before I decided to reach for my flashlight, she snapped something behind me and tossed a couple of pale green sticks ahead. The green glow brightened until they provided a clear zone of pale light for a few feet around each of them. They also shed enough light to let us dimly see the walls stretching around us in a cavern the size of a medium conference room.

At the extreme range of the wan light, a human figure could be seen moving feebly atop a natural stone outcropping about the size and shape of a table. The water from above us splashed down the tiered steps and ran in rivulets to either side of the stone table or altar. At the far side of the cave, the water just disappeared into cracks along the base of that wall.

Nowhere within our sight was another exit, or entrance, or a large and intimidating tree woman. In fact, I could not even guess how she would have gotten into or out of the cave. I said as much to my companion. "She's not here."

"You mean the Baobhan Sith?" Her tone was hushed and cautious sounding.

"A bayou van sith? What the Hel is that? I'm talking about the Hulder witch." I refused to believe she was *that* good. Better and more prepared than I was for the operation *and* smarter than Eachan with the research? Not likely.

"A Hulder? Not in my lexicon Mr. Mouse. A Baobhan Sith is a Celtic nature spirit. Appears as a seductive woman and lures men to their talon-like claws which they use to drain the lifeblood and energy from a victim. Not that I've ever seen one ye ken?" Something about her dialogue bothered me. Then again something about the smooth play of all that female flesh under her leathers bothered me. It was hard to tell if the distraction was coming from my own hormone levels or the seductive whammy of our target. I tried to ignore the distraction and focus on her words.

"I sure hope it's a Baobhan. That's what I came equipped for. Music to counter hers, an iron horseshoe for both her fear of horses and as a cold iron deterrent to the fairy folk. If it's something else then I'm not sure what we'll do about it. If it shows up. Maybe she's out for a hair appointment or something?" She couldn't have given the thing a better straight line if she tried.

"Why? Are my roots showing?" The voice came from above us. As we both looked up, the roots of trees that hung from the ceiling fell in a shower of dirt and the Hulder witch slithered through the earth like it was water or soft mud. She landed in a martial arts movie crouch in front of me. If martial arts actors had glistening green talon-tipped arms long enough to reach their knees.

"This time I take you both and sacrifice the soft one over there." Something about the voice wasn't right. In fact, several things weren't right. She wasn't big enough. Previously when we met she'd been taller than I. Taller, heavier, and somehow more ponderous of aura. The last time we fought there was a palpable sense of age and power about her. She didn't have a sibilant version of a Spanish accent last time either.

Her smaller form was much faster though. While I was still comparing my mental notes from the two encounters, she covered twenty feet so fast that I barely registered that she was moving. And then she was on me. Her first blow knocked me off my feet and onto my back a good three tiers of slick stone behind and above me. I couldn't tell if it was a fist or a kick that hit me. It was just a blur and a sickening thud. With a hiss, she spit incomprehensible words at me, "Quemarte Bastardo."

Once again, I was on fire. It would seem that watered stone should put that kind of fire out. It didn't. If anything, the fire seemed to be drying the water out as little puffs of steam erupted from the rock where I rolled. In a frenzy, I thought of my ally and companion down in the bowels of rock under Austin. I ripped Eachan's amulet from the pocket of my hoodie, I threw it in an arc to the girl. "Maureen! Take it!"

The amulet and the gout of flame from the Hulder hit her at the same time. She didn't need the amulet. The flame came at her like a flamethrower. And she sucked it into her right hand, not through the palm, but through the back of her hand. She cocked that hand downward like some martial arts striking-adder pose or something. The flames hit the skin and disappeared as if it was just so much wind. When she did that, flames sprang from the crescent-shaped blade in her other hand. It looked like a burning crescent moon with the handle protruding back parallel to the outside curve of the moon-shaped blade.

She struck with her fire sheathed blade in the split second between the plant's attack, and its stunned expression when the flames disappeared. The shining blade left a thin line of oozing green along the creature's forearm. The fire appeared to have no effect at all. The plantess hissed with a mocking note. "My own flames are useless against me, as is your puny steel."

A puzzled look followed the tree woman's comment and she turned her arm to look at the oozing wound. Maureen's response was taunting. "Maybe the steel is puny. But the silver seems to sting."

I wanted to cheer as Maureen lunged and took another swipe at her adversary. I couldn't cheer though. For one thing, I was terrified for the girl fighting something old and steeped in its amoral power. For another, cheering would probably give away how effective my runework had been in stopping the fire.

Instead of cheering and applauding my audacious Amazon, I writhed and rolled ever closer to the fray. The girl was fit. She was fairly strong and armed with something that at least had the potential to harm her opponent. On the other hand, it was very clear that she had only rudimentary training with the weapon she carried. Her hand-to-hand work with me had been much sharper. With the blade though, her attacks were wide arcing swipes that she telegraphed a second or two ahead of time. A trained fighter would have had her disarmed and on the way to unconsciousness within seconds.

The tree thing was not exactly Bruce Lee either. She was fast, strong, and tough. That had probably been enough to account for most foes. Then there was the psychic whammy she'd hit me with the first time. And of course, there was no dismissing the magickal flames. Honestly, she'd probably never had to fight until we met last time.

Maybe that's why she never noticed when I got the tomahawk out. She was still keeping a wary eye on the flickering fires of the silver sickle when I rolled to my feet behind her left shoulder and took the arm off at the elbow.

She thrust with the remaining stump of an arm and left a green smear along the front of my hoodie. The blow behind that green smear would have easily crushed my ribcage if it weren't for the chainmail and tactical vest. As it was, she drove me back a good two or three steps. Her good hand was busy with a different task though. With two foes to face instead of one, she threw caution aside. An adder fast strike of her good fist caught Maureen just below her sternum. It was good enough to drive the girl's breath from her audibly. I heard it clearly even above my own breathing and the sounds of our fight. While the girl rocked on her heels, that same fist caught one whole side of her auburn hair and with a wrenching motion sent my Maureen tumbling and rolling all the way down the wide steps. She landed with a cry of pain against the stone block.

Even from dozens of feet away, I heard the impact and the snap of a bone. That caused the red fires of a primitive rage to erupt inside me. The fire in my core was more than a match for the flames still wrapped ineffectively around my torso. I let the rage feed on itself as I drove forward into the tree. She was fast and strong and tough just like before. She was not as heavy as I was in all my gear. Nor was she fueled by a power held sacred by Vikings for centuries. As a bestial roar erupted from somewhere deep in my chest and belly, the tomahawk became light as a feather.

Glittering sparks seemed to erupt from the inscribed runes as I hacked without my previous hard-won skill. In the rage, I just had furious determination and newfound strength. Chunks of bark flew, green ichor splattered. I know she hit me and raked at my flesh. Some of her attacks got through my armor. Most of it was stopped by either armor or enchantment, but some of it got through. More of my swings got through than hers did though.

She dropped to a knee and I grabbed her green tresses in one fist while the other hand prepared to remove pinochio-ettes head. "NO!!"

The sound of that one word was like a round of artillery inside the cave. The volume alone was enough to stun me into immobility. The roiling waves of anger and hate almost drove me to my knees beside my foe. In the silence following that attack, I heard another note. It was a wordless humming with a melody like none I've ever heard. If Freddie Mercury were to take up magic, this would have been who he went to for lessons. The song reached out and tugged at me past my protections. The runes did not stop the siren call, but they dulled it enough to allow me to think and take a deep breath.

When I turned it was plainly obvious why the tree witch tonight wasn't like herself from the previous fight. The one standing over both Maureen and Walter Roy *was* herself. Mine was just a younger, more vicious copy. The older one was even bigger than I remembered.

Her arms were almost as long as the body of the one I held in my grip. Apparently, she had some comic book healing powers too. The hand retrieved by my helpful police buddy had grown back. It looked a little wet and undone. But it was there as real, knotted, and wood-like as the original. The venomous green sap or ichor welled up thick enough to drip off of her claws and land on the stone block beside Walter. He groaned and shifted his weight as if rolling away from the splash of those deadly droplets.

Somehow, she managed to speak without breaking the rhythm of that buzzing melodious hum. "So you still resist. As you still live. It seems I underestimated you." Her voice, aside from the musical and magical component, was quite alien. The tone did not hold interest or fear or even anger. It was a flat statement of fact.

"You will release my young cousin or I will begin pulling pieces off of these two." She was certain of her control of the situation. Even without normal cadences of voice or suggestion of emotion, she conveyed her confidence and her complete belief that I would obey.

"I got a piece you can pull on, you old oversized sex toy."
She might have been as shocked as I was that I could defy
her that much. The surprise and the exhilaration of success
fueled me to a new effort. My every focus went to the soft
holster attached to my vest. I tugged the zipper of the
hoodie down despite the fact that it was glued in place and
weighed more than an anchor. It probably did not take me
the several minutes it felt like.

I could dimly feel the smaller creature struggling weakly
against my grip in her hair. She was too weak from all of the
damage she'd already taken to be effective. I ignored those
struggles and refocused on the gun. At the same time, I felt
the ancient Hulder intensify her focus. The music increased
in vibration. I could feel the buzz all the way to my bones. It
felt like the entire cave was resonating with her seductress
song. Hel, it might actually have been resonating. If Eachan
was right, people had been doing rituals in this cave for
thousands of years.

How likely was it that they'd been doing them to placate
and strengthen a guardian spirit of sorts? Likely enough that
I didn't want to consider what I might be facing. Instead, my
every thought went to the gun. Slowly it came out of its
holster. I saw my arm rise with the gun in my fist. The
resonation increased until I thought my eardrums would
burst. Or maybe it would be the blood vessels in my eyes.

That didn't matter. In a final surge of defiance, I
squeezed the trigger twice. The heavy .45 long colt rounds
thundered in the cave and left my ears ringing. I heard the
thunderclap and saw the splash of color as the bullets
impacted a few feet from the target. White rings of light
radiated from the impacts like water from a thrown rock.
They rippled and faded away until my eyes and ears
adjusted.

She had stopped singing or humming or whatever it was. But she didn't show any harm from the gunshots. Instead, a ring of glowing symbols appeared in a circle around her and the stone block. The bitch was bulletproof.

Okay, that's probably not accurate. To be precise, she seemed to be standing in a circle of power that was strong enough and focused enough to deflect my bullets. I'd heard of such power.

I mean come on, we all grew up on stories of wizards and trolls, magical elves and industrious dwarves. Those things meant a lot more to someone like me than they do to John Doe on the street. Hel, even I could do some of those things. But there was no way I knew how to stop a bullet with Magick. Maybe Eachan might, but at that precise moment, I doubted I'd ever get a chance to ask him.

My hopes crashed as did the last dregs of my berserker style rage. With a groan, I released the weak and shattered creature in my grasp. She no longer radiated her cold cruelty. All she radiated was green sappy blood as she dragged herself down towards the older Hulder and their captives.

In defeat I let my arm fall. I let everything fall. I was too weak to steady myself and ended up rolling down a section of the steps that was a little rougher and not as gently terraced as the rest. It put me on the cave floor to within fifteen feet of the ancient.

Maybe I hadn't hurt her but my inexplicable defiance didn't do anything for her self-confidence. Almost as if she knew fear, she pulled Walter up and used him to shelter the core of her torso. I wasn't ready to risk that though. Her spell seemed perfectly adequate to me. And even if I were to take a shot, the girl and the semi-comatose Walter were in harm's way between the tree and I.

Maureen seemed to be in shock or something. She was sitting back on her heels and swaying with the broken arm cradled in her other hand. I could see Eachans amulet hanging from her injured arm. She must have had her own enchantments too. The amulet seemed to be sizzling at her just like it had at me. The Hulder drew my attention back with a sharp hiss.

"Put down your weapons, warrior of old. You should not be my prey. Things are often not as they should be these days though." She glanced aside at the shattered remains of her younger copy. If I had to guess, I'd say that glance was calculating and dangerous. "Warrior I will make your end glorious. When you die you will be in ecstasy, and I will grow in strength with the power that radiates from you. In exchange, I will let the soft man go. He has little power to feed me. Just his lifeblood. The witch woman and you will give me more magick and more power by far than a dozen such unenlightened creatures as this man."

I had to consider it. Maybe if I could get inside the circle I could try and shoot her again. Chances were that the shots I took at her would be wasted on the very people I was trying to save. If she'd offered me Roy and Maureen both I'd have a hard time refusing. But she only offered me the bar owner. Still...one life saved might be worth it. I was pretty sure I wasn't getting out of here anyway.

Maureen saved me from having to make that decision. She rolled forward to hands and knees but cried out as her broken arm folded under her. She fell into a roll that took her inside the circle but aside from my line of fire. That was almost as good as falling back out of my way.

It was also just the first step of what she must have planned out. From inside the circle, she threw a glass bottle that must have been in her pouch. It had a cloth sticking out of the neck but wasn't lit. All she got for her efforts was a glare from the older Hulder and a whimper from the younger version. With that failure, she looked at me with something like fear in her eyes. But there was also calculation and the flush of success. "Magnus! My bag! Flare stick!"

She tried to roll to her feet and distract our foes long enough for me to scramble back and dig in her pack for the flare. In her attempt, she put weight on the broken arm. She was just too damaged to support her own weight on it. The broken bones kept her up long enough though. She had just enough time to throw Eachan's amulet at the stone block that was the center of that circle of power. I heard the older man's voice and saw his will evoked as a barely visible ripple of energy. In that instant, he must have driven a spike of his own slowly and strenuously gathered power at a piece of crystal embedded in the rock. I saw a hint of the energy and heard the groaning crystal's response before it shattered. With a discordant shrieking sound, the symbols of the circle flashed and sparked chaotically then dimmed completely.

I still couldn't shoot though. In the flashing lights and chaos, I was afraid I'd hit Walt. That's when the chaos resolved itself into a new figure. A stout and heavy silhouette appeared from behind me and charged on thick churning legs to hurl himself at Walter. As the heavy arms wrapped around my dazed boss, Jackson yelled in one of his special stentorian bellows. "NOW!"

Then he was past my line of fire carrying his inert human burden with him. Ancient Hulder reached after him but her reactions were too slow. My adrenaline was pumping again and reinforcing all of the vital juices that had been stewing in me since the fight began with her younger self. The gun seemed to rise by itself until the white-lined blade of its sight was dividing her torso in half from left to right. I squeezed the trigger again, fought the recoil and brought it down to fire the last shot in the cylinder.

The shots weren't a thunderclap. Each one was a sizzling, hissing whoosh, and roar. The dragon's breath .410 shells thumped through the air like an air cannon or a mini-volcano clearing its throat. In the wake of that sound, a lance of searing white light shot across the room to envelop the ancient as well as the whimpering tree girl at her feet. Maybe they were immune to their flame. They weren't immune to superheated magnesium in a cone of fire burning around three thousand degrees fahrenheit. Both females burst into flame in the superheated air. Even without Maureen's Molotov, the tree forms might have gone up like candles. The gasoline she used just added more fuel. Younger and smaller Hulder simply fell and whimpered once or twice more as the fire reduced her to ashy components.

The older tree was tougher. She let out a primal scream then spun and ran at a diagonal. For a minute I thought she was trying to get to the last of the water trickling through the base of the wall. She didn't stop there though. With a horrendous wet crashing sound she tore through the mud wall. This time she did not move through the earth and mud so much as she exploded out of it. The shock was enough to make the cave feel like it was shaking. I'm pretty sure it was just the violence and sound of the impact though.

Racing forward, I caught up Maureen but stopped myself from crushing her to me when she cried out at the pain of her flopping arm. Part of the dragon's breath must have clipped Jackson. He was busy slapping out sparks on his own matte black version of my new tactical gear. Walter, good old oblivious Walter, slept through it all.

Those of us still conscious made sure he was safe behind the block. Then we checked on the little bonfire that was all that remained of the younger tree woman. Finally, we moved cautiously to the new mouth of the cave. Down below us, a large log floated. There were still sparks and embers on top of the log. But that was the only movement visible as it floated slowly downstream with no sign of any directing force. It seemed that whatever animated the tree had left it. Somehow, I was kind of sorry.

If the professor was right, this creature was older than most of the cities in the world. She had been part and parcel of the people, the history, and the very geography of this region for over ten thousand years possibly. It was a shame that she was gone. Imagine what we might have learned from her.

A gasp brought me back to the moment. Where I had been supporting Maureen, she was now supporting me. I wasn't quite sure how that happened. When I looked down though, I was beyond surprised to notice that my nice armor and gear had done its job. Other than some sundered chain links and cosmetic damage the tac vest and chainmail were good to go.

My dark pants were another story. There was just enough left of them to be decent. Ribbons of blood ran freely down both legs. Inside the wounds, a green glint could be seen almost like living worms trying to writhe deeper into my flesh. From what I could see of my arms and legs, most of the henna was gone. Apparently, those vague struggles I'd felt during my blinding rage had been a little more strenuous than I thought.

I heard Jackson ask the girl, "Can you get him out of here and do your stuff with the herbs again? Or do we need to take him to the hospital? For that matter what would a hospital make of him?? We both know he's not normal. If we take him in he might easily end up in a government laboratory. What the hell do we do?"

"It's fine. I have him. We'll have to make it to his house. I have all of my herbs in the satchel." When she tried to move me alone, the pain in her arm made her cry out. I blearily looked around to see her biting her lip in a face gone as pale as the moonlight earlier.

"Magnus, you're going to have to walk." For some reason, she seemed to be crying. Why cry? We'd won. The dragon had gone and taken the treants with him, hadn't he? This was no time for crying. It was time for mead and strutting about. Bragging of your successes and boasting about your next epic adventure.

"Get him to the surface. My driver will be right around." That was Eachan! My friend Eachan was here. He knew the old ways. He would explain to my Maureen how to celebrate a dragon-slaying! When I looked around I couldn't find him. But his voice came from the girl where she was half supporting me. "Magnus, I can't help you. Most of my amulet is gone. There's barely enough left to communicate. Walk with Maureen to the car."

That sounded like a great idea. I hadn't been in the backseat of a car with a beautiful woman since the sixties. And this one was more than beautiful. She was strong and smart and lovely all in one. I reached over to cup her cheek and leaned in for a kiss. Then I kept leaning until I was falling on the slick stone at the mouth of the cave.

The cold water woke me up a little. Then we started climbing. Maureen moved ahead of us holding one of her glowing green chemical lights. Jackson plodded along huffing and puffing with one of my arms pulled up high over his shoulder. Inconsiderate bastard was too tall.

Reminded me of all my brothers and comrades in arms when I was growing up. All of 'em over six foot and laughing jovial assholes. At least Jackson wasn't laughing. Somehow we made it to the top of the bluff and the street nearby. I don't remember much more. There was the car, and Maureen smiling through her tears. Jackson was saying he'd get Walter out and try to cover up any evidence. Something about teenagers and fireworks setting a fire. That was the last I remembered.

## 26

WHEN I WOKE UP, an elegant redhead was looming over me with a concerned look and a cool hand on my brow. Of course, Eachan isn't really my type and his hand reeked of some expensive cologne, but he did look concerned. Behind him, I could see the matte-grey painted walls of my room.

That was almost as relieving as the identity of my nurse was disappointing. The memory of one of my co-rescuers rejecting the hospital trip was foggy but there. They were quite right. If some snot-faced intern had come to check on my wounds there would have been a hue and cry while people tried to figure out how they'd cured me so completely so quickly. After that, there'd be the suits and sunglasses, then meetings and finally basement laboratories until I managed to quit breathing somehow.

That was all provided I survived the first night in hospital hands. I could just picture Eachan or Maureen trying to press their poultices and potions on my doctors and nurses. Mayhem and chaos were the least likely result. Multiple trauma injuries and incarceration were a much better bet before the two rather strong-willed practitioners gave up on me. Let's face it. Their concoctions were more likely than an MRI or the newest pharmaceutical scam to help me survive an unknown venom or whatever the hell that thing had in her claws.

Which is probably why they brought me home and treated me themselves. The secret laboratories and government spooks were real concerns. Surviving to worry about them was a higher priority though. Once more I was certain that my own overcharged healing rate would see me through now that the immediate threat was gone.

Still, I would have preferred an entirely different nurse. Eachan pulled his hand away and scowled down at me. "I thought you were some kind of elite mercenary or some such? You were rescued by a girl with a broken arm, an out of shape old policeman and a crippled college teacher who wasn't even there. Are you sure you've ever even been in a conflict before?"

He barely managed to turn away before his smile cracked the stern frown. "Speaking of which, a young lady is making you breakfast down the hall. For some unknown reason, she feels breakfast would sit better on your tender disposition than a hearty steak and potato. Be warned that it all looks atrocious and the pall of smoke is just contained enough to avoid a visit from fire trucks. The oatmeal is undoubtedly lumpy and the eggs will have runny whites. The toast is more black than golden brown, and the bacon resembles beef jerky. You, sir, will eat heartily and thank her for the tremendous work."

He busied himself tidying the room and making sure I was at least minimally presentable. "I suppose there's no time for a shave and hot shower. I would suggest such a course of action immediately after appreciating the breakfast prepared by someone wearing a brand-new cast. You might mention how amazing she was in the fight. Oh and heap upon her fulsome thanks for the help in saving your life...if that's what we did? You murmured some amazing things before we got the substance in your bloodstream under control. Someday we'll have to talk. Your pronunciation of Icelandic borders upon criminal by the way."

I didn't bother to correct him. Maybe my Icelandic was iffy. My old Norse was spot on though. After all, it was my native tongue. Looking around the room I spotted the ragged remnants of my trousers as well as a pile of clothes and high-tech gear that must have been everything else I wore. My revolver was cleaned and lying on the bedside table within reach. My most comfortable chair from Eachan's divination table had been moved into the bedroom. From the pile of sheets and pillows on it, I gathered that my slumbers had been watched over.

The level of attention was both gratifying and worrisome. I appreciated that they cared enough to watch. I also worried that I might have said a little too much in my delirium. With any luck, neither of my potential sitters understood everything I said. The professor might speak some of the right languages, but he was about the only person I truly trusted these days. While I was pondering exactly *what* I might have revealed in my post-traumatic confusion, a new vision to inspire dreams and hallucinations came in.

She was wearing one of my oxford shirts loosely buttoned to provide decency but not much more. Underneath the hem, I spotted a pair of old basketball shorts that she must have pulled to half the normal drawstring size. Her waist wasn't narrow and waspish, but I was wider and stouter than most men even if I was a few inches shorter than her.

She walked slowly to avoid dropping the tray she

juggled awkwardly on the hard plaster cast that encased her left arm from her elbow to the base of her fingers. Even though she was walking slowly, I had a hard time not checking the sinuous sway of hip that peeked out from the curved hem of the shirt. I guess maybe I have a surfeit of hormones even without ancient floral enchantresses to prod me along.

The professor slipped out behind her as she swayed over and put the tray on my bedside table. I remembered the need to move the pistol first. She took it from my hands and stuck it on top of a dresser across the room. After that, with the room to ourselves, she leaned over with her melting green eyes locked on mine.

With her weight balanced far forward on her good arm, she tempted my gaze with the obvious fact that there was nothing but a very feminine girl under the shirt unbuttoned for two or three of the top buttons. I am a man of strong will though. Besides, the look on her face was as mesmerizing as the potential peep show. When her face was just an inch or two away she closed her eyes and made me meet her partway.

Despite my injuries and some lingering deep pains from all the recent abuse, meeting her part of the way was worth it. For someone I'd already kissed a couple of times, this was an entirely new experience. Her good hand found its way to the back of my head while my own hand cupped the nape of her neck under thick waves of auburn. I don't know how long it went on. It felt like hours of slow languid exploration of each other through that joining of lips and more.

The scrape of wood against the floor outside my room brought an end to it. She leaned back with an easy smile and brushed her hand against my cheek. "The food's not as bad as the old man said. I make excellent oatmeal and the bacon is just crispy, not burned."

She turned and helped Eachan get another chair using her good hand and keeping the plaster-encased arm out of harm's way. Once they were both seated he cleared his throat and nodded to indicate my tray. "Pass the coffee lad and then eat up while I tell you what I've discovered."

Since I had two hands to her one, Maureen let me serve the coffee around. I added brown sugar and a splash of cream to mine. She took hers similarly though with perhaps half the sugar. The professor seemed to have his own ideas for the coffee. He produced an ornately engraved silver flask and added a good-sized splash of amber liquid to his cup along with just a bit of the brown sugar.

In typical fashion, he had different priorities than I might. "Now, should we start with what it took to keep you alive for the last couple of days or go into the really interesting part about the cave?"

Since we were both drinking from the coffee cups, he continued without our input. "The cave seems to be, as I surmised, an ancient ritual chamber. With better light, we managed to discover markings on the walls, the floor, and even the ceiling of the chamber. Closest to the steps I came across newer markings. Cabalistic symbols and other cultural or traditional symbols, as well as some new age manifestations of older religions, were written around the opening into the pond and along the steps. There were similar markings on the altar stone."

He refreshed himself from the "Irish Coffee" while I sampled the oatmeal and bacon. She was right about the oatmeal. It was very good and had some sweetening and flavors I couldn't pinpoint right off the bat.

While I pondered the culinary tricks behind my mush,

the professor continued his discourse. "That stone is a treasure trove all by itself. In addition to factors that only someone like we three might find fascinating; it contained symbology from the present day back to the pre-Columbian era and even further. I suspect that there are faint scratchings on it that might trace themselves to the paleolithic and a contemporary of our aforementioned Leander Lady. Between those oldest markings and the European touches, there were Mesolithic or Epipaleolithic symbols. I even found markings that are very much like things found in Aztec and Olmec ruins. It's truly fascinating."

"Which you can talk about for months on end no doubt." Even Eachan seemed too bemused by Maureen's Gaelic lilt to resent the interruption. She continued while he nodded his gracious consent.

"As for the less interesting information. You've been unconscious a full day and then some. This is the evening of the day after we brought you home. I was concerned about blood loss. However, your body somehow resolved any issues with blood pressure or mortal looking hemorrhage. Someday we'll have to talk about that. We were concerned about internal injuries and vascular damage but the true threat seemed to be whatever she injected with her claws. I made my poultices and used a few tricks and techniques of my own. Eachan cooked up a couple of foul concoctions, burned candles, lit herbs, and hummed his little Scottish ditties over you."

If the professor was offended by her account of his workings and "ditties" he kept it to himself. Instead, he took up where she left off. "We debated taking you to Hospital. Fortunately for you, the girl and I both share the opinion that more than a few yank doctors are more concerned with the health of their bank accounts and the AMA than the wellbeing of their patients. Besides, nurses can be very persnickety about sage and burning candles, not to mention poultices and potions."

Maureen chimed in as if on cue. "So we took care of you ourselves. If the professor had not mentioned how well you responded to my last bandages and herbal work I might have argued for the doctors. As it is, you responded amazingly. I'm not sure if it's your runic skill that makes our work stronger or what. The truth though, is that I've never seen anyone recover from injuries and toxins the way you did with our help."

"What about the cops or anyone else?" My voice was rough and raw coming out. To remedy it I drank some more of the lifesaving coffee.

"Walter Roy was released yesterday afternoon. He called to thank you and tell you to take off as long as you need. He also offered a car and some credit cards if you need to leave town." The professor managed to express curiosity and support in his expression rather than surprise at the statement from Walter.

Before I figured out how to respond, Maureen spoke up again. "Walter remembers part of the cave, but it was very nebulous in his memories. I think he mentioned feeling like he was on peyote for the fight. He is quite grateful even though the investigation is still open. Oh, he wanted to let you know that Consuela and the guys did a great job of covering for his days off. He's giving them all a bonus and might be handing out some promotions. I think there was some question about whether he needed a new head of security."

While I thought about that, Eachan took the refrain up. "As for police. We haven't had a single visit. Not a police car or even your friend Officer Jackson. Maybe he thinks it's better to lay low and not bring any extra attention to you. Perhaps it's in your favor that the whole town is talking about the remarkable new archaeological site discovered through some thoughtless vandalism by unknown juveniles. I, for one, plan to get in on this discovery before it's run over by ham-handed students and faculty. Perhaps there will be another paper to publish after I do my research."

From there the conversation deteriorated. Each of them wanted to discuss their own observations and additions to the magickal mayhem in the cavern. As could be expected, all three of us had recollections that differed. Eventually, the toll of sleeplessness and exertion worked their magick on Eachan. "Magnus m'boy. I do hate to impose. However, I fear I am too exhausted to drive and am hesitant to call one of my collegiate minions at this hour to chauffeur me. Do you suppose it would be too much trouble to allow me a nap on your couch?"

Once more I didn't get to answer. Maureen was up in a flash of very shapely thigh under my shirt and shorts combo. Helping the professor to his feet, she handed him his cane and gathered up blankets and pillows. "You sir will take the guest room. I'm younger and fit and have slept in worse places than a broken-in comfy old couch. Your leg probably aches from angling it out of that chair so you take the spare bed and I'll make do. It seems our patient is stable enough for us to rest through the night and that means it's about time for our break too wouldn't ye say?"

Alone in my room, I shifted up to arrange the pillows in a pile that propped me half reclined and half sitting. With an arm behind my head, I finished my coffee and poured a second cup. It seemed amazing to me that the three of us had become so comfortable that the two of them could tag-team a conversation and I could follow the whole thing without asking a bunch of questions. I thought about that comfort. About that feeling of acceptance, of *home*. It was a comfortable dream. To have a stable place in the world and the people who you knew and cared about. To have people that knew you and understood the things you never talked about.

Those were sobering concepts. It was hard to deny how deeply they rooted into my thoughts. I went to sleep trying to convince myself that I didn't really care about all of that.

I woke up to the sound of some inconsiderate jackass reverberating down the street in a muscle car or motorcycle. I had just rolled over irritably when the door opened quietly across the room. The silhouette in the door was tall, famil-iar, and achingly feminine. She padded softly across the room with her hypnotic eyes on my face again. I don't know how I could tell, but I knew she saw my eyes open and watching her. Without a word she knelt on the bed and bent until her hair hid our faces.

This kiss was different. It started slow and warm and soft. That only lasted so long. Soft and warm turned to heated and intense. From there it escalated to scorching and demanding. It wasn't entirely clear who was moving faster. I know I enjoyed the slow kiss. But I was racing right along when we hit a feverish pace and she moved my hand under the hem of the shirt.

I felt the curve of her hip where the basketball shorts had been. Now there was only soft skin and firm muscle under my hand. With her breath coming out in short moans between kisses, she took a couple of seconds to tell me. "Be careful of your bandages....and my arm."

I tried. The bandages weren't that big of an issue. If it had been two days since the fight, then I should either be dead or well on my way to healing a few cuts. I was more worried about her arm. When I rolled her down beside me she bit back a cry at the pain in her wrist. I pulled away an inch or two and whispered. "I don't know. I want this. I want this more than I can tell you. But is it the right time? I don't know if I can do this without...Look I don't want to hurt you."

Her good arm pulled me back against her and there was a low throaty growl as she bit my lip. She twined her calves behind mine and writhed against me in a way that made me reconsider the risk to benefit ratio. "Then you better get creative mister."

## 27

IT WAS LATE when I woke up again. It was hard to put my feelings into categories. Don't get me wrong, I've had lady friends and some very satisfying relationships as far as they went. For that matter, an air hostess stopped by every two or three weeks on her circuit and usually spent a couple of days enjoying the food and music available in Austin. We tended to enjoy each other quite a bit during those stays too. She stayed at my house whenever she was around.

This did not feel like any of those relationships though. Some part of me always knew that the other girls would be gone someday. They would find someone else. Some would get tired of waiting for more than I was willing to give. Others would just lose interest after a while. And that was fine with me. I enjoyed them.

There were none that I didn't enjoy from casual dating to intimacy when it happened. Austin is a fairly progressive city despite the cowboy reputation of the whole state. Some talented ladies could make even an experienced man blush. They weren't all pros either. Back before I swore off the young ones, a college girl or two from UT had taught me exactly how open-minded and truly skilled a twenty-year-old could be in the erotic arena.

Yet despite some of those very fond memories, none of them made me feel like I would be ready for the current relationship. This just didn't seem like a casual entertainment. And I didn't have a place in my life for commitments like this. In mid-thought, my attention was dragged back to the present. I smelled gas. Not gasoline but natural gas. Had the girl left my stove on to leak somehow? The newer models generally won't do that. That's what they say at least. I wasn't sure.

I decided to roll over and get my oxford off the floor where it had fallen sometime during the night. I remember being surprised that it fit over the cast so easily. There were other surprises during the night that meant a lot more to me. I rolled...

Check that. I started to roll over. All I managed was a weak shudder. For a minute my heart raced to new speeds and I tried to draw a deep breath. That didn't work either. What I got was a ragged shallow inhalation followed by a vaguely mumbled profanity. Was the venom still doing its work? That didn't make any sense at all. Oh, I guess all of the exertions might have dragged some remaining molecules of the toxin into my system. For a while there my heart and blood had both been pumping rather vigorously before we fell asleep curled around each other.

Still, my body could metabolize some potent things given enough time. With the help of the professor and my lovely Maureen, there was no reason there should be any danger from the claws of our defeated foes. From a corner of my eye, I could see my calf past where her own much nicer leg was draped over me. The bandages were in complete disarray and already the ragged gashes were just thin lines. They were still an angry red, but they had a look of fresh wounds well on the way to healing. There were no radiating lines of sickly color to indicate a spread of the venom.

The voice that slithered out of the shadows behind me was all smug silk and exotic spices. "The sugar covers flavors very good no? No, no vaquero, don't try to turn. Even you ain't gonna be moving until manana. If you was still gonna be alive manana."

Her chuckle was throaty, self-indulgent, and utterly at odds with the chilling effect of her words. "Here senor, let me turn you over. You gotta see what I planned for you people."

Soft hands tipped with perfect nails rolled me over to see her silhouette in the soft light coming through my window. The first thing I noticed though were the eyes. Even with her back to any light source, they seemed to be reflecting a reddish glow. Jacque Brewster from the bar reached into a bag at her side and pulled out a familiar sickle-shaped blade. With Maureen's blade at my throat, I might still have made a move against the witch. The only problem was I couldn't move more than a few twitches of any part of my body.

She grinned down at my helplessness. "Oh, this is going to be fun! But we don't want to hog all of the fun do we?"

Removing the blade from my throat she used it to prod Maureen's shoulder where she lay on her side facing both myself, and the dark silhouette of the dead drummer's widow. Maureen's eyelids fluttered and opened to about half their normal width. It was apparent that she had even less strength than I did. I saw her chest shaking and it occurred to me that she couldn't even get a deep enough breath to scream or cry. Right then I put every possible effort into forcing my body to obey me despite any poisoning. My muscles weren't getting the message.

My weak grunts and useless twitching were apparently a ripe source of amusement for our tormentor. She clapped her hands like a little kid despite having a razor-sharp blade in one of them. "Yes...make it fun for me!"

With the blade, she made a long shallow cut from my shoulder to my wrist. It was barely deep enough to hurt. The fact that I could feel it at all though told me that we were probably dealing with some sort of paralytic. The knowledge wasn't much help. In the dim light, the oozing cut looked more silver and black than red. She found it delightful. "You have so many other scars. They're beautiful but confusing. Your wounds from my pet are already healing. So what did it take to make the other scars? Ay, I wish you could talk, Mister Wolf. You're a fascinating guy. I might even seduce you if I didn't have to kill you tonight." She pronounced the word "keeel" but it didn't sound any less final.

"You people really should not have keeled my pet and her ancient ancestor. I loved having her. And when I found out that she was the key to the older one...ay ay ay. I had the young one since I was a little girl. My Abuela used to take me out in the moonlight and teach me the mysteries. Abuela was a Bruja Blanca, a white witch. She also knew the art of the curandera. She taught me the herbs that heal and which ones to be careful of because they could kill or take away the arms and legs. They are good herbs, no Mister Wolf? The spell is better because it leaves no trace. But you gonna burn up anyway so..." Her shrug was expressive and dismissive both at once.

"Anyway, when I was a teenager hunting herbs for my Abuela, La Sayona found me. She protected me from some bad men who were sneaking through the woods to grab some women in our village. I hid while she made the magick that makes men thick-headed, easy to sneak up on. She told me to hide and not watch. But I wanted to see. It was beautiful and terrifying both. When she was done, and the screams had died down, she came and told me it was safe to go home. But I hugged her first and thanked her. After that, I could always find La Sayona in the woods. She taught me another kind of magick. I learned enough to do darker things. That was my first step into becoming a Bruja Negra. I liked it more." Jacqueline moved around the room rearranging things. From the splashing sound and the crystal thud of bottles, I decided she was spreading my meager supply of liquor around the bed. Maybe she would awaken Eachan.

Eachan might not be my first choice to brawl with a very healthy and exotic looking young Bruja with her blade. On the other hand, his ability with magick had made quite an impression on me lately. I hadn't even taken time to consider how he did what he did through that amulet. It was nothing I could have done or even worked out. He could probably shut this witch down and turn some of her evil magicks back against her. I just needed to keep her talking. Bullies love when the victims are terrified. I forced a few more shuddering muscle movements and whimpered to get her attention. "Oh, you are such a good boy! You have no idea how happy you make me, Mister Wolf."

She drew the blade down my thigh and left a deeper cut from groin to knee. "I don't know yet. Do I want to do to you what La Sayona did to my cheating asshole husband Abel? It would be a shame. But soon you will be dead so it won't matter to you eh?"

I suddenly had a startlingly clear mental image. The

mangled and messy remains of The Niddhoggs drummer laying in a pool of his fluids. That must have been what originally drew the Brujah down. Vengeance against her unfaithful husband. Now that I thought about it, most of that damage was centered around his groin. It spread out viciously, but the genitals were the epicenter of that storm of violence. Somehow, I could not summon up any enthusiasm about the same treatment for my own nethers. Another test of my paralysis told me enthusiasm wasn't the only thing I couldn't summon.

"I'm pretty sure I can make you dead with just the knife here." She hefted the sickle-shaped athame but then traded it for a much plainer dagger with a black obsidian blade. It was probably the same one she had used on her Abel.

. "We ain't gonna take any chances though. Besides, I want you to know what's gonna happen to your friends too. You took my Sayona away. And the Ancient one was just defending her home. I'm going to take your girl and the old man away too. He's gonna be an unlucky accident when you keel the murderer with your fire gun. I found the bullets in the bag I took from the policia. OH! I almost forgot to tell you. I keeled your policia friend Jackson after you left the cave. A stab to the kidneys with some of my special curandera poison on the blade. Then I cut his throat and threw him in the lake like you did the Ancient one. He should not have involved himself. Old men are easy to keel."

I watched helplessly as she took one of the normal rounds out of my revolver and replaced it with a dragon's breath. "It's a real tragedy, Senor Lupo. You just gonna defend yourself and the whole house gonna explode in flames. The weak old cripple...he just too weak and too drunk to escape. You too weak from the blood loss and wounds the keeler gives you and she just too cooked to get out of the burning house."

Her giggle was enough to drive me crazy. Which may be why I doubted my eyes at first. Just out of the witch's line of sight, the door to the bedroom crept open a foot or two. Just as silently as any ghost, a red fox padded into the room. I felt the blade start to cut through the muscle of my abdomen. It hurt more than most things even I had experienced. The sheer terror was the worst part as the blade made its slow way down through my stomach muscles towards my groin. That was when the fox made a little yip. It was the first sound I'd ever heard it make. It caught the Brujah's attention and made her pull the sharp blade out of my flesh. I would have cried in relief if I had control of my diaphragm and vocal cords.

That damned make-believe fox sat down with the shadows of the door behind him and curled his bushy tail forward over his feet. In the most expressive look I'd ever seen from an animal, he grinned at her, tilted his head to one side, lolled out his tongue comically, and then yipped again.

The young Brujah was instantly on alert. "What's that? You got a familiar Senor Wolf? No, it don't feel like a familiar. I don't know what that thing is. I don't think it can stop me though. She took a running step and kicked at the much smaller vulpine, and the shadows in the doorway exploded in a yellow mass of fur. Grimmr didn't growl or bark or make any sound in his initial rush. There was just the thunder of his big paws as he cleared the door, and then he hit her at the chest and drove her back to the floor.

I didn't see that fight but I did hear it. There were low pitched female words that I assume were Spanish curses. The dog fought with low rumbling growls while the fox never made another sound. I heard the Brujah cry out a few times as fangs found their mark. I also heard the wet slicing sounds that drew a yelp every time she cut my dog. Finally, I heard her curse explosively and then her feet appeared beside the bed. They catapulted my dog across the room to crash against the far wall.

Grimmr was bleeding from several places. The crash into the wall had probably knocked his breath out too. I saw him stagger to his feet and then Jacqueline was standing over me with the revolver in her fist. She must have known something about guns. She managed to spin the cylinder to one of the normal rounds instead of the dragon's breath. At that range, the dog would be lucky to escape even one of the three .45 caliber bullets she could put into him. Grimmr froze with his hindquarters bunched to leap across the bed and back into the fray. I had to wonder if he knew what the gun meant. He certainly didn't try and ignore it for a new attack. For the moment, it looked like the proverbial Mexican standoff. I was hoping the fox would intervene. Instead, he bounded out of the line of fire.

Maybe he could wake up Eachan. There was obviously something supernatural about the thing. Maybe he had the power to wake the professor up. At least he might escape. The witch made sure I knew that Maureen and I weren't going to be that lucky. "I'm gonna shoot your dog, Senor Wolf. Maybe he won't die. But I'm gonna shoot him bad enough he can't escape. And then I'm gonna go out that window and shoot your fire bullet. The gas from the kitchen....it's gonna catch the whole house on fire and all of you are going to burn up without being able to move. That's how you're gonna pay for what happened to La Sayona and the Ancient."

She thumbed the hammer back. Her movements were

slow but competent. I was more certain than ever that she was going to shoot Grimmr two or three times. Before she could squeeze the trigger though, a blur of black swept in on thunderous wings. I saw the blackness speed between us so that her face was hidden. Then there was a wet rending sound and a scream. The gun fell to the floor and Grimmr left his frozen posture to charge back out of sight behind me. This time there were no female curses. There was a single scream that cut off into a wet gurgle even as that same sound of wet suction repeated itself. A horror of black and scarlet with coffee-colored skin lurched back into view. Her throat was a red ruin from Grimmr's jaws, and her right eye was simply missing. Jacqueline the Bruja fell limply back to the floor. All I could see from our angle was the pool of blood spreading away from the bed. I heard something wet hit the floor and I knew where she'd lost the eye. My guess was confirmed when I heard the voice by the window. "Dumbass."

## 28

It was daylight before we started regaining control of our muscles. Maureen was just starting to cry, and her breath was hoarse but steady. I heard a clatter from the other room that sounded like Eachan's cane falling to the floor. For my part, I was sitting up with my feet off the bed. Part of me wanted to walk out and check on the professor. Another part was pretty sure I'd fall on my face if I tried. For some reason, the prospect of rolling around in Senora Brewster's blood wasn't exactly unappealing to me. Call it an unorthodox upbringing.

I twisted to check on Maureen again. My voice was hoarse, and it broke up from all of the weakness going around. "You okay?"

This time she managed a nod and weak kittenish sounding whimper that I was sure was a yes. I managed to lean over and brush my lips across her forehead. "Okay, sweetheart. You rest. I'm going to check on the prof."

It was approximately as rough as a stormy sea crossing from Denmark to Scotland. Somehow though, I made it through the bedroom door and was halfway down the hall when there was a very soft and polite sounding knock at my back door. I didn't know what to make of that. Nobody ever came to my back door. Maybe the fox that wasn't there needed in? Maybe it was another evil creature from another place or time.

I wanted to go back for my gun. It would take too long even using the walls to stay on my feet. Maybe I could ignore it? The next knock was just as gentle but somehow conveyed the thought that it would not simply go away. I grabbed a chef's knife on the way through the kitchen and held it out of sight in the hand supporting me against the wall. My left hand fumbled with the knob and opened the door.

The second thing I saw was around a dozen bikes scattered across my yard. The first thing though was a leather-skinned and fierce-looking biker. The reason I noticed him first is that we stood eye to eye even though he was on the ground while I was in the doorway above three concrete steps.

I did the math quickly. My porch steps were each a shallow five inches high. That made the total 15 inches plus the thickness of the floor. Add that to my height and...this guy could have been in the NBA when he was younger.

Not that he was ancient, but there were definite streaks of iron-grey in his beard and hair. The hair he wore long and shaggy around the enormous face with its sharply angled jawline. The beard itself wasn't long nor was it particularly well-groomed. Instead, the dark brown and grey silhouette of whiskers formed an uneven or coarse texture to his face. He turned to me and I saw his nostrils flare as if he detected an unpleasant odor.

Without breaking the stare he had pinned to me, he

nodded respectfully to the figure standing on the steps. "Viejo, she is there."

I broke the stare first. Not because I was intimidated, but because I wanted to see this "Viejo". What I saw was the wizened face of my old cellmate Theo. He shook his head and graced me with a faint smile that turned into a mournful and sad look within seconds. "Si, she is here. And we are too late."

The old man politely gestured and I didn't even hesitate to step aside and let him in. I stepped around to clear the door for the old man and ended up bumping into the solid and immovable shape of his biker bodyguard. It irked me that he padded up behind me unheard. It also irked me that he wasn't even inconvenienced when I bounced into him. He steadied my balance with one hand and never bothered to look at me when he did it. *Arrogant oversized jerk. If I weren't half-killed and then poisoned you wouldn't be sneaking up on me and dismissing me out of hand.*

I revised my opinion shortly. He was several steps down the hallway and moving like a shadow before I noticed he was moving. I had no idea how somebody that size could move in my small house without shaking the walls. He walked into the room behind the old man and stood over him while they both looked down at the red splashed lump of meat that had been Senora Brewster. Without a word the old man nodded.

"Tall and silent" over there grabbed the rug she was laying on and rolled it around the body as if he'd done similar things before. He even tucked the ends of the ruined rug in like a big bloody burrito before he lifted it to his shoulder with no visible strain. Okay, the girl wasn't a heavyweight, but still, I'm no weakling. I'd have to puff up a little and grunt in a manly fashion if I hefted her up over my shoulder with one hand.

Even with the awkward burden, he strode silently down my hall and didn't even bang his grisly package into the walls or door frames. I'd say he moved like a big cat but that wasn't quite the feeling I got. When he got to the back door he passed the burden to two or three of his biker brothers before turning back to pat the old man on the back respectfully and then murmur. "Lo Siento por su pérdida Viejo."

That's when I remembered our conversation in the jail. He was trying to keep a young relative from getting in trouble! Suddenly I didn't feel as victorious about the way Jacqueline died. I stepped down and gently put my hand on his shoulder. "Lo Siento too Theo. I'm so sorry that this happened. There was nothing I could do though. I am sorry my dog killed your granddaughter."

There were tears in the old clear blue eyes when he looked at me. He just shook his head and patted my upper arm in return. Then he turned and let one of the other bikers in my yard help him into a sidecar.

"It wasn't your dog" The voice came out like gravel in a barrel. Or maybe like a stone giant might sound. I glanced over to where the giant of a biker leaned against my fence with his arms crossed on his chest and his feet crossed to support him lounging there. It took a minute for the words to register.

"What do you mean it wasn't my dog? It sure as hell wasn't one of us. You saw. That was animal attack damage. She poisoned us and then came in to finish the job for fun. I don't want to hurt the old man's feelings, but his granddaughter was a fruitcake." I wanted to be angry, but mostly I was just tired and sick of the whole mess.

"Wasn't your dog. And that wasn't his granddaughter."

This time he grinned and I suddenly knew why he didn't remind me of a big cat after all. That grin showed a mouthful of sharp teeth and amber eyes that didn't belong on a man. "That baggage we're disposing of lured his girl here and caused her death. It wasn't a dog that killed her. It was fire. Some *really* hot fire. But you know that don't you? I smelled you all over that cave and the garden above it. Smell the fire in that gun in your bedroom too. Don't sweat it though. He doesn't blame you. He blames himself for not getting to her sooner. I guess he blames the dead witch too. Don't worry about it. We have a plan to make sure none of this comes back on you. It's too bad you had to kill Sayona, but she wasn't herself anymore. That witch had turned her into something she was never meant to be. The old man is sad, but he's not angry."

It was a bunch of information to assimilate in a very short time. I could go over it better when I had more time to think about the whole confusing mess. For now, I focused on the immediate priority. "So we're okay? I don't have to worry about you or your buddies showing up to trash the house or the bar or catch me alone in an alley?"

Again I got that wolf grin. "I wouldn't say that, Warrior."

The way he said "warrior" made ice slither around my spine and settle in my stomach to do flips. There was something way too knowing in his eyes for my comfort. He didn't help my frame of mind when he continued. "You think about it boy. I know you, and you should know me. I used to watch you and the other fodder drink yourselves stupid and make fumbling passes at girls that were practically goddesses. I know you. I bet the all-father would love to know where you've been hiding down here. Always wondered why Kara didn't drag you around by your cod anymore. So I figure maybe you want to do me a favor and I forget I ever saw you."

Misbegotten flea-ridden sheep shagging *wolves*...I should have known. I didn't know which this was. I never could tell Freke or Gere apart in wolf form. In human form, it was just as hopeless.

"And you won't tell him? Some night when you're laying there at his feet with your tongue out and he offers a haunch of boar you won't let it slip to gain favor? Sure thing, you can probably get me a good deal on the Bifrost bridge too I bet." Maybe it was stupid. Maybe this creature that was a companion of gods could crush me like a bug. Certainly, he could give the news back to Blinky. He couldn't make me cower though. I hate bullies. That's probably the biggest reason I didn't want to go back to Valhalla.

He laughed at my anger. If he had a single worry about being on my doorstep in my home ground, it didn't show. "That depends on you...Warrior. I'm willing to develop some amnesia and take measures to forget where I saw you. It will just cost you a little errand."

He paused to judge my reaction. I'm pretty sure he saw both anger and maybe hopeful curiosity. "See, my brother is getting into trouble down south. I'll give you a guide. You'll go down there and disrupt his scheme without getting caught. Easy as rabbits in a trap."

His tone became smoother and charming. "He's too caught up in his own fun down there. Won't know to look for you. Gere was never particularly perceptive anyway. Unless you screw up bad, he'll never think to question your origin. You do this for me. I'll make sure you get some reward *and* I'll make sure the memories of you here disappear from my mind as if we'd never met. If not...well, there's still a couple of murders unsolved. I've got the murder weapon and can arrange some things to point at you and the cute redhead in there. So we got a deal?"

Dammit, I hate bullies and I hate those wolves and the ravens that go with them. But I hated the idea of Maureen behind bars even more. "Deal. Where do I meet your guide?"

The wolf and the old man were good to their word. They covered our tracks like pros. Maybe they were pros of a sort. None of them flinched at carrying a corpse out of my house. Even the old man only watched with his sad eyes.

Of course, he wasn't really an old man. La Sayona turned out to be a legend almost two hundred years old. If that was his "young" relative, then he wasn't a wizard or even human. I don't know what the Hel old Theo was. Maybe his version of Biker "colors" was a clue. He had a large Mexican style skull on his back. Around the skull, both owls and bats flew carrying guava fruit. I found some interesting references in one of Eachan's books on pre-Columbian indigenous people of South America. I'll let you do your digging though. I just know I have no plans to cross the old man's path again.

I didn't hear from the police for a full day after the bikes disappeared from my backyard. Green young officer Chuy showed up with Jackson's nephew in the car. Agent Dixon never got out of the police car. For the most part, he sat stiffly upright in the passenger seat while Chuy debriefed us. I did catch a glare or two from the young fed. If what the Bruja said was true, I couldn't blame him. We might not have killed his uncle. But we didn't exactly take care to watch his back either. I didn't want to think too hard about that part of the ordeal. I was going to miss that generous and funny old cop.

Chuy's story was short and sweet. He never stopped looking around suspiciously while he talked. They'd discovered Uncle Joe's squad car still at the cave site after he never showed up for work. Nobody was in it nor had been for days from the state of a coffee cup in the cupholder. They hadn't found his body but people were expecting the worst. The firefighters had been the last to talk to him about the "fireworks".

I was off the hook for the murders. They'd found the Brewster widow with her brains blown out in the country-side. Wolves and coyotes had gotten to her before some bikers found her while they were out raising hell at a bonfire. She had one of the murder weapons with her. There was also a suicide note explaining why she killed her husband for sleeping around. She said she'd had to kill his bandmate when the elder McKinnon became suspicious. The guilt finally got to her and she put a gun to her own head. It was an easy solution to a messy few days. The cops decided to go with it. Besides, they were busy trying to find their missing brother in arms. I wanted to tell them where to look, but that would have just opened a new can of worms to no point. If Senora Brewster was telling the truth, he was well out of the fight now.

Maureen was staying with me. We'd decided after she firmly vetoed all other options, that I would stay in Austin and keep my job. For the time being, she was content to recuperate in my house and read up on some of the books I had that were different than her own sources. It was way too comfortable for my comfort level if you can wrap your head around that. We could share a kitchen without bumping into each other. There was no argument about politics or restaurants or even the television remote. That was just unnatural. On the other hand, I hadn't laughed or smiled so much in years. I couldn't even remember the last time I woke up grinning and anxious to see what the world held for me that day.

It was probably too good to last.

A couple of weeks after everything settled down, we were coming back from the lake. It had been a full day of paddleboarding and picnicking with some discreet hands-on exercises that weren't as fulfilling as they were teasing. We were both looking forward to a hot shower and some quality time behind closed doors when we got home.

I unpacked the car while Maureen took the shower first. In the middle of washing the picnic dishes, my phone rang. I thumbed it open and answered even though the number wasn't even an area code I was familiar with. Probably just a salesman trying to get a commission off of installing a new security system. I get those calls a couple of times a week.

This wasn't one of those times. A vaguely familiar bass voice rough and raw in its tones rumbled out of the phone. "Your guide will be in Del Rio four days from now. Ask for Perro at the bar in Doc Holiday's between seven and midnight. Don't miss him."

The phone went straight to dial tone without another word or even a goodbye. Oddly enough my first thought wasn't about the rude son of a bitch. First I thought, *Maureen isn't going to be happy about this.*

After that, I called the rude son of a bitch several things under my breath. A deal's a deal though. And I certainly didn't want another wolf, or raven, or valkyrie, or that damned horse with legs like a spider to show up.

Maureen stepped into the kitchen wearing only a towel. She must not have heard the phone ring. She didn't ask about the call at least. What she did say was, "you better hurry. I used most of the hot water. If you take too long you'll end up taking a cold miserable shower. They tell me guys do that to help with...tumescence?"

She turned away from the door then turned back with a mischievous grin and suddenly dropped her towel. "If that happens what are you going to do about this!?"

She ran down the hall with laughter bubbling up from her belly into very unladylike guffaws. I was more concerned with the way the water glistened on her firm and bouncing hindquarters as she ran. She was right, I needed to hurry if I wanted to be clean and still ready willing and able to do something about that sparkling fanny.

I hurried with the shower. Despite all the boat and board paddling, I turned out to be more than ready, willing and able. Twice.

## 29

CHAPTER The Last

It was dark in the ICU. The nurse that came in didn't bother turning on a light. She just looked up at the monitor and watched the green and pink lines scrawl across the screen. She nodded to herself and then went to check on the machine pushing air into the patient and letting him breathe it out on his own. He wasn't trying to breathe. He wasn't even conscious. The lungs just did that whether he was aware or not.

Once more the nurse nodded at her findings. Finally, she lifted her hand and a light shone out barely visible from beyond the curtained doorway. The charge nurse dozing at her desk looked up and made a note. Looked like a new nurse. Maybe she didn't know the rules about cell phones in patient rooms. Some people kept the devices and claimed they were just there for flashlights. Rules were rules though, she'd give the girl a quiet and unofficial warning. No need to give them verbal counselling on their first shifts.

Inside the room, the light shined down to illuminate the tube pushing air into the old man. It also showed his greying hair, leathery skin with a sickly pallor, and the thick pad of bandages that were still showing some blood as the wounds refused to cooperate.

He'd come in on an ambulance without a stitch of clothing. He was covered in mud and they were having an ungodly amount of trouble with his blood pressure and the wound in his throat on arrival. There was kidney failure and possible drug overdose to consider as well. The Narcan had helped. He quit having runs of V-tach. After that, it was a race against blood loss and exposure. The race was still running its course but most of the staff were betting on the guy in black robes to win this one. The part that had them shaking their heads was his lack of identification. If they knew who he was, they could call family in to say goodbye maybe.

They might not know who he was. But behind those closed eyes he knew. He knew who he was and he remembered things.

*That had been one helluva fight. Joe Jackson was shaking his head at the memories. It was hard to believe he'd seen any of the things that happened down in that cave. Even harder to believe that he'd squared off against some ancient deadly tree creature and come out alive.*

*The thought of that reckless charge made him want to break out in a cold sweat. The success of that same reckless charge made him grin to himself. Fat, old, slow, and closing fast on retirement, but I still managed to get the helpless civilian out of trouble. Gave old Mag's his shot too. The boy wouldn't have had a chance without me. Not bad for a washed-up old flatfoot.*

*He'd already been to his car and called in about out of control kids and fireworks. The bar owner was on his way to the hospital with a story about a spiked drink gone wrong. That was one Jackson planned to follow up on. The way this case had shaped* up so far, the doctors would probably find some unknown toxin in the guy's system that would put the medical circles into cold sweats of excitement.

Austin was full of enough old-style hippies, herbalists, and holistic healers that it would probably be the center of thousands of animated conversations once word got out. That would revive the old zombie pufferfish dialogue and next thing some kids would be experimenting with stuff that sent them to the ER. The old police officer grimaced but then shrugged it off.

The job was always pretty much the same. Even amazing pyrotechnics and supernatural creatures would fade into the background within weeks or days. Just the cycle of people finding new things to talk about. Kids finding new ways to try and express how "special" and emotional they were. And paramedics and cops picking up the pieces, so the cycle could go on.

Sitting in his patrol car, Jackson sipped at the Donut Shop coffee in its Styrofoam cup and looked out at the stars. Emergency services had been by and made sure no human casualties were lying around. The fire department had a few bored people out in their distinctive yellow-banded baggy protective pants with suspenders over blue polo shirts. There wasn't a lot of risk but who was going to tell them that the biggest burning tree had run through a wall and fallen into the lake?

They were starting to fade back to the ladder truck anyway. Maybe half an hour more and they'd head back to the station. They probably had breakfast laid out to cook when they got there. One young firefighter had mentioned their cooking after joining the old cop on the sidelines.

The young man in his protective gear looked over with a grin. "You oughta join us flatfoot. Had Gumbo and Etouffee last night. We cook all the time in the house. Those twenty-four-hour shifts can be boring as hell. Every house has something. We do cookouts and have a pool table plus a dartboard. Chief doesn't like it much.

Say's we probably hide the keg and dancing girls whenever he pulls up to inspect."

The look of pure evil enjoyment on his face indicated that they weren't particularly concerned that the chief did or did not like their pool table. Sometimes Joe thought he should have gone the fireman route. Other than that whole thing about running into a burning building as other people run out.

By the time he finished his coffee and "energy bar" from the same donut shop, Sergeant Jackson was watching the youngsters pile into the ladder truck and roll away. A few motorcycles coughed into life in the bar parking lot. They circled around the now cordoned-off building. Train wrecks and fires always drew the onlookers. After a quick pass around the parking lot, the bikers lost interest and roared off in the same direction the truck had gone.

That left Officer Joe a few hours before the official end of his shift. As far as he was concerned it couldn't end soon enough. For several days in a row, there hadn't been a quarter as much sleep as his older thicker body craved. Be good to end this one and spend some time away.

He had a four-day weekend coming. He'd probably spend a little of it with his sister and pass on the message from their nephew Drew. He was a good kid. Sure, he could be odd and compulsive, but those were some good schools he went to. You didn't exactly sneeze at a job with the agency he was part of either. Of course, there were whispers that he was a maverick and they would be downsizing his position as soon as there was a good reason. Good kid though. Just a little weird.

With everybody else out of the area, Jackson got out of the car to do one more sweep. He checked the yellow tape around the fenced area and the new cave mouth below. No doubt tomorrow it would be gone. If the snippets he heard from that weird assed *amulet were true, then there would be university people arguing over who had precedence for a new archaeological find.*

*He shrugged and headed back to his car. Those eggheads could get all excited and argue all they wanted. He'd kept people in his town safe and got rid of something he couldn't even talk about. Oh, there were always stories from cops. Weird shadows, perps that disappeared impossibly, people surviving impossible odds, they were all like campfire stories to cops. Trusted anecdotes to get a round of drinks or secure your few minutes of the conversation.*

*Nobody was going to believe in supernatural warriors or ancient evil tree witches though. Maybe he could just talk about the weird person-shaped bonfire and the symbols and crystal in the rock? Yea the guys would eat that up at the bar.*

*Jackson opened his trunk and pulled out a rucksack with the amulet and a couple of weapons. The tomahawk and weird scythe would go back to their respective owners. He wasn't sure who got the amulet that everyone seemed to have carried at one point or another. He was closing the trunk when a whisper of sound started to turn him around.*

*The old cop never finished his turn. Pain, fire and ice, and sharp agony ripped into the side of his lower back. Gasping for breath he tried to turn, tried to free the handgun snapped in his holster. Another hot wet agony ripped at his throat. He felt the warmth spreading down his chest as two slender arms slipped around him and started laboriously dragging his now weakly struggling body.*

*The splash of cold water woke him. It didn't give him any strength to move though. He felt the numbing cold seep into the areas around his back and the tattered edges of his ruined throat. That was some relief. It didn't do anything for the deeper burning agony in his kidney. Maybe it was better when consciousness went away, and a dull cold numbness carried him into the darkness.*

*His last thoughts were. "Nobody will even miss me until I'm absent from Roll Call next week. Aww hell, I'm gonna miss my fishing trip for the weekend. Drew's gonna be disappointed we didn't talk about tonight too dammit."*

Outside of his cycle of memories, Joe was barely aware of the alarms going off on his wall monitor. The charge nurse down the hall saw the monitors and the numbers reflecting a spike in blood pressure and heart rate. She decided the Reaper was on his way.

The nurse at the bedside didn't completely agree. She moved her empty hand closer and leaned over so the light from her palm illuminated her high cheekbones and piercing blue eyes as well as the patient. Her voice was a crooning whisper directly into the old man's ear. "Well met Joseph Jackson. I am Gondul. When you get tired of this race let me know. I will take you with me to a much better place.

"Some of my sisters would leave you with your wounds and just fix your muscles and your skeleton. Aren't you lucky you got me? When we leave, I will erase your scars, restore youth to your frame, and clear sight to your eyes. When we get to Valhalla you will be at your prime again with clean limbs and heavy thews. And I will take you and love you for your first night in the halls of the gods. What say you to that old Joe? Aren't you happy it is Gondul and not one of my colder sisters here for you? Just let go when you're ready and I will catch you."

The End

# INTERESTING TIDBITS INDEX

IA DRANG- A VALLEY in Vietnam and scene of a historic battle. It was one of the few times a commander called in fire on the position of his own men. One platoon had been overrun by a much larger force of enemy troops who were engaged in hand to hand with the smaller American force. As Hal Moore watched his men being chopped down he called in an airstrike on the position. One source later said the strike was intentional to take out the enemies butchering his men. Other sources claimed the strike was for "Danger Close" and overlapped the American position. In any event, a number of G.I.s received that fire. I include as the origin of Magnus in modern time. On a personal note, the research was already done because I helped an Uncle look up what the history books said. Troyce Ray Stacker was my uncle and was there on that fateful day. He never confirmed to me that it was where he received either of his purple hearts or the chemical burn marks over a lot of his body. One can make some guesses though.

Leanderthal- In 1983, road work being done in Cedar Park Texas uncovered a skeleton. She has been nickname the Leanderthal Lady or even Leane in deference to the nearby town of Leander. The lady in question is one of the oldest complete female skeletons ever discovered in North America with diagnostic dating placing her remains between ten thousand and thirteen thousand years old.

**Dragon Rounds**- Yes you can buy the dragon rounds that produced Magnus' fireball in .410 shotgun shells. I haven't tried one and am not sure how good they are for your weapon though so beware!

## ALSO BY STEVE CURRY

For more in The Saga of Mouse, aka The Valhalla AWOL series.

Start with book one

Austin Wyrd, Book One

Wyrd Gere, Book Two

Freke Wyrd Voodoo, Book Three

Yule, Have a Wyrd Christmas, The holiday Novella.

## ABOUT THE AUTHOR

Steve Curry is a fledgling author just beginning to use a wide spread of experiences and careers. His current forays into writing are Urban Fantasy infused with Culinary tidbits from a decade as a Le Cordon Bleu chef. Military weapons and protocols plus realistic medical and physical descriptions abound from his work with Uncle Sam's Army NBC branch and time as a Licensed Respiratory Therapist in ICUs across the nation. Toss in lots of mythology, new age religion, supernatural goodness and real world history along with a soupcon of Jim Butcher's humor, and a few pinches of Robert Parker's character building traits to see how he'll entertain you. He currently resides in West Texas under the management of a yellow hound dog with claims on most of a large bed. Others in the hierarchy are an imperial princess and rainbow unicorn riding granddaughter, his wife, the imperial queen and mistress of eyerolls, and an uncountable horde of invading mongrel cats. You can join others interested in his work at Steve Curry's author pages

https://www.MyWyrdMuse.com

https://www.facebook.com/MyWyrdMuse/

Made in the USA
Columbia, SC
03 August 2021

42871732R00164